Praise for Angela Roquet's
Lana Harvey, Reapers Inc. Series

"Darkly comic and wildly imaginative. Angela Roquet gives us an afterlife we've never seen before."

-Kimberly Frost, best-selling author of
The Southern Witch Series

"*Pocket Full of Posies* has just enough laughs, lots of mystery, tons of action, some great romance, a cast you can't help but love, and a story that never lets you rest!"

-Literal Addiction

"*Graveyard Shift* is an impressive feat of imagination built on a broad knowledge of world religion. It's also great fun! No small accomplishment."

-Christine Wicker, best-selling author of
*Not in Kansas Anymore: The Curious Tale of
How Magic is Transforming America*

"*Graveyard Shift* is sacrilicious. Roquet's first book in the Reapers Inc. series will be a huge hit with fans of authors like J.K. Rowling and Neil Gaiman. I look forward to getting my hands on the rest of the series."

-Lance Carbuncle, author of
Grundish and Askew

"I love sci-fi and fantasy. Horror is also one of my favorite genres. I have had a lifelong love of mythology in all it many varied forms. It is rare to find a book that combines more than two of those with both a joyous wickedness and intelligence. Angela Roquet has managed it beautifully in her novel *Graveyard Shift*. She has artfully woven many different religions and mythologies into a believable afterlife."

-D.E. Cook, author of
Fairy Exterminators

by Angela Roquet

Lana Harvey, Reapers Inc.

Lana Harvey, Reapers Inc. short stories

other titles

FOR THE BIRDS

LANA HARVEY, REAPERS INC.
BOOK 3

Angela Roquet

ISBN: 1484087690

ISBN-13: 978-1484087695

For my supportive husband,

who dresses up like the Grim Reaper

at my book signings.

You big weirdo.

What did I ever do without you?

I love you.

CHAPTER 1

There was blood everywhere. It dripped from the bannisters and splashed across the deck floor, pooling near the door to the captain's quarters, where my trusty hounds waited with their tails tucked between their legs. They were both covered in bloody chicken feathers. Saul looked more innocent than Coreen, but I had a feeling that was only because he didn't know any better. What he lacked in brains, he made up for in loyalty. This little mishap wasn't entirely their fault today.

Kate Evans and Alex Grayson, my two least favorite reapers, lounged against the railing on the far side of the deck. Alex was taller by half a foot, but Kate was the one who emanated confidence, the sort that always seemed to beg or threaten a double-dog dare. She shook her head, tossing her bangs back and crooked her finger, motioning Alex to tilt her head down so she could whisper in her ear. Alex grinned and covered her mouth with her fingertips as I approached.

Kate tossed her bangs back again. It was a painfully juvenile gesture that I really couldn't stand. "Your ex-boyfriend stopped by for a visit, but the mutts got hungry," she said, sending Alex into a fit of roaring laughter.

Kate had not been thrilled when I was announced as the new captain of the Posy Unit. Not that anyone had been particularly thrilled, but she seemed to take it the worst. She had been on the unit the longest, and I think she had honestly thought that the promotion was in the bag for her. She very well may have deserved it, but it wasn't my problem.

I didn't say a word. Instead, I carefully made my way to the closet beside mine and Josie's quarters and fetched a mop and bucket. The culprits were still snickering when I returned, until I thrust the mop in Kate's hands and shoved the bucket into Alex's gut, drawing a satisfying grunt out of her.

"Have fun kids. If you're lucky, there might be some souls left to harvest when you're done."

Kate scrunched up her face, tossing back her long, side-swept bangs again. "You won't clear that list of souls if you keep us here."

Josie Galla and Kevin Kraus, my roommates and fellow unit members, laughed behind me. I hadn't heard them come on board. They froze suddenly and looked around the ship, taking in the remains of the chicken that Kate and Alex had set loose for the hounds to massacre. Josie narrowed her gaze. Her upper lip curled back. "What the hell happened here?"

"A little practical joke, but it's being taken care of. Think you can handle a little extra workload today?" I raised an eyebrow.

"Oh, if it means they have to clean up this disaster, then absolutely." She folded her arms.

Kate huffed.

I turned back to face her and Alex. "Better shake a leg, ladies. I'll be back to check on you around noon."

We left them scowling on the deck of the ship and took the ramp back down to the dock, where the last member of the team, Arden Faraji, stood waiting with his hands folded behind his back.

Arden was a rarity among the reapers, in more ways than one. For starters, he was black. His skin was such a dark hue that it had blue highlights, streaking over his shaved head and across his high cheekbones.

I think the reason Grim made most reapers white was because his mythology originated in Europe, but somewhere along the way, he decided having reapers of different flavors could be beneficial to the harvesting process. So there's Jenni Fang, another roommate of mine and Grim's new second-in-command, who's Asian; Santos Consuelo, the Latino captain of the Lost Souls Unit; Arden Faraji, a.k.a. the African Posy; and Arden's sailing partner, Asha Dipika, who's Indian.

I wasn't sure if Arden and Asha were more involved than just being sailing partners, and I wasn't about to ask. Arden hadn't said five words to me since I'd joined the Posy Unit. He'd wait for his assignments, give me a nod, and coin off to his first harvest site, just like that, every morning. He wasn't rude or anything, but he wasn't exactly trying to make new friends either. He had a solemn, sorrowful attitude about him, but it was hardly surprising.

The Posy Unit hadn't been Arden's first team. He'd gotten his start on the Mother Goose Unit, collecting the numerous child souls that died from malnutrition and starvation in Sub-Sahara Africa. While other members of the Mother Goose Unit were collecting child souls that had had some semblance of a decent life, the child souls Arden collected spent most of their short lives waiting for his arrival. That sort of work takes a toll on one's psyche, but he seemed to handle himself well, as far as I could tell anyway.

By the time he transferred to the Posy Unit, the child souls of Africa weren't just resulting from malnutrition anymore, though their numbers had increased. Thousands of child soldiers joined them in meeting Death. Arden also added adult victims of war and starvation to his resume by joining the Posy Unit.

Over in India, Asha Dipika also harvested the souls of starving children, as well as a good chunk of the victims from the wars raging in Iran and Afghanistan. Her and Arden's ship was a floating contradiction. The hold was equipped with chambers to separate soldiers of various armies, and the deck looked a bit like a carnival, with a carousel set in the center. I was tempted to ask about that too, but Asha's demeanor was even more solemn than Arden's, so I kept my mouth shut.

"Hey, Arden," I said, coming to a stop in front of him. He was nearly a foot and a half taller than me, so I had to look up to make eye contact. "Think you could make a stop in China today? There's a factory fire scheduled around two o'clock in Jiansu. It was on Kate's list, but she's going to be tied up most of the morning."

Arden nodded slowly, maintaining his neutral expression. I sometimes wondered if he was even capable of smiling, or frowning for that matter. Maybe one morning I would suggest that he harvest a strip club massacre and see if I could get a new expression out of him.

I pulled my handy dandy soul list out of the pocket of my robe and looked it over. "Great. That leaves a plane crash in Tulsa, a six-car pileup in New York, and a gang related shooting in L.A."

"I'll take the pileup," Kevin said with a shrug.

"Plane crash!" Josie chirped.

I frowned at her. "Fine, I'll take the shooting."

With a plane or automobile accident, the bodies were usually pretty easy to spot. With a shooting, there was some hunting involved. Sometimes a stray bullet will find a home

4

in someone three blocks down the street from the scene of origination. Sometimes a fatally wounded gang member will scurry off to die somewhere less public. If that happens, it can take hours to find every last soul involved.

When the harvests were divided amongst the team, I gave them each a coin for traveling in the human realm. After the terrorist attacks on Limbo City last spring, Grim had deactivated coin travel in the city. Travel was now regulated through a handful of booths stationed at busy junctions, like the Reaper Academy and the Three Fates Factory. However, the dock at the harbor was a free travel zone, so Reapers could take off for work with the roll of a coin. There were nephilim guards stationed at the entrance to the dock, so it was still regulated.

Saul and Coreen nuzzled against my legs, merging our auras so that they could travel through the realms with me. I waited for the rest of the team to coin off before taking my leave.

A few months ago, I would have dawdled. I would have done my best to convince Josie that we had time for coffee or breakfast first. Then, I would have found something entertaining to occupy my time in the human realm until a casket arrived at a burial site and I could grab the soul before the body was lowered into the ground. It was a tidy routine that didn't pay well, but it was easy and there were minimal complications.

While I wasn't fond of the unpredictable nature of my new job, the money was outstanding. I was also pleasantly surprised, and almost embarrassed, at how much I was enjoying the new level of respect that came with being a captain of a specialty unit. Not that that respect didn't come with a heap of resentment most of the time.

I arrived bright and early at my first harvest site. L.A. was not my most favorite place to collect souls. Of course, most of the souls needing to be harvested there were not in the nice parts of town. Sirens pierced the air. It was only seven a.m., but there were nine bodies lying haphazardly around several jalopies in an alley, spanning between a few buildings that I was almost certain were condemned.

I looked down at the hounds and sighed. "Welcome to the city of angels."

CHAPTER 2

"If you die in an elevator
be sure to push the Up button."
-Sam Levenson

The lobby at Reapers Inc. was always busy. While Reapers Inc. headquarters only utilized the seventy-fifth floor, there were dozens of other businesses that rented space in the executive high-rise. The Afterlife Council dining hall and conference rooms were located on the seventy-third floor. I had the privilege of dining with the council at the last Oracle Ball, just before I found out that I was an anomaly among the reapers.

A more positive approach would be to call myself special or one of a kind, but it's hard to be optimistic about something that could get my head chopped off if the general public found out about it. There weren't very many people who knew the truth about me. Hell, there weren't very many people who knew the truth about how Grim was running Eternity.

From the beginning, war raged in the afterlife. With so many religions forming in the human realm, it was inevitable. The first original believer of every faith spawned the deities, heavens, and hells of that particular religion. In the beginning, there were no boundaries. Afterlives overlapped each other in Eternity, and deities fought viciously to claim and keep their territories and the souls they held.

Around the time that Islam was founded in the human realm, Grim was out harvesting souls. He happened across a Muslim woman named Khadija. Khadija was the Prophet Muhammad's first wife, and she was also the first person converted to Islam, making her an original believer.

Grim seized the opportunity. He took Khadija to Eternity and showed her the mayhem and suffering. Her compassion compelled her to help. Her will and true knowledge of the afterlife gave her the power to tap into the collective soul matter that fueled the worlds beyond the grave, and she created a power hub of sorts, the Throne of Eternity. Grim wrote up a peace treaty, and Khadija separated the afterlives and formed their boundaries. The Afterlife Council was founded to sort out the finer details and laws needed to maintain the peace.

It seems simple and innocent enough, but common knowledge does not include the part about Khadija. Grim hoarded that little tidbit of information. Khadija was the skeleton in his closet. Her will was the only thing keeping the boundaries in place, and as long as only he knew about her, he didn't have to worry about anyone else swooping in and taking over.

He had her create Limbo City in the center of Eternity, and then he had her create a secret pocket realm for herself. After that, he established himself as the unofficial king of Eternity. He launched Reapers Inc. and formed a monopoly on the soul harvesting business by convincing the council to allow him to create the race of reapers. As the president of the Afterlife Council, he secured an indefinite term by forfeiting his voting privileges. Although, I'm really not sure how he's managed to keep them from questioning his ability to maintain the territory boundaries. It seems generally accepted that that power is something he wields personally. I'd probably still assume that myself, if I didn't know any better.

I just so happen to be the one and only reaper who has actually met Khadija, because it's her fault that I'm so damn special. Being the actual force behind Eternity's peace and maintenance, Khadija was the one responsible for creating the new reapers Grim required to further expand Reapers Inc. The problem was, even the soul of an original believer does not possess boundless power. After more than thirteen centuries, Khadija was losing her edge. An unauthorized island materialized out in the Sea of Eternity where Seth, a crusty old Egyptian god determined to take over Eternity, gathered rebel forces, mostly from the Abrahamic hell regions and Duat, the dwindling Egyptian underworld.

Khadija had been urging Grim, several centuries prior to this incident, to find another soul to replace her. He ignored her requests. That's where I come in. In 1709, Khadija was busy baking up a new batch of reapers, the eighth generation, when she had the brilliant idea to make an extra special reaper fully equipped with Grim's ability to see the potency of a soul. That's right. Me.

Grim hadn't harvested a soul in nearly a thousand years. He spent most of his time carefully manipulating the council so that he could still reign supreme, even without a vote. Not that he would have gone out looking for a replacement even if he wasn't an invalid in the field. His absence would have been noticed by all the wrong people. The risk of exposing his secret was too great, so he ignored Khadija's pleas.

When she could take it no longer, she revealed her own little secret to Grim. He didn't have much of a choice at that point. He could either send me out to find a replacement, or wait and watch Eternity cave in on itself.

So I got promoted. I'd spent the first three hundred years of my existence harvesting low-risk souls, and then suddenly, I was entrusted to harvest the highest of high-risk. No pressure, right? And to top it off, Grim tried to pull off the whole gig without explaining the truth of the matter to me, but Khadija eventually requested a meeting. After the death of Coreen Bendura, the captain of the specialty team I was assigned to, I was ready for an explanation. Things haven't been the same since.

So began the search for a replacement soul. Horus, the Egyptian deity on the council, had worked out a deal with Grim allowing for the harvest of souls with past lives of Egyptian Royalty, as long as Horus was permitted to take the rejected soul candidates back to Duat. Duat so rarely saw new souls anymore, now that their territory was a sliver of what is once was.

I eventually found Winston, or the child king formerly known as Tutankhamun, to take Khadija's place. King Tut wasn't an official original believer. He only restored the old Egyptian faith after Akenhaten tried to destroy it, so his power on the throne was already dwindling.

It was just as well. Horus was not thrilled with the outcome. Tut was one of his favored descendants. Using his supreme powers of deduction, he came to the conclusion that I was special. Then he threatened to out me to the council if I didn't help him find another replacement soul.

The peace treaty specifically states that no new deities are to be created. I'm not technically a deity. At least, it's really difficult to perceive myself as one. I don't even really consider Grim a deity, but by all rights, I suppose he is. I was made outside of the restrictions set in the treaty either way, and that would mean a very definite and prudent execution. Some of the council members would even be disappointed about it, but that wouldn't stop them from doing what they were required to do by law.

Let me make this perfectly clear, since we're talking about the devious structure of the political beast. The members of the council are not a stupid bunch, not in the least. They consist of nine very old, very powerful beings from the most esteemed faiths, ancient and current. But they do have a way of tiptoeing around the elephant in the room, all for the sake of keeping the peace or manipulating said elephant into joining their circus. There was a lot of circuses in town lately, but I've never been much of a juggler. The tightrope balancing act I was pulling off was top notch, however.

One by one, the council members were finding ways to indebt me to them. After a demon rebel burned down my apartment last spring, Holly Spirit rented me a discounted condo at Holly House, the most Holy abode in Limbo City. Meng Po patched me up, more than once, after several close calls on the job, and off the job. I even dated one of the council members for a short while.

Maalik, the keeper of hellfire, was the Islamic angel who guarded the gates of Jahannam, the Islamic hell. He eventually became painfully controlling. I imagine he thought he was being protective, since he was one of the few who knew the truth about me. Things didn't end so well. And like a first rate harlot, I very quickly found myself in the bed of none other than the Lord of the Flies.

Beelzebub was commissioned by Cindy Morningstar, another council member, to instruct me through a two week demon defense course. At the time, Grim had not yet replaced Coreen Bendura, his second-in-command. After he promoted me to head of the specialty team, many of the council members assumed he was grooming me for the vacant position. Instead, that promotion had gone to Jenni Fang, one of my new roommates. I was instead promoted to captain of the Posy Unit, courtesy of Horus. He pulled some strings within the council to get the placement proposal drawn up to be voted on.

Grim was not pleased. I really think he had hoped I would disappear back into the bottom of the barrel. Originally, that had been my plan, but Horus threw a great big monkey wrench into it. Being captain of the Posy Unit would put me in contact with the most souls possible, thereby expediting the search for a new replacement soul.

So here I was, with a fancy new job that I really didn't deserve. I was giving it my all, and not just to save my ass from the wrath of Horus, but because everyone else was expecting me to fail. Nothing is so motivational as the desire to prove people wrong. I wasn't a real go-getter my first three centuries, and that alone was enough to make most other reapers resent me for getting such a hefty promotion. Also though, I needed to convince Grim that I was serious about my new job. He was suspicious of Horus's motives, so he was just waiting for an excuse to demote me, which is precisely why I showed up twenty minutes early for our weekly meetings and hadn't let a single soul slip past my team.

As a captain of a specialty unit, I also had a fancy pants office at Reapers Inc. It was meant to be a place of solace where I could go to sort out my paperwork and plan the next day's harvest schedules. But mostly, I just sat in the stiff chair behind my empty desk, staring out the enormous picture window and at the blank walls. The other captains had tastefully decorated spaces, but I was still stunned by the whole concept of having an office at all. Plus, the idea of finding solace when Grim was just down the hall was preposterous. So I did most of my paperwork from home and days in advance.

After a long ride up in the elevator, I checked in with Ellen, Grim's secretary, and took a seat in one of the stiff waiting room chairs. My reports were perfectly arranged in my portfolio, but I looked over them again anyway. This sort of dedication would have served me well during my classes at the Reaper Academy. It would have also kept Josie off my ass. She was the only reason I passed my classes at all last semester. Hopefully, it would be another three hundred years before I needed to take another one.

"Lana," Grim grumbled, poking his head out of his office. "Come on in."

I stood and smoothed a hand down the front of my work robe before following him.

Grim was ancient, but like the deities, he had aged well. There were a few lines around his eyes, but his hair was a glossy black and combed back into the standard seventies businessman helmet. His trademark gray suit was as identifiable as a reaper's robe and scythe.

"Take a seat." Grim snatched the portfolio out of my hand and flipped through it, lazily glancing over my weekly reports, while I tried not to look too uncomfortable in one of his torturous office chairs. The leather squeaked beneath me.

Grim glanced up and sighed heavily. Our meetings were tense lately. Not that they were ever friendly in the past. His demeanor was just a little icier since Horus went around him to have the council vote on my placement. They didn't usually have any interest in the reaper hierarchy.

"Did you know that Kate Evans filed an official complaint against you?" he said, tossing the portfolio on his desk.

"No, but I can't say that I'm surprised. She's having trouble accepting my authority. It's still early. I'm sure she'll adjust eventually."

Grim frowned. "How are *you* adjusting?"

"Just fine." I tried to smile, but smiling in the face of Death is never an easy thing to do.

"Are you sure?"

"Yes. Absolutely. Why? Is my work not up to par?"

"It is, actually." He relaxed back in his chair, but the frown was still there. "I'm surprised. I was sure you would be too busy consorting with Horus—"

"I haven't spoken to him in months."

13

"Or running all over Eternity with your latest hell-born consort."

"Maalik isn't technically hell-born. He's an angel—"

"My point being," Grim raised his voice, "I don't know how you're managing to keep up with the requirements of this position. I suppose Josie and Jenni are of use—"

"They have their own careers to attend to. They were plenty helpful with my last round of classes at the academy, but I've managed to figure out this captain gig all on my own, thank you."

Grim sighed again and reached up to massage the back of his neck. So far, our little meeting circled more around my personal life than my work performance. With the effort I had been making, it was hard not to take offense.

"Is it so hard to believe that I've turned over a new leaf?" I asked.

Grim laughed and gave me a skeptical grin. "It might not be as hard to believe if you had actually accomplished your promotion without the unwarranted aid of a council member."

I nodded. "True, but I'm sure Horus and the other council members were just garnering my favor, assuming that I would be your new second-in-command. They haven't been as attentive of me since you appointed Jenni Fang."

"Is that so?" He still didn't look convinced.

I cleared my throat and sat up straighter. "Is there some other reason you don't want me in this position?"

"You mean besides the fact that your five centuries younger than any other unit captain and not half as qualified or experienced?"

"Is my performance lacking?"

"No." Grim's frown creased so deeply that his jowls looked like they might slide right off his face. "Let's try to keep it that way. You're being entrusted with more souls than any other reaper. I don't have time to deal with a clusterfuck if you screw this up. I might just be tempted to terminate you."

My teeth clenched so tight that I could hear them grind inside my skull. I took a careful breath and gave him a strained smile. "I'll keep that in mind."

Grim flashed an insincere smile of his own and tossed my portfolio across his desk. "You do that."

I left Grim's office in a grim mood, and almost didn't notice Ellen Aries, Grim's secretary, until she was practically on top of me.

"Lana," she squealed in a whispery voice. "You got a delivery during your meeting." She gave me a schoolgirl grin and silently clasped her hands together. "From Hell."

She followed me back to my office, bouncing excitedly. Everything about Ellen was bubbly. Since she was less active than most reapers, she had put on a few extra pounds over the years. Of course, that could have also had something to do the fact that she kept enough chocolate stashed in her desk to survive an apocalypse. Her style hadn't changed much since the sixties, and with her full hips and breasts, she looked like a vintage pinup girl. Her dark curls coiled even tighter than my own, and they bounced around her ever-cheerful face. She looked a lot like I imagined I would have looked if I were more girly and twenty pounds heavier.

The other unit captains seemed to glaze over Ellen. It was like they didn't know what to think of her. She was a first generation reaper like my late mentor Saul Avelo and Grace Adaline, professor of the wandering souls course at the Reaper Academy. The difference was that Ellen was a terrible reaper. So Grim gave her the secretarial position. And while she couldn't tout the esteemed reputation many reapers strove for, she was still quite ancient, as in over a thousand years old.

This puzzled the younger reapers as to whether they should address her as a superior or an inferior. So most of them decided to avoid addressing her altogether. I, on the other hand, chose to address her as a peer. The new notion tickled her, and she quickly decided that we were girlfriends. I wasn't exactly sure how I felt about that just yet.

We entered my pathetically undecorated office, and Ellen closed the door behind us. Setting atop my desk was a crystal vase overflowing with daisies in multiple shades of blue. A matt black box sat next to it, tied with a shiny red ribbon.

"Open it! Open it!" Ellen bounced on her toes and nestled her hands under her chin.

Her excitement was contagious. My hands trembled as I untied the ribbon. The corner of the box was embossed with the image of a serpent coiled around an apple. It was the logo of Lilith Enchanted, the most regal dress boutique in Hell. Butterflies took over my stomach. I gently shook the lid loose and peeled away several layers of red tissue paper.

"Oh, my." Ellen's jaw dropped.

I swallowed and lifted the dress out of the box. The material was slinky and sparkled, despite being dark navy in color. The top was strapless, and the skirt was asymmetrical, with a cutout slit that would run from my left knee to just below my right hip, exposing a layer of black tulle framed by a black lace hemline. There was a small tag dangling from the back zipper.

Ellen reached for it. "Oh, my," she said again.

My eyes followed and I came back with an, "Oh, my," of my own. Bub had expensive taste.

I laid the dress back in the box and noticed a little black notecard tucked down in the daisies. It held Beelzebub's delicate handwriting in silver ink, and simply read, "No panties allowed." There was a little fly doodled in the corner.

"Oh, my," Ellen whispered once more, peeking over my shoulder.

CHAPTER 3

"Hear no evil, speak no evil—
and you'll never be invited to a party."
-Oscar Wilde

I didn't care for Beelzebub's flat in Pandemonium. I didn't care for the perpetually nigrescent skyline, or the sulfuric smog that managed to billow all the way to the rooftop of the sixty story skyscraper. More than anything though, I didn't care for the hoity-toity people Beelzebub surround himself with and called his friends. The flat was full of them tonight.

There were six dozen demons in sparkling evening attire lounging around the sitting room. Despite the low lighting, everyone twinkled. Most of the women were in dainty little cocktail dresses, heavy on the glitter and sequins. Plunging necklines and thigh-high slits were all the rage, in addition to suicide stilettoes and over-polished pouts. With the dress Bub had bought for me, I wasn't too far off from blending right in. I think maybe that's what he had been going for, except I wasn't nearly cutthroat enough to complete the ruse.

I sipped at a glass of champagne from a quiet spot near the open balcony doors and watched a pair of harlots in matching red minidresses fawn over Bub while he mixed himself another drink. He smiled politely at them and nodded at whatever they were saying. It really didn't matter how he smiled.

Everything about him whispered sex, from his messy black faux-hawk down to the tastefully snug cut of his pinstripe suit. It had taken some effort, but I'd learned to manage my jealousy for the most part. I knew I was the only one who would be sharing his bed tonight, and that alone gave me the courage to peel my eyes away and glance over the rest of the room.

I knew less than a quarter of the guests, and the only one who had said more than two words to me was Amy, Gabriel's girlfriend. Dating an angel, and an archangel at that, did not do much for her reputation in Hell. Half the crowd was snubbing her, and the other half were feigning interest in the hopes of catching a juicy tidbit of gossip that they might be able to skew to their advantage later on. I had learned to keep my lips sealed when it came to these charade-infested events. That was probably another reason why no one was speaking to me. Amy was an acrobat when it came to tiptoeing the line between sharing too little to be considered interesting, and sharing enough to compromise herself.

Bub slid up beside me and tilted his head down to lay a soft kiss on my neck, tickling my ear with his goatee. "I can't wait to tear that dress off of you later tonight, love," he whispered against my skin with his light English accent.

I stifled a shudder and grinned. "Are you sure about that? I saw the price tag. A bit much for such a tiny thing, don't you think?"

"It's brimsilk, some new manipulation of brimstone, mixed with zinc and copper particles. That's what makes it appear to glow."

"Fancy."

The party chatter softened, and I stole a glance across the room, just in time to catch a slew of sour looks. Bub's reputation wasn't faring so well lately either. He wasn't receiving as much flak as Amy, but then again, he instilled more fear in their kind than she did. Plus, I wasn't an angel. Still, there were plenty brave enough to shoot a dirty look while they enjoyed Bub's high dollar champagne and caviar.

"I think a set of horns and a spiked tail would have endeared me a little more to your guests than the dress," I said.

Bub glanced over his shoulder. "Hmmm. Maybe. Shall we step out on the balcony for a bit of fresh air?"

"Fresh?" I rolled my eyes but let him lead me away from the brooding crowd.

Bub's flat was on the top floor of one of the tallest buildings in Hell's capital. While the view was spectacular, it had lost its appeal for me in a very short amount of time. My nose crinkled at the smell of sulfur emanating from the bowels of the city below. The roar of tortured souls was muted to a dull hum this high up. It sounded more like the gentle whistling of wind, although there was none to speak of. Luckily, the heat wasn't quite as unbearable on the sixtieth floor either. I still preferred the volcanic countryside where Amy's Inferno Chateau was located, when it came to Hell. Bub's country estate in Tartarus, the Greek hell, was also nice.

I leaned over the balcony and gazed down through the smog, trying to make out the Cocytus, the river of wailing, that curled around the city.

"I'm sorry you're not enjoying yourself." Bub folded his arms over the iron railing next to me. "These little socials are necessary though."

"Really?" I laughed.

"Really. I mean, I suppose I could employ a few dozen spies, spend countless hours in meetings with them, and then still have to worry about the quality of their work and their loyalties, but I'd much rather spend a quarter of that on champagne and party favors and form my own analyses."

"And if the guest in question doesn't show up?"

"Well, even that can be analyzed." He grinned.

"Aren't you a clever devil?"

"Oh, you have no idea." His hand found the back of my waist and trailed down lower. "I see you obeyed my little love note."

"No, I just didn't want to risk panty line. This fabric is so thin."

"Of course." He grinned and moved his hand up to the back of my neck, running his fingers through my curls before pulling me in and pressing our mouths together in a surprise kiss. It left me breathless and aching for him.

When he broke for air, he nuzzled his nose playfully against mine. "Why don't you wait for me upstairs? I won't be much longer," he whispered huskily.

"Hmmm, okay." I stepped back from him and downed the last of my champagne before handing him the glass. "Go make nice with the fiends, and then come make nice with me."

Back inside, I stopped to say goodbye to Amy, and then again to thank Jack, Bub's butler, for all his hard work. I liked Jack. He had helped Bub train me in the art of demon defense. Jack gave me wink and bid me goodnight. I didn't even bother to make eye contact with anyone else as I made my way to the circular staircase leading up to Bub's lofty master suite.

Bub's Pandemonium bedroom gave me the chills. It was a far cry from the setup at his country home. The walls were deep red, and the massive, circular bed was covered in black satin sheets. The floor to ceiling windows that made up two entire walls were left bare and open to the fading night sky. Even knowing that it was one-way glass, I still hesitated before undressing and crawling beneath the covers.

Incense burned from a metal orb hanging in one corner above a stone pot that was home to an oversized black orchid. The petals were glossy and turned a deep red when they met in the center. In the opposite corner where the windowed walls met there was an eight foot white marble statue of Eve, depicting the scene just after she ate from the tree of knowledge. Red and pink veins ran through the marble apple in her hand and through the juices dripping from her mouth and chin. Her pupilless eyes glowed a haunting, crystalline blue. She was eerie and seductive, and I couldn't help but wonder how many women she had watched disrobe for Bub in this very room.

I wasn't usually a jealous lover. A long and sordid past is to be expected of an ancient demon, but still. I was only a three-hundred-year-old reaper. I couldn't help but wonder how I measured up to Bub's other conquests. We had only been together for a few months, since the beginning of summer, and I was already guessing at how long it would take before he tired of me.

Soon, the hum of the party below began to fade, and Bub quietly slipped into the bedroom with a bottle of wine and two glasses. He gave me one of his devilish grins and came over to sit next to me on the edge of the bed. He handed me the glasses and one-handedly loosened his red tie.

"You're already undressed. I wanted to do that," he pouted.

"I know. I just really like that dress. Couldn't risk you ravaging it." I grinned and held our glasses out as he uncorked the wine bottle.

Bub filled them to the brim and then set the bottle on the night table before removing his loafers and jacket. He was slower about removing his dress shirt and pants, unabashedly enjoying my ogling. He knew exactly how to accelerate my pulse.

I didn't blush as much as I used to, but it was something I had to work at to achieve. My last lover, Maalik, had been more subtle and modest. Of course, he had been an angel. Dating a bad boy was definitely more exciting, but as the saying goes, the light that burns the brightest usually burns out the quickest.

I wasn't under any delusions about our relationship. It wasn't going to last. I wasn't looking forward to the end, but I wanted to be prepared for it. I was too old to be sobbing over lost love, if you could even call what we had love. We were very much in lust, but beyond that, I couldn't really say. We had a good time, mostly in the bedroom. And we had stimulating conversations, usually after our bedroom adventures. I found myself looking forward to our late night pillow talk more and more.

Bub finished undressing and slipped under the covers, but instead of his usual innuendo-laden banter, he let out a heavy sigh and snuggled in next to me, wrapping his arms innocently around my waist.

"What's wrong?"

He frowned apologetically. "I'm exhausted. These parties aren't as easy as they used to be." He laid his head on my shoulder, letting his breath rush over my skin. "I didn't find out anything useful tonight. My meeting with Cindy is not going to go well tomorrow morning."

It wasn't like Bub to unload his work worries on me. I rubbed a hand down his back. "What were you trying to find out about?"

"Hades' manor was broken into last week."

"In Tartarus? Just down the way from your place?"

"Yes," he said softly. "Another reason for the party locale tonight. I'd like to know whether the rebels are targeting Tartarus, or if the attack was random."

"Are Hades and Persephone all right?"

"Yes. They weren't home. Their vault was broken into and several valuables were taken though. Everyone in all the hells knows that I'll be here tonight, so my estate would be a perfect target. I had Jack put out several replicas of the valuables I keep there, so we'll see if anything is missing tomorrow."

"Did you suspect any of your guests?"

He groaned. "Everyone I invited with a grudge against Hades or with a history of thieving showed up, and furthermore, they all seemed genuinely surprised and concerned when I mentioned the incident. Unless the culprit makes a go at my place and is caught by a surveillance camera, I've got nothing."

"I'm sorry." I ran my hand over his back a few more times, and he was soon snoring.

I grinned to myself and closed my eyes. So much for tearing my dress off. This was definitely a first. I couldn't say that I minded much. It was nice to see that he could let his guard down around me. No one likes to be the only vulnerable one in a relationship. Besides, I had a big day coming up too.

There was a tsunami that had just hit an oblivious yacht club off the east coast of Australia earlier in the day. Come morning, about a hundred souls were going to be floating around in the ocean, waiting to be harvested.

It sounded more like a job for the Recovery Unit to me, but Grim had issued a permit to take the ship over, so I felt a little better about it. It seemed like a good job to take Kevin on too. He didn't really need my guidance very often, but it was still best to give him the easy jobs this early in his apprenticeship. It would also keep Grim from blaming any of Kevin's mistakes on me for not spending enough time training him.

CHAPTER 4

*"While I thought that I was learning how to live,
I have been learning how to die."
-Leonardo da Vinci*

Bub was all apologies in the morning. He brought me breakfast in bed, with gourmet coffee, fresh strawberries, and the promise of a spectacular makeup date that didn't involve hoards of cutthroat demons. I started the day off with a spring in my step and even caught myself humming on the way down the dock to my ship.

Saul and Coreen trotted on either side of me, their tails wagging in time. They were going to have a blast today, herding the hundred-plus souls on board. They had really been an asset on the Posy Unit so far, and they loved their work.

I dished out the harvest jobs without acknowledging Kate Evan's grunts of disapproval. I didn't say out loud that I knew about the complaint she had filed, but I'm sure she could figure that out for herself, considering I gave her all the shit jobs for the day. Mass food poisoning, anyone?

Josie was a little bummed that she wasn't going on the harvest with Kevin and me, but we all agreed to meet up for lunch at the Phantom Café in Limbo City.

Josie and Kevin seemed to be doing well together. I had really expected their age gap to become a problem over time, especially with Josie's superiority complex when it came to reapers younger than herself. I guess Kevin didn't mind letting her boss him around. Of course, he was a goody-two-shoes like her, so maybe he didn't require that much bossing.

Once everyone had coined off to their harvest sites, Kevin and I prepped the ship for crossing over to the Pacific Ocean. The permit was actually a spelled slip of paper with an incantation written on it. It was designed to open up a portal, and it held just enough juice for one round trip to and from the mortal realm.

"Anchors aweigh!" Kevin shouted from the bow of the ship.

I made my way to the forecastle deck and pulled the permit from my robe pocket, clearing my throat. Incantations made me nervous, especially ones that I only had one shot at to get right. If I screwed up, the best case scenario would be that the permit became void, and I would have to get a new one, throwing our whole schedule off. In the worst case scenario, the ship could be split in half, and then we would have to decide which realm we wanted to sink in. I took a shaky breath and sent up a tiny prayer to whoever was listening, before painfully tackling the Latin verse.

"Patefacio porta quondam mihi in mortale saeculum," I said to the vast nothingness before the ship.

The air was suddenly full of static. My hair crackled in my ears as it lifted upward, and a seam opened in the emptiness, giving me a view of a similar setting just outside of Eternity. A wind that hadn't been present before filled our sails, and we were propelled forward.

Kevin appeared beside me, looking a little green around the edges. Sailing was his least favorite part of the job, but he managed to keep his breakfast down this morning.

"Have you done this before?" he asked, frowning at the narrow opening into the Pacific Ocean.

"Nope."

The ship slowed and creaked as the hull rubbed against the edges of the portal.

Kevin turned to me. "Are you sure you did the incantation right?"

"Nope."

"Fuck." He looked back at the portal and held his breath as it widened to accommodate the size of the ship.

It occurred to me a little late that Grim might have issued me the permit in order to sabotage my perfect record as a unit captain. As the widest part of the hull slipped free of the portal and into the Pacific, it also became feasible that he simply did it to scare the bejesus out of me. Either way, my pulse slowed as the portal closed behind us. I sighed a breath of relief as Kevin retched over the side of the ship.

"I hate you," he groaned.

I patted his back. "You wanna open it on the way back through?"

He retched again. "I think I'll pass."

"Suit yourself." I shrugged and went to ready the ship tenders, which were just a couple of small motorboats, large enough to hold maybe a dozen souls each if we crammed them in. If everything went smoothly, we would be able to gather everyone up within a few hours.

The sky was overcast and the air was salty and thick with the smell of wreckage and regurgitated sea life. A gust of wind circled the deck, tugging at the hem of my robe and blowing my black curls over my face. Another storm was brewing. I just hoped it held off long enough for us to finish our harvest.

For about half a mile in all directions, bloated human remains and chunks of fiberglass littered the Pacific. It was the peak of summer, so the bodies were already decomposing. I noticed one of the closer victims was missing a leg. This day was traumatic enough without having to navigate through shark-infested waters, but I couldn't think of another fish that might take a bite that big. With all the storms plaguing the area, I was honestly surprised any fish would be brave enough to risk life and fin for a snack.

Kevin finally pulled himself together and joined me at the first tender. His brow furrowed as he took in the davits and pulley system that suspended the boat a good twenty feet above the water.

"You know how this works, right?" I asked.

"Not really. Have you used these before?"

"Nope."

"Great." He looked green again.

I sighed. "Look, it's not brain surgery. Hop in the boat and use the winch in the center platform to lower it. Once you've reached the water, unhook the ropes at either end, and you're good to go. How hard can it be?"

Kevin's jaw clenched, and for a minute, I thought he might retch over the side again.

I rolled my eyes. "Let's do this first run together, and then you're taking a boat out on your own. We don't have a lot of time before the next storm is supposed to hit."

"Thanks, Lana." His shoulders sagged and he waited for me to board the boat first.

It was almost as easy as I made it sound. The ropes hanging from the davits were stiff and crusted with decades of salt buildup. They caused enough concern that I made a mental note to have them replaced soon. The motorboats were electric, which was a good call on Josie's part. She had insisted that we forgo gas-powered tenders, since the fuel could stale and leave us stranded. She had also been the one

27

to install the boats, and I never got around to testing them out myself.

Kevin's confidence surged again after we reached the water. He steered the boat over to our first catch. It was the legless body I had spied from the deck. She was facedown, like everyone else. Her skin looked like a wrinkled sheet that just barely kept her innards from spilling out into the ocean. She was missing her bikini top. The bottoms were leopard print, and they matched the strap of the wedged heel attached to her remaining foot. Kevin nudged one of the boat oars under her arm and flipped her over in the water.

"Oh, good god," he groaned, taking a step back in the boat.

Our catch was missing more than a leg. Her lips and eyes lids had been nibbled away by smaller fish. I had a feeling most of the bodies would have similar B-movie qualities about them. Kevin's shoulders heaved, and I wondered just how much he had eaten for breakfast. I gently pushed him aside and reached down, pressing my fingertips through the doughy flesh of our catch's chest.

Her soul shuddered free, and I gasped as she reached up with a ghostly hand and took my arm. I pulled her aboard the boat. Kevin found an abandoned towel and threw it around her shoulders. It was an odd concept, but whatever clothing a person happened to be wearing when they died, copied over to their soul once we harvested it. From the looks of things, we were going to have a ship full of half-naked souls by the time we were done. I could think of a few towels and some spare clothes in mine and Josie's cabin, but it wasn't going to be enough.

The new soul blinked a few times, which was easier to witness now that she had eyelids again.

"Some party," she giggled and then sobered as she took in her surroundings. "What the—"

Kevin placed a firm hand on her shoulder. "It's okay. You're safe here." He led her over to a bench at the back of the boat while I used an oar to poke at another floater.

This one was missing half of his toes and a good chunk of his face. I could see the edges of his eye sockets. Death was never pretty, but drowning in the ocean had to be near the top of the list for worst post-mortem makeovers.

After another twenty minutes, we had a full boat of disoriented souls. Most of them were still trying to convince themselves that they were just too hung-over to make sense of what had happened. A portly little redhead kept commenting on how God must have heard her prayers, since there were so many survivors. I didn't have the heart to break the truth to her just yet. Plus, she seemed like the type that could inflict mass hysteria.

After we herded the first lot down into the ship's hold, where the hounds took over guard duty, Kevin found the nerve to take a boat down by himself so that I could make use of the second tender. Since the souls were friendly with one another, we were able to pack them in even tighter, reducing the harvest to three additional trips, using both boats. The assortment of sofas and picnic tables scattered around the hold were filling up fast.

We were on our last run when the clouds shifted. The sky fell dark and the wind whistled across the water, rousing the waves. It almost sounded like a girl was singing in the distance. Maybe the redhead had switched from prayers to hymns. The small circle of souls on my boat huddled in against each other. I had one more to collect.

Kevin was already lifting his last lot out of the water. He turned his face into the wind, letting it blow his hair back as he frowned at the encroaching storm on the horizon. "Shake a leg, boss lady!" he shouted over the rumbling thunder.

My boat bumped the last body, a lanky kid who probably wasn't even drinking age yet. I reached out for him, but just before I could make contact, a slender hand shot out of the water and coiled around my wrist. My resolve shattered, and I let loose a screech that could be heard for miles.

A bubbly laughter boiled to the surface, and a head soon followed. The mermaid was not of the storybook variety. Her dark hair was tangled and matted with seaweed, and her teeth were green and caked with muck. It looked like she had just eaten a mud pie.

"My mistress would like a word, child," she said in her haunting, siren voice.

"W-what?" I croaked.

Three more mermaid heads broke the surface of the water, but paused halfway, revealing only their tangled hair and glassy, fish-like eyes.

"Eurynome, daughter of the ocean," the mermaid announced, just as the sea bubbled and sprayed a mist into the air.

Eurynome, the Grecian mermaid goddess, rose from the water, suspended on the back of a wave that continued to crest without actually moving from its fixed place beneath her. She was more or less the vision most little girls conjured when they thought of mermaids, with glistening scales and golden hair, topped with a white coral reef crown.

"Y-you're not supposed to be on this side," I said, almost in a whisper.

The goddess frowned at me. "And why is that? Because some new rule was implemented? And you really suppose I, a deity of the boundless sea, would be confined by such rules?" She smirked.

"What do you want?" I asked, taking my eyes from her long enough to frown down at the mermaid still squeezing my wrist.

"Nothing much. Your consort has been sticking his nose where it doesn't belong. I thought I might discourage that behavior by sending him a little message."

"Message?" I echoed.

She nodded to the mermaid holding my wrist, and the sea hag yanked me from the boat. I barely had half a breath in my lungs before she pulled me under, wrapping her arms around my torso as we sank deeper. I kicked until the muscles in my legs burned and my chest felt like it might explode. The water grew colder and darker, and just as the light began to slip away, an arrow zipped past me, slicing through the mermaid's pale shoulder and releasing a purple cloud of blood into the water. Her grip didn't slack at first, but then a second arrow torpedoed past me and lodged itself in the thick of her tail. She screamed under water, and it was beautiful. The siren pull of her voice was magnified, and I was almost tempted to drown, right then and there, for the chance that she might speak again. Instead, she pushed away from me, wincing at the arrow stuck in her tail as she hurried to put distance between us.

I mustered what energy I had left and kicked for the surface. Kevin's hand shot through the water and grabbed my shoulder. He had coined himself from the ship to my boat in record time. Josie's spare bow was strapped across his back. He pulled me up and into the boat, just as another mermaid surfaced, screeching in his face. Kevin curled his hands up over his head and squeezed his eyes shut, and then I saw the blood in his ears. His moans echoed out over the water, vibrating in tune with the nearing thunder.

Eurynome was gone, but her mermaid minions were still lying in wait. I could hear them whispering beneath the waves. They weren't finished with us yet.

"Kevin!" I choked up water and gasped for air. "Kevin! Can you hear me?" I pulled him back away from the edge of the boat, and fired up the engine.

My last catch bobbed in the water, just a few feet away. I clenched my teeth, knowing that a mermaid was probably waiting for me to take the bait. I'd be damned if some sea wench was going to ruin my perfect harvest record as captain.

31

There was a coil of rope under the center platform of the tender. I tied it to a boat cleat and fashioned a noose out of the opposite end. Then I very carefully looped it over the head of my last harvest. Once he was secure, I opened throttle like the kraken had been released.

I could hear the disgruntled mermaids behind us, and I just knew they would give chase. Kevin was still curled up on the floor, moaning in agony. Keeping one hand on the tiller, I reached down and squeezed his shoulder as tight as I could. I needed him to snap out of it. There was no way I could pull this stunt off on my own. He finally blinked up at me. The blood from his ears trailed down his jawline and throat.

"Can you hear me?" I asked him again.

The confusion streaked across his face was answer enough. I pointed to the ship and then to the winch in the center platform. He glanced behind us, and then slowly nodded, pulling himself upright. I didn't bother looking back. The mermaids would be underwater so they could have the element of surprise.

I didn't kill the engine until we were almost on top of the ship. Kevin set to work reattaching the davit ropes, while I reached over the stern of the boat to harvest the last soul. I couldn't afford to be gentle. There was no telling how close the mermaids were. I reached down and ripped the soul from his body like it was a shuck on an ear of corn. He tumbled on board and fell flat on his ghostly face.

"Holy shit! What's your problem?" he snapped.

The other souls on the boat, who had been shell-shocked and silent since Eurynome and her mermaids appeared, moved to help the new arrival. I ignored them and went to tie up the other end of the boat. Kevin took hold of the winch and wrestled us into the air. He cranked the handle for all he was worth, pulling us further and further out of the mermaids' reach.

Frantic splashing from below drew my attention. A trio of mermaids were taking turns throwing each other up out of the water. They were too far away to reach the boat, but the dangling body of my last catch was an easy grab. One latched onto his legs, throwing the boat off balance. The souls clung to each other as we rocked back and forth, knocking against the side of the ship.

"Shit!" I fumbled with the knot tied around the boat cleat, until I remembered the hunting knife in my boot. After everything I'd been through, it was little wonder that I found myself more heavily armed these days.

I sawed at the crusty rope, not quite severing it before one of the mermaids of doom pulled herself up onto the side of the boat. She gave me a victorious snarl, but it was short-lived. I slammed the palm of my hand up under her chin, throwing her head back. She lost her grip on the boat railing and just barely found the rope again. After another split second of hacking, that gave way too, sending the mermaid plummeting back into the ocean along with the dead body. Kevin's ears were still bleeding, but I could have sworn I saw him smile.

Saul and Coreen were waiting when we reached the deck. I left the souls for them to herd down to the hold and made a mad dash for the bow of the ship, hoping that I could get the incantation underway before the mermaids dreamed up some new way to sabotage our harvest.

"Patefacio porta quondam mihi in spiritum mundo," I said, all in a single breath.

The portal split open again and the ship lurched forward. I only hoped the mermaids stayed behind. Of course, the portal spit us out only a short distance from the harbor, where a couple nephilim guards waited.

The temperature was cooler on the Sea of Eternity. I was still soaked from my little swim with the mermaids, so my teeth began to chatter. Kevin stepped up beside me and touched my arm. He didn't look so good.

"I still can't hear anything," he said awkwardly.

"Meng Po?" I mouthed.

His nose scrunched up, but he nodded his head.

CHAPTER 5

*"Never take a solemn oath.
People think you mean it."
-Norman Douglas*

I really didn't like Meng Po. She was crabby and hateful, and I still owed her a favor for the vote she had cast to help me get on the Posy Unit, which is probably why she slammed the door in my face when we showed up at her temple along the southern edge of Limbo City.

"Damn it, Meng! Open up!" I pounded my fist against the door.

Jai Ling, Meng's child soul servant, opened the door and threw her arms around me. "Lana! It's good to see you."

"You too," I laughed, returning her squeeze. "What's gotten under your boss's skin today?"

"The same as usual." Jai Ling shrugged. "She's upset that we've been here for nearly a year, and she still hasn't made any significant changes to the soul purification system at the factory. Your name might have come up a time or two also."

"I bet." I gave her a strained smile.

"So what brings you all the way out here?" She opened the door wider and welcomed us inside.

"Kevin got his eardrums blown by a siren this morning."

"Wow. Really?"

"Yeah. Looks like we're still popular targets among the rebels. Do you have a tea that might help?"

"I'm sure I could whip something up." She grinned at my surprise. "Meng says I'm a natural."

Jai Ling was the only youth living in Limbo City. The Fates didn't employ child souls. It had something to do with their time here not being long enough to fulfill a factory contract before they needed to be installed back into the mortal realm. And since only souls who worked at the Fates' factory were allowed to live in Limbo City, there were no merry-go-rounds in our park and no kid menus in our restaurants. Grim had given Jai Ling to Meng Po after she was voted onto the Afterlife Council. The old hag had to leave her current soul slaves in Diyu, the Chinese hell, and settled for the aid of a single soul servant for her century long term in Limbo City.

Jai Ling was a timid little thing when I first met her. She seemed more at home now, bouncing around Meng's creepy temple in her pink dress.

"Make yourselves comfortable in there." She waved her hand towards one of the rooms adjacent to the foyer. "I'll be just a few minutes."

Kevin plopped down on the corner of the bed, and I took a seat on a wicker bench against the far wall. The room was familiar, with its bamboo paneling and big paper lantern in the corner.

Usually I was the reason for the visits to Meng's temple. I still had a grayish handprint on my neck from where a demon had tried to strangle me after she set my apartment on fire last spring. The rebels have always been a nuisance, ever since the peace treaty went into effect, but I had never really noticed them until I started working my way up the corporate ladder.

While we waited, I slipped out my cell phone and called Josie to update her. She was not thrilled, but agreed to pick up the rest of Kevin's souls. I was just glad that we wouldn't have to ask for Kate's help. She was smug enough without the encouragement. She and Alex had a ferryboat for delivering their souls. It was a good thing too. The ten minutes I had to see them each morning always seemed to max out my brat tolerance for the day.

When I hung up with Josie, I slid out the phone's keyboard. Bub was probably still in his meeting with Cindy, but I knew he'd want to know as soon as possible about Eurynome. I hated texting. There was something that felt sacrilegious about butchering language in order to squeeze a conversation into a bite-sized format, but I felt obligated to, since Bub had bought me the fancy little gadget.

U pissed off mermaids. They attack. I'm OK.

The phone dinged almost immediately.

???

I tried again.

Eurynome and co. said u r nosy. Tried 2 drown me.

I added one of those little yellow cartoon heads, the one with the crossed out eyes and hanging tongue.

Where r u?

Meng's. Kevin can't hear.

???

Xoxo.

Bub hated it when I ended a text conversation that way, but really, he was lucky I had held out that long. He would call me later for the rest of the details.

Jai Ling was back before we knew it, carrying a cup of steaming tea. Like most of Meng's healing concoctions, it smelled worse than sewage. At least Kevin had already gotten rid of his breakfast. Otherwise, the tea would have done it for him. He staked me with a hopeless frown as I stood.

I pulled my soul docket from my robe and tore off a blank page so I could scribble a note for him before I left.

Josie will be by later to check on you. I have to get back to work. Great job today! I couldn't have asked for a better apprentice.

He laughed when he read the last line. I hadn't asked for an apprentice at all. I was barely qualified to have one. I still felt lucky that I had ended up with Kevin, and not just because he had saved my ass today. He graduated from the academy at the top of his class. Honestly, he deserved better. But since Grim had dumped him off on me after his original mentor, Coreen Bendura, had died, we were both trying to make the best of it. He was currently the only reaper from his generation working on one of the specialty units, so being my apprentice wasn't a complete loss.

I left the temple and ran into Meng at the pond in the front garden. She was bent over the railing of an arched bridge, feeding breadcrumbs to fat goldfish as they kissed the surface of the water with gaping mouths. She dusted her hands off and gave me the stink eye as I approached.

"Worthless girl. Oath breaker," she grumbled under her breath.

I stopped to glare back at her. "I haven't broken any oaths. You asked me to mention your request to Grim, but he already knows what you want."

"Of course he knows! I told him. You were to remind him. Keep it fresh!" She poked a crooked finger at her temple for emphasis.

I winced away from her screeching. "Today. I'll tell him again today. All right?"

"Humph." She turned her back to me and began feeding the fish again, grumbling to herself in Chinese.

I hated owing deities. They always wanted to collect at the most inconvenient times. I sighed and hurried off down the gravel path that led back into the city. There was a tornado in Kansas that needed to be harvested yet today.

CHAPTER 6

*"We have no reliable guarantee that the afterlife
will be any less exasperating than this one, have we?"*
-Noel Coward

Grim's eyes looked like they had caught on fire. I'm not sure I had ever seen him so worked up. I just hoped that the other captains had gone home for the day, because I was sure if there was anyone left on the seventy-fifth floor, they were getting quite the earful.

"What the hell am I going to do with you?" Grim paced back and forth before the wall of a window behind his desk. "You're by far the biggest liability this company has ever seen."

"Hey, I didn't lose any souls today," I protested.

"You have rebels on your tail at every turn. If that wasn't bad enough, you bed men in powerhouse positions, making yourself a secondhand target for their enemies as well. Then you consort with council members in order to obtain the most compromising position a reaper can hold. And I know, I KNOW, you've got something going on with Horus."

I cleared my throat, too tired to argue with him again.

Grim sighed. "So you didn't lose any souls *today*. Forgive me if I'm not overcome with gratitude and newfound approval for your increasingly hazardous lifestyle." He rolled his eyes and plopped down in the chair behind his desk.

I cleared my throat again, trying to build up the nerve needed in order to stick my foot in my mouth.

Grim looked up from his paperwork. "Why are you still in my office?"

I crossed my legs and tried not to look as nervous as I felt. "I spoke with Meng today, when I dropped Kevin off to be treated."

His upper lip curled back. Grim didn't particularly care for any of the council members, but Meng Po was his least favorite by far. He despised her even more than he despised Horus.

"And?" he growled.

I swallowed. "And she wanted me to remind you about the meeting she requested to have with the Fates."

"Since when do you care what Meng wants?" Grim's eyes were beginning to glow again.

"Since she doctored me up after the demon attacks last spring."

"Don't you mean since she voted you onto the Posy Unit?"

I folded my hands in my lap. "Well, that too."

He gave me a vicious smile. "Sounds like maybe you made a promise you were expecting me to fulfill? That's really too bad. I'm busy making good on my own promises. If you want to help Meng out so bad, go talk to the Fates yourself." His face fell back into an annoyed frown. "Now get out my office, Ms. Harvey."

"Gladly."

I hightailed it out of Reapers Inc., not bothering to stop by my office. I couldn't stand to be there for another minute.

The rest of my day was progressively worse. The tornado harvest had been miserable, especially without Kevin's help. I had run into a couple members of the Recovery Unit, who were harvesting souls in the same area. One reaper actually had the nerve to accuse me of poaching his souls. Oh, how I had wanted to tell him off, but I was short on time and minus a reaper, so I called his boss instead. Right in front of him.

Bub still hadn't called, which was unusual for him. After a long ride down the elevator, I flipped open my phone and tried his number again. It went straight to voicemail. I had already left him a message, so I hung up and pushed through the glass double doors of Reapers Inc.

I blew out a frustrated breath I hadn't realized I'd been holding. The air was crisp and the sidewalks were nearly empty. It would have been a great day for a long walk with the hounds around the park, but they had already gone home with Josie. Usually Kevin was tasked with the duty, since Grim didn't want them in the office. I thought about taking a walk by myself anyway. I needed the fresh air. Not a minute after the thought hit me, my pocket began to vibrate. I groaned. My cell phone was still on silent, so as to not upset Grim any more than necessary during our meeting, which meant that it was the spelled coin Winston had given me. It was his extra special annoying way of summoning me for a meeting. Like I needed another one of those today.

I slipped into the park and ventured a safe distance into the rose hedges before flipping Winston's coin in the air. Coin travel had been deactivated in Limbo City last spring, but Winston had found a way to spell a special coin, just for me. If Grim found out about it, or found out about our little visits at all, I was so beyond screwed.

The coin sucked me through to Winston's private pocket realm, the Throne of Eternity. The sky was brighter there than it had been in Limbo, which wasn't too terribly surprising. It was perpetually noon in his realm. Grim thought it made the little cottage more secure. I thought it was a farce. A dozen of the Nephilim Guard would have made the place more secure, but to Grim, that would have just been a dozen more people who knew how to undermine his rule and take over Eternity.

Winston wore a pair of faded blue jeans and a green tee shirt. He leaned against the open doorway of the cottage with his arms folded gently over his chest, looking older and not quite as comical as when he had first arrived in Eternity. Holding the afterlife together was taking a toll on him. It was hard to see any residual soul matter leftover from the small, cancer-ridden boy I had harvested from a Cleveland hospital, not quite a year ago. After drinking one of Meng's teas, he had reverted back to an ancient past life, King Tut. His skin was darker now, and he had a full head of black hair that he kept tied back in a low ponytail. He was also man sized, although just barely. Tut had been eighteen when he died. To me, he would always be the ten-year-old Winston.

"Lana, it's been awhile." He smiled as I walked up the front steps and welcomed me inside with the wave of an arm.

"How are things?" I asked, knowing I would probably get a vague answer before he jumped in with the same lecture I'd heard half a dozen times over the past few months.

"Things suck. So pretty much the same as always." He laughed and plopped down on a sofa in the living room.

I sat down across from him and crossed my arms and legs, readying myself for a conversation I almost knew by heart at this point.

Winston gave me a pleading smile, but it soon dissolved with a sigh. "I don't suppose you've come across any potential replacements lately, have you?"

"I promise, you will be the first to know when I do."

His eyes glossed over, and he swallowed hard. "I don't know how much longer I'm going to hold out. Things... have been happening to me." He rubbed his hands together slowly and then turned them upward to examine his palms.

"What things?" I sat up straighter and unfolded from my defensive posture.

Winston tucked his hands between his knees and looked down at the floor. "Any time I try to alter the fabric of Eternity, even in the smallest way, I can see through myself. It's like... it's like I'm fading."

"Fading?" I whispered.

Khadija, the last soul who had served on the throne, had lasted well over a thousand years. Of course, she was an original believer. All this time I had been comparing the difference between her and Winston to the difference between a new tire and spare. Now it was starting to look more like the difference between a new tire and rubber band. It was an uncomfortable analogy, but the throne job wore away at a soul like the road wore away the tread on a tire. It was the most accurate way to put it.

I reached out and put my hand on Winston's knee. "I'm really trying to find a replacement. It's just harder without the Fates' help this time."

"But you can't ask for their help without drawing too much suspicion. We have to be careful. I haven't even told Grim about my... problem. He ignored Khadija for centuries, until she had to take matters into her own hands. I don't have centuries. I'm not even sure if I have months left in me."

"There has to be some way to speed up the search."

Winston shrugged. "You could always ask for Maalik's help. He's the only other one who knows about the Throne of Eternity. He understands the importance of this position."

I cringed at the mention of Maalik and dodged the subject. "Maybe I can find a way to check out the Fates' records without them knowing. Meng Po wants a meeting with them, and Grim's refusing to set it up. Maybe I can arrange the meeting myself."

Winston grabbed my arm. "I don't think that's such a good idea, Lana. The Fates don't take deception lightly."

I sighed. "I don't really have much of a choice, and tempting fate seems to be a specialty of mine lately."

CHAPTER 7

*"Fate is for those too weak
to determine their own destiny."
-Kamran Hamid*

I am not a very good liar. I know how it's supposed to be done. I know that lies should be spoken with confidence, and eye contact should be maintained, but I have a really hard time following these rules. Luckily, I was able to skip making eye contact with the receptionist at the Three Fates Factory since I spoke with her over the phone. The uncomfortable conversation I'd had with Grim came in handy too. I was able to stretch the truth, almost to its breaking point, in order to secure an appointment with the Fates on Thursday afternoon. I mean, Grim did say that I should talk to them myself, right?

I watched Meng shuffle herself out of a cab as I waited across the street in front of the factory. The old bag had put on her most formal and elaborate dress, and she was wearing makeup. Sort of. The colors all seemed a bit off, and I wasn't sure if it had more to do with the fact that they were outdated or if it was because I had never seen rouge on a bulldog before. She noticed me and smiled a big awkward smile, full of yellowed teeth splotched with pink lipstick. I didn't even try to smile back at her.

The Three Fates Factory loomed above us, and I was sweating bullets under my work robe. I had left it on, since it looked more professional than the jeans and tank top I wore underneath. I'd come straight from my last harvest. Kate was in a better mood with me today. I'd cut myself some slack, in order to make the early afternoon appointment, so she got a fuller harvest docket. It would help balance out her and Alex's little mishap on Tuesday with the chicken and the hounds.

Kevin's hearing was still a little iffy, so I'd paired him up with Josie for the day. They had both been giddy about it, so neither had bothered to question my early leave. I told them I had an appointment and left it at that.

As Meng and I walked through the front doors of the Three Fates Factory, I decided that no matter how the meeting went, I was not coming back. No way. The Fates gave me the heebie-jeebies. I just wanted to find out something useful and get the heck out of there. Hopefully Meng would be a good enough cover, and my promise to her would be fulfilled too. Killing two birds with one stone was always nice.

A semi-circle desk spread out in the lobby of the factory, where two souls were furiously typing and chattering into headsets. Down a wide hall to their right sat half a dozen baffle gates leading into the heart of the factory. Staggered office doors stretched down a hallway to the left. The ceiling was high and the walls were bare, save for several draped coils of fabric hanging behind the receptionists, probably intended to reduce echoing in the cave of a room.

"Do you have an appointment?" One of the receptionists noticed us and slipped off her headset.

"Meng Po, escorted by Lana Harvey," I announced.

"Ah, yes. The reaper." She grimaced. "Atropos will meet with you in her personal office, third door on the right." She pointed down the hallway of doors.

I nodded my thanks, since I'd lost my voice, and apparently my senses.

Atropos was not the Fate I wanted to see. She was the oldest of the sisters and the most grim, deciding the when and how of a soul's demise by snipping their life thread with her abhorred shears. Of course, the shears were more of a metaphor these days. She kept them proudly framed in a shadowbox behind her desk, the bleached bone handle and silver blades contrasting against a soft black velvet backdrop. She still decided when and how humans died, but that was all programmed into souls nowadays, not by the spinning and cutting of thread.

When Meng and I reached Atropos' office, the door was open, but I paused to rap my knuckles against the doorframe anyway.

"Enter." Atropos was seated behind her desk with a pair of wide frames sitting low on the bridge of her nose. She motioned us inside with one hand, never taking her eyes from the file she was reading. Her desk was stacked high with them. All four walls of her office were floor to ceiling shelves, mostly stuffed with thick volumes containing faded Latin titles along their spines. Occasionally, a bronze or marble bust would peek out from a gap in the stacks.

Meng nestled herself into one of the plush chairs in front of the desk, but I remained standing behind her, like a good escort. Even so, I felt out of place, not at all like the fly on the wall I had hoped to be. This was a room for gods to convene in. I had no business being here, and when Grim found out, he was not going to be amused.

When Atropos finally looked up, she gave us a bored sigh and slipped off her reading glasses, letting them dangle from a cord around her neck.

"Lana Harvey, I must say, I'm surprised to see you. Grim did say that you had balls though." She gave me a lopsided smile and stood.

As the most business oriented of the weird sisters, Atropos knew how to present herself. She was a classic beauty, in modest pumps and a black pencil skirt. Her navy blouse brought out the blue of her eyes, and her shiny black victory rolls were straight out of a glamour magazine from the forties. She made her way over to an oversized globe in the corner and flipped a latch along the equator, revealing a minibar beneath the top dome.

"Drink?" she asked, pouring herself a lowball glass full of vodka.

"No, thank you," I said. My throat felt like sandpaper.

Meng's nose curled upward, but she echoed a polite, "No, thank you."

Atropos looked down at her for the first time. "Lady Meng, we finally meet. I suppose it was bound to happen sooner or later."

"Sooner would have been better," Meng grumbled, "but today will do."

Atropos chuckled softly and sipped at her vodka. "And what, pray tell, is your business with the Fates?"

"Your purification method no good. You need my teas," Meng said matter-of-factly.

"Is that so? How did we ever get by these past... what is it now? Thirteen? Fourteen centuries?"

"By skin of teeth, you ask me. Too many souls go into sea. They come out, they know something, not solid, but enough to keep them from believing. We need them to believe if they to fuel the afterlives, and not just your factory."

"What exactly are you suggesting?" Atropos set her vodka down hard on the desk.

Meng cackled, flashing her lipstick stained teeth. "You think I don't see what you doing, girl? You think I am only one concerned?"

"Well, won't my sisters be disappointed to hear that you don't approve of our methods. If they're on schedule today, they should be in the roost. Shall we go see what they have to say about your teas?"

Meng stood and smoothed the front of her dress, waiting for Atropos to lead the way. We followed her out of her office and back down the hall. As I walked behind the two deities, I took in as much of my surroundings as possible, taking particular note of a door boldly labeled RECORDS. If there was a file cabinet somewhere containing details about high priority souls, that room was as good as any.

We passed the receptionists in the lobby and pushed through the baffle gates leading to the other side of the building.

The factory was a busy little hub. Several hundred souls worked for the Fates. Their duties not only replaced what the Fates were once responsible for, but also what many other deities used to do in order to prepare souls for reentry into the mortal realm.

Some deities were retired due to a reduced number of followers, and some were retired simply because they wanted to be. They welcomed the Fates takeover. There were a few deities who still took care of souls personally, but only if they were considered worthy and important to their particular faith. It was the same way with soul harvesting. Grim's business took care of the vast majority of souls leaving the mortal realm, and the Fates took care of the majority of souls entering the mortal realm. It was a tidy little process that simplified things in Eternity for everyone.

Reincarnation is a pretty big deal among the deities. Aside from Christianity and Islam, it's accepted by most other faiths as a part of the soul cycle. Buddhism, Hinduism, Paganism, and even some tribal and traditional folk religions depend on reincarnation. Many Orthodox Jews believe in reincarnation as well. It's one of the deeper teachings found in the Torah. Although Christianity and Islam do not promote belief in reincarnation, after a soul's been in a hell or a heaven long enough, they're more or less ready to go back to the other side. Even some of the deities prefer the mortal realm from time to time. Immortality can become unbearable if one doesn't have something to continually occupy their time in a meaningful way.

Atropos led us to the end of the hall where it bloomed into a cavern of a room half exposed to the sea, pushing in through a domed cage wall. Two giant concrete faces resembling Greek gods projected from opposite walls, spewing water into the interior pool, where it was churned into the soul matter by a rustic water wheel. The wheel scooped up bucketfuls of the mixture, sloshing it into a steaming trough on a conveyor belt. A dozen souls on either side raked through the solution, separating the soul matter with silver combs, before it disappeared into a fiery oven.

Atropos pointed haughtily at each element of the process, starting with the faces on the walls. "Water from the Lethe, the Greek river of forgetfulness, imported from the Hypnos Caves. The elbow buckets of the wheel are a modified version of Hygieia's bowl. The steam bath trough is a design of the Aztec goddess, Tlazolteotl. The purifying fires in the oven were provided by the Celtic goddess Brighid." She looked back and raised an eyebrow at Meng. "Still doubting our intentions here?"

Meng harrumphed. "Still room for improvement."

Atropos sighed. "The roost is this way."

We followed her up a set of stone stairs at the back of the room that led beyond the wall the oven was built into. On the other side, another room full of factory workers was busy gathering the soul matter after it passed through the oven. They handled it with great care. When I looked closer, I could almost see forms taking shape in the blobs of soul matter. Each blob was taken to another station, where it was scanned by a gadget that looked like the kind of thing used at a crime scene to find hidden blood evidence.

Atropos waved a hand over the room. "This is where the souls are imprinted with their destinies."

More factory workers waited to take the imprinted little soul blobs up another set of stairs opposite of the set we were climbing.

The roost was a circular room, sitting atop the factory. Arched, Grecian windows opened on all sides above a tall ledge. The two sets of stairs emerged out of hatch-like openings along the outsides of the room, as the center was occupied by a shallow pool. Clotho, the youngest of the sisters, stood at the other hatch entrance, signifying the end of the factory assembly line. She more closely resembled the ancient paintings of the sisters, draped in a simple Grecian toga. A clipboard was gripped in one hand, and she wielded a pen in her other like a baton, directing the factory workers as they carefully placed the new souls into the pool.

The roost was called so because it was full of storks. They were luminous beings that were nearly transparent. I, along with most of Limbo City, was familiar with this part of the process. The ghostly storks that delivered souls to the unborn could be seen coming and going from the factory all day. I watched as one dipped into the pool, drawing a soul into its beak. It suddenly became more visible. The creature looked to Clotho, and they exchanged a nod before it took flight, leaving through one of the arched windows.

"The storks were a gift from Venus," Atropos continued. "The pools they nest in here are filled with ancient Nile waters, brought by Keket, the Egyptian goddess of childbirth. And the big cat napping under the lookout perch is one of the goddess Shashthi's, the Hindu protector of children."

Meng seemed to pale at the sight of the panther sized kitty. It wasn't much bigger than my hounds, so I didn't feel quite as concerned.

Atropos popped both hands on her hips and turned to us. "So tell me, now that you've toured the whole facility, where exactly do you suppose our sneaky betrayal is occurring?"

Meng shrugged, and her dress scrunched up on her shoulders. "My tea would still be asset."

Atropos rolled her eyes. "And what exactly can your teas do that our factory isn't doing already? We already have plenty of water being imported from the Lethe—"

"Ha! The Lethe," Meng sneered. "My tea is special recipe."

"Is there a problem?" Clotho asked, circling around the pool to our side of the roost.

"Old Lady Meng here thinks the best way to persuade us to include her nasty tea in the reincarnation process is by insulting our methods and accusing us of foul play." Atropos raised an eyebrow at Meng. "Does that about sum things up?"

Meng was stunned. She huffed her unease and spewed a few Chinese obscenities, trying to regain her composure. "How my fault if you find truth insulting?" she grumbled. "You cannot deny that my tea good for this job."

An amused grin spread over Clotho's face. She stepped forward to lay a gentle hand on Meng's arm. "Dear Meng, please, forgive my sister. Perhaps you would like to explain to us where you think your tea might be of most use?"

With that tension dissipating remark, I decided to make my move. "I hate to interrupt, but could you direct me to your restrooms?"

Clotho turned and blinked at me, as if she were seeing me for the first time. "They're just past the receptionists' desk."

"Thank you. I'll return shortly." I gave the deities a small bow, which only seemed polite in the company of so many, and hurried off to make my mischief.

The factory souls would be busy working for at least another hour, so I didn't run the risk of being spotted by one of them. The receptionists were really my only concern. They smiled politely as I passed the front desk. I could feel them watching me as I ducked inside the ladies' room. This was going to require a little more stealth than I had planned on.

I hated to do it, but it was my best shot at sneaking into the records room. I shut myself into the very last stall, clicked open my cell phone, and dialed Horus's number.

"Yes?" he answered on the first ring.

"I need a favor."

"Yes?" he answered again, but less cheerfully.

"Call the factory. Insist that you need to speak to Council Lady Meng immediately. Tell the secretary to take the phone directly to her."

"Okay. And what should I say to Meng once I have her on the line?"

"I don't care. Make something up. Tell her you need one of her teas desperately. She'll like that."

"Hmm. All right then." He wasn't even going to ask why.

"Good. Thanks." I hung up before he had the chance to change his mind.

I tiptoed out of the stall and pressed my ear against the restroom door, waiting until I heard one of the receptionists answer his call.

"Councilman Horus, how are y—oh! Oh, dear. She's in the roost with the sisters. I'll just page her—of course. Right away." Her heels clicked as she scampered around the desk and down the opposite hall.

I nudged the restroom door open and stole a glance towards the desk, making sure that the other receptionist was busy staring after her partner, before tiptoeing across the hall and down to the records room.

I could hardly believe my luck. The door was unlocked. I took a moment to do a happy little jig once I was safely inside. Then I set to work. The records room was no joke. This was surely what hell looked like for the cubical confined workers of the mortal realm. The cabinets in the room were divided into what I could only assume were files on souls currently in the mortal realm and souls residing in Eternity. There was a method to the Fates' madness, I was sure of it. Although, it was lost on me. Everything was in Latin, too. Sucktacular.

After entirely too long, I deciphered that the cabinets for the mortal realm were organized by date of death. I hurried to the front of the row, where the upcoming harvests would be listed, and opened a file drawer with sweaty hands. The files were arranged by time of day. I groaned and rested my forehead on the top of the file cabinet.

If I couldn't figure out which souls would be assigned to my unit, this was all for nothing. Even at that, there were too many files to read through each one in the next two minutes, which is about how long it would probably take before someone came to make sure I hadn't fallen in.

I quickly scanned the files until I noticed a section all marked for ten-thirty. I was guessing they went by Eastern European Time, the same time Greece was on. Surely those files were for a harvest that would be assigned to the Posy Unit. I pulled out the stack and fanned them across a long table behind me. My heart ached in my chest, it was beating so hard. I slipped my phone out of my pocket again and opened each file, snapping a quick picture of their first pages before closing them back. When I finished, I gathered up the files and stuffed them back in the drawer, quickly scanning for another large section marked with the same time.

I had just finished my fourth round and was busy cramming files back into the cabinet when I heard a throat clear behind me. I gasped and spun around, shutting the drawer with my back.

Lachesis, the middle sister of the Fates, stood in the doorway with her arms folded beneath her breasts. Her white summer dress was the epitome of graceful cheer, but her expression was full of malice. Tuffs of strawberry blond curls trembled around her face as she fumed. "Just what do you think you're doing in here, *reaper*?"

"I, uh, took a wrong turn?" I stammered.

"Try again."

I sighed. "Look, I just wanted to see what my schedule was going be like next week." I held my hands up innocently.

"Leave. Now." She stepped aside, leaving a narrow passage for me to slip by her on my way out the door. I held my breath as I did.

"Oh, and reaper?" she addressed me again.

I froze and looked over my shoulder.

"Don't let me catch you in here again. Do you understand?"

"Of course." I nodded sheepishly and continued on down the hall.

The receptionist gave me an odd look, but she didn't say anything as I passed her desk and pushed through a baffle gate to rejoin Meng and the other two Fates. I was ready for our visit to be over.

Apparently, Meng was too.

Clotho's sweet disposition had worn off. She mirrored her sister's defensive stance, with both hands grasping her hips and her chin pushed out in defiance. "The souls are like slumbering infants after being churned in the waters of the Lethe. They're easier to handle that way. Do you really expect us to wake them and force them to choke down your wretched concoction?" Clotho snapped.

Meng snarled back at her like a rabid lapdog, shaking the phone the other receptionist had brought to her in the air. "My tea good enough for Horus. Lazy girl! You sacrifice quality to keep job easy?" The phone slipped from her fingers and plunked into the pool.

Clotho cheeks puffed up as her eyes widened. "Lazy? Lazy! Why, I'll show you lazy, you old heifer—"

"We should really get going." I looped my arm under Meng's and steered her away from the furious Fates. They gaped after us, as if amazed that I would have the nerve to lay my hands on a deity, even one as loathsome as old Lady Meng.

"Thank you for your time," I called over my shoulder, trying to muffle Meng's cursing until I could get her out of earshot. Once we were down the two flights of stairs and she didn't need my aid any longer, Meng jerked her arm out of my grasp.

"Stupid girls. Stupid factory. Stupid excuse for lousy reincarnation job!" She turned and waved her fist in the direction of the roost, but we were a safe distance away now.

Just then, a whistle blew, and the souls in the main room began to stir, preparing to leave for the evening. Meng cringed at the oncoming hoard and let me take her arm again, leading us back down the hall and through the baffle gates. Luckily, Lachesis wasn't waiting in the lobby. I gave a quick nod to the receptionists as Meng and I exited the factory. Her taxi waited patiently.

Meng looked up at me and sighed, losing some of her fury as the creases around her eyes sagged. "Thank you. This meeting no good, but you keep your oath."

"You're welcome," I said slowly.

The thank you felt weird coming from Meng. It felt even weirder when she pulled a little teabag out of a pocket in her dress.

"For bad day," she said, stuffing it in my hand. "Not like fresh brew I make, but still good in pinch."

I helped her inside the cab and had barely closed the door, when my phone rang. "Hello?" I answered on the first ring.

"Miss me, love?" Bub said on the other end.

"You have no idea." I turned my back on the cab and the factory and made my way towards the nearest travel booth.

Bub sighed. "Sorry I didn't phone last night. After your text, my itinerary became substantially more complicated."

"Tell me about it."

"Apparently, your fishy visitor has been poaching Persephone's sirens."

"Really? So was one of the mer-hags responsible for the smash-and-grab at Hades' place in Tartarus?"

"I'm not entirely sure yet, although she does seem awfully offended by the accusation, hence the attempted drowning."

"How do you suppose she knew where to find me?"

"Well, you are rather popular lately, and your permit to take your ship over wasn't exactly top secret. I don't think she was sincerely hell-bent on killing you though. It was more for show, to prove a point, I think."

"Drama queen, much?" I grumbled.

"Exactly." Bub sighed. "I'm terribly sorry. I haven't made many friends during this investigation."

"I'm not making many friends lately either. Join the club."

Bub chuckled softly. "Let me make it up to you. Meet me for dinner tomorrow night?"

"Hmmm. I don't know. Will there be another assassination attempt?"

"Anything is possible."

"When and where?"

"The Hearth. Eight sharp."

"The Hearth?" I paused. "Are we just asking for trouble now?"

The Hearth was the fanciest restaurant in Limbo City. It also featured great big open windows on all sides. It was perfect for the paparazzi, which meant we would be on the cover of *Limbo's Laundry* in no time. We would also be nice and visible for anyone wanting to crash our dinner, or you know, kill us dead.

"I'm bringing a few undercovers with me," Bub said slyly.

"So I'm bait now?"

"No, pet. I just don't think we should allow anyone to keep us from having a good time."

"Mmm hmm." I wasn't convinced.

"I'll take you shoe shopping if anything bad happens."

I grinned. "You like shoe shopping more than I do."

"So it's a win-win." I could hear the smile in his voice.

I hung up giggling, but reality had not escaped me. Dinner at the Hearth was a really bad idea. I was most definitely being used as bait. I just hoped we could make it through desert before someone ruined our night.

CHAPTER 8

"True friends stab you in the front."
-Oscar Wilde

I really should have gone home after the nerve-shattering meeting with the Fates. I had fully intended to. Promise. But Purgatory Lounge was just too inviting. A shot or two of whiskey didn't sound half bad either. I immediately regretted the impulse the moment I stepped through the front door.

"Well, well! Look who we have here."

Gabriel was tanked. He was trying to hold himself upright with a pool cue, but his wings fluttered sporadically, trying to make up for the difference in his balance... or lack thereof.

I smiled tightly and took a seat at the bar. "Hey, Gabe."

Gabriel was my best friend. At least, he had been. We weren't on the best of terms lately. While he hadn't been thrilled about me dating Maalik at first, he had eventually warmed up to him. He was outright outraged about me dating Bub, and he hadn't even begun to thaw on the subject. What irked me the most was the fact that he was dating a demon too. I don't do double standards well.

Purgatory was fairly empty, but it was only Thursday. There were a few nephilim scattered around the pool tables, doing a little better job of staying upright than Gabriel, and a handful of souls, minding their own business in a corner booth. The place reeked of cheap cigarettes and barbeque, and the jukebox droned out sorrowful Elvis tunes, like it was lonely for the weekend crowd to come back around.

Xaphen, the owner of Purgatory Lounge and father of Gabriel's better half, appeared behind the bar and lit a cigarette by pressing it to the halo of flames dancing around his temples. It was a nifty little party trick that I'd seen too many times to count.

"What'll it be, missy?" he asked in his gravelly voice.

"Two shots of whiskey and a chicken basket with fries. To-go, please."

Gabriel stumbled up next to me. "I'll have some o' that whiskey to-go, too," he laughed and followed it up with a hiccup.

Xaphen glowered at him. "The only thing you're getting to-go is a thump'n, boy. Ain't my girl got you straightened out yet?"

"Can't a guy get any peace around here? I shoulda just stayed in Heaven tonight, but I can't get a decent drink there to save my -hic- life." His tangle of blond curls was especially unruly tonight, and he smelled extra ripe. He was on a drinking binge. I was half tempted to ask what was eating him, but the surety of a smartass reply kept me at bay.

Xaphen kept a stern eye on Gabriel as he slid my shots of whiskey across the bar. Then he slipped off to the kitchen to fill my food order. I slammed the shots before attempting a conversation with the drunken archangel.

"Crashing with us tonight?"

Gabriel snorted and waved a finger in the air. "I have my own room at Holly House tonight. Ms. Council Lady, her holiness, one of my feathered brethren, er, sistren... Holly

Spirit hooked me up good. Got a great deal on one of her studios for the week." He nodded his head, agreeing with himself.

"That's nice."

Xaphen appeared with my order and I slipped him a hefty coin. He gave me a nod and a two-fingered wave as I stood to leave. I liked Xaphen, but like most other demons I knew, he had begun acting differently around me since I'd started dating Bub. I couldn't quite grasp what it was. It felt like some strange combination of curiosity, respect, and caution. I wasn't sure if I cared for it.

Gabriel frowned as I tucked my food order under one arm. I sighed and tried to smile. "Guess I'll see you around."

He struggled to pull his bloodshot eyes up to meet mine and licked his chapped lips. "Yeah. See you around."

I left Purgatory Lounge with a growing pit in my stomach. I didn't feel like eating anymore. I hated being on the outs with Gabe. We were both pretending not to give a shit, and we both knew it. A three-hundred-year-old friendship is not so easily thrown away. The big question was all about who would break first and apologize. I wasn't the one being a big fat hypocrite, so I'd be damned if it was going to be me. That meant waiting it out for him. I'd done it before, and so had he. It didn't make things suck any less. Immortal or not, three months is still an awfully long time to be without your partner-in-crime.

The condo was quiet when I got home. Josie and Kevin's door was closed. They were probably already tucked in for the night. I'd given them quite the harvest list so that I could take off early to be Meng's escort. Jenni's door was cracked open, but I could see that her bed was still neatly made. Grim was working her all kinds of odd hours. I was still relieved she had gotten that particular promotion rather than me.

The city lights twinkled distantly through the living room window, turning the white sofas and rugs a dusty blue. I pulled off my work robe and threw it over one of the dining room chairs before kicking off my boots. Then I thought better of it and put everything neatly away in the coat closet. The classy condo at Holly House made me feel like a shmuck anytime I got lazy about tidying things.

I put my dinner in the fridge and poured a glass of water from the tap before heading back to my bedroom. The hounds were already snuggled up at the foot of my bed. Saul thumped his tail against the ivy bedspread in greeting, and Coreen tipped her nose up for a pat as I walked by. I changed into an oversized tee shirt and grabbed one of my old history books out of my closet. Then I crawled under the covers and clicked open my phone to scan through the risky pictures I had collected from the records room at the factory.

The notes from the Fates' files were more extensive than the ones Grim handed out with the harvest dockets. I had been counting on that pretty heavily. There was a serial number for each soul in the upper right-hand corner of the page. The first table revealed mostly basic information about the soul's current life, like their location, date of birth, and a brief death classification. Most of the files I had snapped pictures of were marked either as natural disaster or mass murder.

The second half of the page had the details I was really interested in. The soul's current beliefs were listed, along with their assigned afterlife. There was also a time line that charted the soul's previous religious affiliations along the bottom of the page. It didn't seem possible that several thousand years could be condensed down into a time line that only spanned the width of a single page, but there it was. Each of the soul's lifetimes wasn't necessarily marked. Sometimes half a millennium would be sectioned off and labeled Christian or Muslim or Hindu. There wasn't a lot to go on, but I had enough sense to figure out that I needed to find souls who believed in any given faith just before it gained some margin of popularity. I also needed to select souls that were destined for the Sea of Eternity, like atheists, agnostics, and the generally non-religious or neutral. I couldn't risk anyone noticing the tracking bracelets Horus demanded I place on potential candidates. If I dumped the souls out in the middle of the sea, I didn't have to worry about any of the gods' spidey sense tingling when I made a delivery.

I'd managed to snap photos of fifty or so files. Between zooming in and out with my phone and cross-referencing with my old history book, it took a good two hours to go through them all. I don't know why I expected to find some epiphany-inducing bit of information. It's not like the Fates kept record of which souls were original believers, and Grim would never ask them to—not in a million years. That would jeopardize the great mystery of his supreme rule.

The souls in the files seemed pretty run-of-the-mill to me. There were only a couple that looked like they might possibly be worth checking out, and they happened to be in Arden's territory. It was going to take some creative logic explaining why I should harvest those souls instead of him. Of course, I might finally get more than a nod out of Arden.

One of the souls was scheduled for in the morning, so I ignored my grumbling stomach and clicked off the bedside light. I liked to be nice and rested before fulfilling my blackmail duties.

CHAPTER 9

*"I'm sick of following my dreams. I'm just going to
ask them where they're goin' and hook up with them later."*
-Mitch Hedberg

Friday morning started off like an apocalypse. I woke up
covered in sweat, right after a night long quest for a soul that
I never found, while being chased by demons that I was too
afraid to fight. My stomach felt like a cement block, and my
chest ached like I had just run a marathon. I stumbled into
the kitchen to find Jenni, looking about as rough as I felt,
rummaging through the cabinets in a frenzy.

"What are you looking for?" I asked.

She jumped and spun around with a snarl. "Where the
hell is the coffee?"

My jaw dropped. Jenni never snapped, and she certainly
never swore. Her expression softened at my shock.

"Sorry. It's been a rough week," she said awkwardly, the
words rolling off her tongue like she wasn't quite sure how
to put them together.

"No kidding. The coffee is in the refrigerator." *Where
we've always kept it.*

"Thanks."

Jenni found the coffee and fired up an extra strong brew, while I filled the hounds' dishes with Cerberus Chow. I dug my cold dinner out of the fridge and picked at it with far less vigor than the hounds munched at their breakfast. Purgatory fries were just never as good the day after. I tossed them after a few bites and fixed a cup of coffee. I was somewhat surprised that Jenni hadn't offered to fix one for me, but she didn't seem herself this morning. She gave me a forced smile as I reclaimed the barstool next to her at the breakfast bar.

"Any big harvests planned for today?" she asked.

"You tell me," I laughed.

She cocked her head to one side and snorted. "Oh, right. I guess I should have paid better attention. Grim has me running in circles."

"I bet." I took a sip of my coffee and gagged. "Wow. Trying to raise the dead today?"

"Sorry, I didn't get any sleep last night." She shrugged. "I better go get a shower."

"Yeah, me too."

I waited for Jenni to leave the room before dumping another spoonful of sugar in my cup and topping it off with creamer. Then I went to get the day started right by washing away the nightmare funk with an extra hot shower. After brushing my teeth and pulling on a pair of snug blue jeans and a green, silk blouse, I was feeling better about the day.

Kevin and Josie were choking down Jenni's brew when I reemerged in the kitchen. I snickered at their sourpuss faces. Josie looked grumpier than usual. She liked her coffee black, so it wasn't as easy to fix as mine had been. She dumped half her cup in the sink and filled it back up with water before popping it in the microwave, glaring at me the whole time.

"That was totally Jenni's fault," I said.

She blinked in surprise. "You mean she finally came home? It's been two days."

"Really? Guess Grim's getting his money's worth. He probably shouldn't have waited so long to hire a new second. Hard telling how much work she has to catch up on."

"I guess." Josie shook her head and ran a hand through her spiky, short do. "It's just not like Jenni to let anything get her down. I mean, she's the one reaper known for being able to chew everything she bites off. That sounded way better in my head." She laughed and fetched her coffee out of the microwave.

The extra dark brew filled the condo with the smell of morning. It mingled with the hounds' woodsy musk and the odor of their kibble breath. They waited patiently by the front door, black tails thumping a cheerful ditty on the hardwood floor.

Kevin yawned and rubbed at his stubbly cheek. "Am I hanging with you today, boss lady?"

"Maybe for a bit. I think I'm going to take you on a foreign harvest this morning."

That got a frown out of both of them.

"Sometimes there's an overflow and a reaper ends up harvesting outside of their territory. You should be prepared for something like that."

Josie folded her arms over the counter and propped her chin up with one hand. "That very rarely happens anymore."

"Well, Kevin is also fresh out of the academy. So he might like to sample a few of the different territories before deciding what classes he'll eventually need in order to harvest in his preferred area." I pulled my work robe out of the coat closet and rolled it up before stuffing it in a duffle bag along with the day's harvest docket.

Josie's suspicion didn't wane. "Did you really just suggest that he take more classes at the academy?"

Kevin snickered and reclined back in his barstool, kicking his bare feet up on the counter. "Next she'll be telling us we need to synchronize our watches, like you do."

"And what's wrong with that?" She shoved his feet off the counter with a glare.

Kevin laughed sheepishly and chugged down the rest of his coffee. "I'm off to the shower." He gave Josie a quick peck on the cheek and hurried out of the kitchen.

Josie watched him go, and then turned her gray, penetrating eyes on me. "Sample a few different territories, huh?"

"Yeah, what's the big deal?" I sat down on one of the dining room chairs and pulled my boots on.

"I've known you for a few centuries now. So pardon me if I question your so-called authority." She finished off her coffee and rinsed her mug.

"See you on the ship," I said, ignoring her unspoken questions as I slipped out the front door with the hounds.

Since I was running pretty early, courtesy of the nightmares, I decided to walk to the harbor instead of using the travel booths. It was only three blocks, mostly up Market Street, where the market venders would be setting up for the weekend. Shopping is always a good pick-me-up.

The streets of Limbo felt safer since Grim installed the travel booths, but it still annoyed a lot of the citizens who were avid worshippers of convenience. I probably would have been more annoyed too, if I hadn't been one of the prime terrorist targets last spring. It was nice being able to come and go as I pleased, without having everyone breathing down my neck, reminding me to look both ways or to just play it safe and stay home. That had been Maalik's catch phrase.

I hadn't seen much of Maalik over the summer. Grim kept the council busy, but Maalik seemed to really take the job to heart. It had been a big part of our undoing. He had managed to keep my secrets though, which I appreciated. Maalik knew about Khadija and Winston. He knew that I was made differently. He didn't know that I had killed the goddess Wosyet or that I was doing an illegal side job for

Horus. He had his suspicions, but like a bad girlfriend, I lied through my teeth to preserve those secrets. He had enough to hold over my head. I sometimes still wondered if the fact that I relieved his prophet's wife from her centuries-long stint on the Throne of Eternity was the only reason he didn't turn me over to the council as a breach of the peace treaty, demanding my head. He and Grim both gave me the feeling that they were afraid I might unveil the big secret of Eternity if they turned on me. If Grim ever decided that I was too big of a liability, I fully expected him to have me assassinated in my sleep.

I brushed away all thoughts of secrets and betrayal as the market came into view. I passed a tent full of saints and a table of faerie cakes before I stopped at a booth selling Muslim hijabs. The silk scarves danced in the breeze, mingling with patchouli incense coming from a neighboring tent. It made me think of Khadija, and I wondered how she was faring in Firdaws Pardis, the Islamic paradise.

Scarves had become a regular staple in my wardrobe after having my throat burned up by a fire demon. The scar was hardly noticeable anymore, but I still liked to wear a nice scarf every now and then. I picked out a pretty blue one and tied it around my neck before tossing the vendor a coin.

The blue looked nice against my green blouse. Too bad I would have to put my black cowl over it all before harvesting any souls. Grim was a stickler about our traditional dress code. At least I would look good when I divvied up the harvests for the day. The hounds fell in close to me as we passed the guards at the entrance of the harbor. The two nephilim nodded at me. I recognized one of them as Abe, who had been assigned to me during the big terrorist scare. He recognized me too.

"Morning, Captain Harvey," he said, giving me the briefest of smiles.

"Morning, Abe."

He seemed surprised that I remembered his name.

The hounds took the lead once we were on the dock, playfully nudging each other closer to the edge, where the soul infused water slapped and sloshed, misting into the breeze over the harbor. Several reapers lingered near their ferries, sharing coffee or reading the *Daily Reaper Report*. A few looked up to frown at me as I passed by. I smiled at them anyway. I was used to being notoriously unpopular by now. It was a bit more than jealousy, I had to admit.

I had not earned my position like the other specialty unit captains. I was too young. I didn't have nearly enough experience, and I hadn't taken nearly enough classes. I didn't blame them for hating me. On top of my luxurious residence at Holly House and my devilishly delectable love interest, I was more often than not thought of as the spoiled brat of Limbo City. What everyone didn't know was what it had cost me, and what it was still costing me, to keep my head on my shoulders. I sincerely doubted that a single one of them would have traded me places if they could have seen the whole picture.

I took the ramp up to the deck of my ship to find Kate and Alex waiting. They hated me as much as any reaper, if not more, but they were being more subtle about it since I'd given them a better harvest list the past few days. Kate raised an eyebrow at my outfit, but she kept her mouth shut. Saul nudged Alex's leg, and she set her coffee down on the ship railing to pet him with both hands. The traitor. Coreen was more reserved. She tilted her muzzle in the air and sat on her haunches next to me.

Soon we were joined by Arden. I motioned for him to follow me up above the captain's cabin to the quarterdeck where we could talk in private. If Arden disliked me as much as everyone else did, he was doing one hell of a job of hiding it. I wasn't even sure he owned another expression besides the one of neutral indifference he'd adopted for all occasions. When I was sure we were out of earshot, I pulled the harvest docket out of my duffle bag.

"I'm taking Kevin to a few different areas for harvests today to give him a little more variety. I think it will be good for his apprenticeship. One of the stops is in your territory, so if you would like first choice from the rest of the list, you're welcome to it." I handed the docket to him.

Arden blinked at me and took the list. He scanned it briefly and handed it back. "The daycare fire in New Mexico."

"Really?" I frowned. "Seriously, you can take whatever harvest you want. You don't have to settle for the bleakest lot on the list. The harvest in Paris has fewer souls, but they're worth more coin."

Arden looked down at me, fixing his black eyes on mine. "I am good with children, and I do not do this job for the coin."

"Fair enough. It's yours." I marked his initials next to the harvest and flipped the page back on my clipboard to pencil it in on his docket before tearing the page free and handing it to him.

Arden nodded his thanks and left to begin his harvests. It was the longest conversation we had ever had, and I still hadn't gotten a new expression out of him. I suppose I should have just been thankful that he didn't throw a full-blown tantrum like Kate would have.

When I made it back down to the main deck, Josie and Kevin were lounging against the railing opposite of Alex and Kate. Coreen had nestled herself between their legs, and Saul made his way over to greet them too. I fairly divided the rest of the harvests and passed out everyone's dockets. Josie was still watching me with narrowed eyes as she coined off to her first harvest.

I don't know why I was having such a hard time being honest with her. She already knew why I had joined the Posy Unit, for the most part. I had told her about Horus's secret side job, although, I had left out the part about it being illegal and unsanctioned by the council. We hadn't really talked about it since I confessed, and I guess part of me was really hoping she would magically forget the entire conversation. When I looked at people who knew my secrets, it was hard not to envision a guillotine in the distance behind them.

The harvest where the throne candidate waited took place in an African village with a name I couldn't pronounce. When we arrived, the place reeked of chaos. Women and children rushed past us, screaming and covered in blood and dust. There were a dozen people dying a slow death in a clearing in the center of the village, and another few dozen already waiting to be harvested. Several huts were burning, and gunshots called out from every direction.

Kevin had harvested a couple of gang related shootings before, but that was a little different from gathering souls in the heat of battle. He pulled his scythe in closer to his chest as he stepped out of the path of a small horde of children busy making a dash from a burning hut into one that was still intact. The leader of the group, a young teenage girl, caught my eye, and I knew she was who I had come for. I pointed Kevin off towards a growing pile of bodies and turned to follow the girl. She didn't have much time left, according to her file.

The new hut the children had disappeared into was one of few left untouched. It didn't take long before a man with a rifle and a torch marched by to finish the job. He heard their screams and hurried to drag several empty poultry pens in front of the door, trapping everyone inside. He seemed rather pleased with himself, and I quietly prayed that there was an extra special place in one of the hells reserved for him.

The hut was small and it burned quickly. Half a dozen charred little bodies with gaping mouths poked through the ashes as the fire died down. As seasoned a reaper as I was, it was still hard to witness. I didn't know how Arden could do these kinds of harvests on an almost daily basis. He had a stronger stomach than I.

I nudged my way through the ash and held my breath as I pulled the first soul free from its remains. A little boy, no more than five years old, came screaming out into the open. I wasn't specially trained to harvest child souls, but it didn't take an expert to figure this one out. I pushed my hood back and dropped to my knees, wrapping my arms around the boy.

"You're all right. It's over."

He didn't understand a word I said, so I rocked him until he caught his breath and stopped trembling. When he had calmed down, I held him back by the shoulders so he could see me. Then I placed a finger to my lips and pointed at the ground in a silent gesture to stay put.

The other souls had enough time to settle, and they were a few years older, so it didn't take as much coaxing to round them up. I saved the eldest girl for last. She shimmered a blue hue when her aura stepped out of her remains, but she quickly faded to the normal pallor of the others. She didn't seem at all surprised by my presence. Instead, she nodded to me and went to the others, taking the small boy's hand.

The lot of them followed me quietly through the havoc, not taking notice of and not being noticed by the raging assault still plaguing the village. Kevin met us in the clearing with a swarm of souls. His jaw was set in a tight line and his eyes glazed over as he spotted us through the smoke.

"All accounted for?" he asked.

I took a quick head count. "All accounted for. Let's move out."

The sound of gunfire was suddenly sucked out of the air. A tunnel opened in the clouds above and swirled around like a bathtub trying to drain us away. Our new souls clung to each other, watching as mine and Kevin's robes frantically flapped around us in the descending storm.

Kevin turned to me, his brows pinched together. "This wasn't in the forecast," he shouted.

I shook my head slowly, still eyeing the sky funnel.

"Leaving so soon?"

I didn't seen her come out of the sky, and maybe she hadn't. Maybe it was all for show in order to make her appearance all the more alarming. She was one of the sirens, the kind that had stayed true to the Greek histories, with the dark blue-gray wings that Demeter had sprouted on their backs to search for Persephone when she first ran off with Hades. The feathers didn't stop there. They spread over her like a cloak, up her neck and over her head, growing bluer where they dipped into a widow's peak and where they tapered off over her shoulders. She was naked otherwise, with supple white flesh and small round breasts, punctuated by budding blue nipples. Her eyes were glowing, pupilless orbs that seemed to look at everything and nothing all at once.

She cocked her head to one side and purred at us. "I don't see anything particularly special about you."

It was impossible to tell who she was looking at, but I wanted it to be me. She couldn't know about the soul. She couldn't. No one could. I hadn't told a soul, or otherwise. I had to fight the urge not to turn and look back at the girl behind me.

The second scenario I had to dismiss was that she was affiliated with Eurynome's minions and was here to finish the job of sending Bub a message, but it was too unlikely that the sea deity would consort with the winged beings.

The purr of her words resonated and echoed, like a bowl had been tipped over, trapping us inside with the storm and the siren's song. Kevin began rocking next to me. His eyes rolled back in his head, and he began to whimper, struggling to fight off her spell. The souls didn't stand a chance. They fell away from each other, their whimpers soon shifting into a soft, humming background chorus, like musical zombies.

74

All except for the girl. Her eyes were on me, hard and piercing, accusing and pleading. I gasped and turned back to the siren.

She smiled at us with sharp, blue teeth. "Well, what have we here?"

I didn't think. I couldn't think. My body snapped into survival mode, and I let it. I wrenched Kevin's scythe from his lax grip, tipped the blade to the ground, and stomped on it. The end snapped and broke off, leaving a jagged tip behind. I heaved it back and threw it with an Amazon war call that razorred its way up my throat.

The siren's song broke as the makeshift spear found her heart. It cut through, just above one of those perfect breasts. Her gray skin split and blackened around the handle, leaking dark blue blood. She sobbed out a broken note and fell to her knees, fluttering her speckled wings.

"Move!" Kevin was the first to shake the spell. He rounded the souls up, linking them back together, hand by hand. With big blinking eyes they let him position them like dolls. Then he turned to me, waiting for the signal.

The siren gurgled, choking up thick, blue blood. She tried to stand, not ready to give up the fight. She pointed to the girl, sucking in a watery breath as she rose to her feet again.

"We need to go, Lana. Now!" Kevin's voice cracked, desperation taking over.

But we couldn't go. Not yet. Not while she was still breathing with my secrets trapped in her bloodied mouth.

My Latin was shoddy, but I had practiced a few incantations enough to commit them to memory, as required by the demon defense training Bub had schooled me through. I held a hand out, directing my palm towards the siren.

I closed my eyes and focused my senses. "Sanctus Incendia."

It was just a little phrase, meaning *holy fire*, but boy, did it pack a punch. The siren burst into flames. She dropped back to her knees before falling dead on her face, sending a cloud of dust up around her.

The storm rippled away, leaving an empty blue sky. The gunfire had quieted too, creating a heavy silence that no one seemed to want to jinx. Kevin put a hand on my shoulder, just a quick, gentle touch. I turned to face him, lifting my arms up on either side to direct the souls to gather round so we could coin out of there.

When we were safely back on the ship, and the souls had been tucked away in the hold, Kevin found me on the forecastle deck. He slipped up beside me and leaned against the railing, folding his arms to mirror me.

"So," he cleared his throat, "when you plan on teaching me *that*?"

I gave him a small grin. "Soon, grasshopper. Soon."

I sent him off to a milder harvest that he could handle on his own, then I slipped down to the hold.

The girl was nestled in the middle of a heap of dozing child souls. She saw me in the doorway and carefully extracted herself from the puppy pile before tiptoeing her way over to me.

She looked to be maybe fifteen, with a short tangle of black braids that hung loose around her full face. The rest of her was all lanky and thin, but her face was soft, still clinging to a youth that her eyes couldn't match. Her plain green tee shirt and ragged jean shorts were decorated with stains and the gentle sort of wear and tear that accumulated on clothing that survived through several generations of hand-me-down wardrobes. She searched my face for answers I wasn't sure I could give her, and even if I could, there was the language barrier.

I reached into my robe pocket and found the case of tracker bracelets Horus had given me. She watched as I held up one of the bracelets, and then she silently held out her hand, tilting her wrist up to me. I snapped the bracelet on and watched it melt away, fading beneath the surface of her ashy ghost skin. She reached up and pressed two gentle fingers to my cheek. Just the faintest of smiles brushed her lips, then it was gone.

I knew right then that I couldn't put her in the sea, but I couldn't take her to one of the afterlives either. There was also no way I was going to be able to get her into the city. My tongue felt like sandpaper against the roof of my mouth as a very bad plan formed in the back of my head. I found Winston's coin in my pocket. I held my hand out to her, and she took it. I'd done dumber things, I told myself, as I flipped the coin in the air.

CHAPTER 10

"Behind every great fortune
lies a great crime."
-Honore de Balzac

Even Winston was surprised by our arrival. He was speechless, which doesn't happen very often. At least he was able to communicate with the soul. Perks of the throne job, I guess. He said he'd be able to figure something out, so I left her there, not quite feeling like I had washed my hands of the situation.

I finished up my last harvest for the day early, and I let Kevin and Josie take the rest of the souls across the sea to their afterlives. I needed to clear my head and figure out what I was going to tell Josie after she cornered me to play twenty questions. I was sure Kevin was filling her in on all the events of the day by now. The hounds had stayed with them to entertain the child souls in the hold, now that their fearless leader was missing. That question would most definitely be at the top of Josie's pop quiz.

I was halfway down Market Street when two nephilim guards approached me. I didn't recognize either of them. They were male, fair-haired, and full of some superior arrogance that most of the guards I had encountered up until this point hadn't possessed. They loomed in my path, taking wide stances so as make sure I knew they were there for me.

"Captain Harvey, the Fates require a meeting," said the shorter of the two.

My shoulders dropped and I stuffed my hands in the pockets of my robe. Apparently, that was the wrong thing to do. Their spears slanted in unison as they crossed them over the breastplates of their armor.

I pulled my hands back out of my pockets, slowly lifting them in the air. "Whoa, there. Look, I'm kinda busy tonight. Maybe they could just call me and set up an appointment?"

"We're not here to deliver a message. We've been sent to retrieve you." The taller one dipped his spear, pointing towards the factory, silently ordering me to lead the way.

It really wasn't a good idea to deny the Fates, but I wanted to anyway. I did not want to go back to the factory, and I had a date to get ready for and plenty of unsettling thoughts to mull over while I primped. I didn't have the time or the nerve to face the sisters, but it looked like I didn't have much of a choice.

I glared at the guards. "Fine. Just watch where you're pointing those things."

We paraded back up Market Street, stopping briefly to take the travel booth near the harbor. It spit us out into the booth across the street from the factory. It was still an hour until the souls would be lining up to head home for the night, and I really hoped I would be able to get out of there before then.

The guards led me right past the receptionists' desk and Atropos' personal office, all the way down to a set of double doors that opened into another passage. It was narrower and darker than the main hall. I was led through a plain, nameless door, into a room with nothing but a couple of metal chairs and a table.

"Wait here," one of the guards said before closing me into the small space.

The concrete walls were bare, and I noticed a wide mirror along the far side of the room. I glanced back at the door, half tempted to try it, but I was almost certain that it was locked. This was not looking good.

Clotho was the first to come into the room. Her toga was wrinkled and her eyes were wide and tired, like she had stayed up one too many nights on a coffee binge. She was all smiles as she sat down across from me and folded her small hands over the table. "Lana, how are you doing?"

I frowned at her. "I'd be doing a hell of a lot better if I knew what this was all about."

"Of course." Her smile faltered. She tucked a chestnut coil of hair that had fallen loose from her bun behind her ear. "After your visit yesterday, something turned up missing." She paused, watching my face intently for any trace of guilt.

I raised an eyebrow. "What?"

"I said, something turned up missing after—"

"I heard you. I meant what turned up missing?"

"Oh." She sat up taller and pulled her hands off the table.

I should have probably been minding my manners, but I hadn't sent a pair of guards out to force her into an interrogation room to make groundless accusations.

Clotho mirrored my frown and cleared her throat. "I'd rather not say just yet."

I sighed and folded my arms over the table. "Look, I'm no thief. I wasn't even here that long. What makes you think I took whatever you're missing?"

It was at that moment that Lachesis chose to come blazing into the room. "Because I caught you snooping around in the records room unattended! That's why," she snapped, throwing her arms around like she had just come from a Jerry Springer set.

I leaned away from her, a little taken back by the outburst. "Yeah, but I didn't take anything. I was only looking."

"You could have done it before I found you." She leaned over the table, putting her face right in front of mine. I could smell the coffee on her breath. Her hair was in worse shape than Clotho's. Frizzy strawberry curls shook with every word she spat at me.

The fury of the goddess had me trembling now. "Ask the receptionists. They saw me go into the restroom. I was only gone for a minute."

"We know," Clotho sighed. She put a calm hand on her sister's arm. "Lachesis, we're wasting time. Please, let me finish here."

"Fine." She jerked herself away from the table to go pace in a corner.

Clotho turned back to me and tried to smile again. "We're not laying blame on you —"

"Yet, anyway," Lachesis sneered from her corner.

Clotho shot her a look and she fell silent again.

"We were hoping that maybe you saw something that might help us. Was there anything that seemed unusual to you? Anyone you saw who seemed out of place?"

I took a moment to really consider my short visit, and then I shook my head. "I'm sorry, nothing is coming to mind. Honestly, I didn't think going into the records room would be such a big deal. The door was unlocked."

"Liar!" Lachesis hissed.

"Please, sister," Clotho sighed, closing her eyes. "Lana, are you sure that you didn't see anyone else in passing?"

"No one besides her," I said, nodding at the grumbling goddess.

"Maybe it was Meng," Lachesis said.

I rolled my eyes. "She was with Atropos the whole time."

"Maybe she put you up to it," she snarled.

I held my breath as the door flung open yet again, slamming into the concrete wall. Atropos threw herself into the room, knocking me right out of the chair. Her lipstick was smeared, and her black pupils filled her eyes completely as she took me by the throat, pressing the back of my head into the concrete floor. "Just tell us where it is. Just tell us. It doesn't have to end this way for you," she said, in a neutral whisper that freaked me out way more than Lachesis' ranting had.

The other two sisters sprang on her, each latching onto an arm in an attempt to keep her from crushing my windpipe. I gurgled against her grasp, crying out when her nails scored my throat as they pulled her off of me.

Atropos' voice was still eerie calm as she tried to reason with her sisters. "She has to know. She has to. We just need to be firmer. I can make her talk. I can reach into her chest and squeeze her heart until she spills every secret she's ever known."

My stomach turned at the suggestion. I had a lot of secrets to hide, and I really didn't want to know how effective her techniques were.

"Is everything all right here?" Asmodeus stood in the open doorway, looking confused at the lot of us sprawled across the floor. I almost cried, I was so happy to see him.

The demon was Bub's best friend, and I never really had much of an opinion about him before. Now I thought he was just dandy. He was a peach. He was my ticket the hell out of there.

The goddesses froze, shame washing over them due to their graceless state. Well, except for Atropos. She had stopped her rambling and now hummed, gazing wide-eyed at the ceiling like a loon.

On a better day, they would have rushed to fawn over Asmodeus, like most warm-blooded ladies did. He was sex incarnate, all firm-bodied and carefree charm. He didn't even have to try. He wore loose fitting slacks and an orange tee shirt with the logo of a demon rock band splashed across the front. A faded blue fedora rested on his head, an accessory that Bub relentlessly teased him for, but it looked right on him.

"I was just leaving," I said, standing up and inching away from the goddesses. "Think you could walk me home?"

"Not a problem. I'm just waiting for the receptionist to finish up some paperwork for a lot of souls I delivered for reinsertion. Thought I'd drop in and say hi to the ladies in charge, but it looks like you all have your hands full tonight." He chuckled nervously at the pile of goddesses and held his hand out to help me step around them.

Lachesis looked like she might protest, but Clotho cut her off. "Thank you for coming, Lana. We appreciate your help," she said tightly, still clinging to her possessed sister.

"Yeah," I said, not looking back as we left. My heart didn't slow down until we had stepped out of the travel booth on the opposite end of town.

Asmodeus put a hand on my shoulder as we walked. "That was dumb luck. If that secretary had been more organized and ready for me, you'd still be back there with those crazy broads." He gave a short laugh. "So what'd you do to light the fire under their asses?"

I shook my head. "They're missing something. I don't know what, but they either think I'm the thief or that I know who is. They can't quite seem to make up their minds."

Asmodeus took off his hat and ran a hand through his scruffy short hair before plopping it back on his head. "Well, I suggest you steer clear of them for a while."

"They sent guards to escort me to the factory," I groaned. "Trust me, I don't want to be anywhere near that place."

We stopped in front of Holly House, and I turned to face him. "Thanks for the rescue. I doubt any other friend of Bub's would have helped me out."

"Yeah." He grinned. "You're the fly in every demon's ointment these days. You've taken the golden boy of Hell off the market. And here I thought that would just mean more ladies for me."

"You mean you don't have enough?"

He wagged his eyebrows.

Asmodeus was the demonic prince of lust. He saw after the souls of adulterers and prostitutes in the second level of Hell. I think the overabundance struck him bored after so long. While he was still desirable to many, he himself seemed to lack desire. I didn't see him out with women often, but I'd heard stories of his illicit love affairs, centuries past. Maybe he was just taking a break, hoping to rediscover his flame eventually. I knew enough reapers who had done the same.

He gave me a friendly pat on the shoulder and tipped his hat. "Stay out of trouble, ya hear?"

"Sure." I smiled. "Have a nice night."

"You too, doll. You too." He stuffed his hands in his pockets and headed in the direction of the travel booth we had just come from. I watched him go, wondering why Bub didn't invite him to more parties. It might be nice to see more friendly faces for a change.

CHAPTER 11

*"You sleep with a guy once and before you know it
he wants to take you to dinner."*
-Myers Yori

The interrogation session with the Fates had shaken me, not to mention the run-in with the siren earlier. I was half-tempted to cancel my date with Bub, but I knew how busy his schedule was. He prided himself on the fact that he made time for us. He would be crushed, and rightly so. I couldn't do that to him, even if he did have ulterior motives. I still managed to enjoy myself most of the time, even when I knew we were essentially on a business outing.

The Hearth was on Market Street, just off Council Street and to the north of the harbor. The restaurant's dining area was set up on the second and topmost floor of the circular building, with a spectacular view of the Sea of Eternity. The kitchen was on the floor below, and the waiters accessed it through a pair of see-through elevators along the side of the restaurant that faced the parking lot. A ramp curled up to the other side, where a set of polished marble steps led up to the front doors.

The driver of the limo Bub had sent to collect me opened my door and held out his hand. I let him help me stand and thanked him before carefully making my way up the steps in my white skyscraper heels. Besides the questionable footwear, I had chosen a matching white sheath dress. It was strapless with a knee-high slit up one side of the fitted, ankle-length skirt. The Hearth had a strictly formal dress code, and it was ungodly expensive. I had only dined there a handful of times, and only for the most special of occasions. It felt strange not having any real reason to be there other than a spur-of-the-moment date with Bub. Two attendants opened the doors, and I stepped inside.

The reason for the kitchen being on the lower level was so that the beautiful panoramic view would be entirely unobstructed. A low-rise stage opened in the middle of the room where a nephilim sat behind a baby grand, playing subtle mellow tunes. Droplights hung in a random pattern from the dark ceiling, giving the illusion of a starry night sky. A hostess led me over to a table on the seaside of the dining floor where a tuxedoed Bub stood to greet me.

"Gorgeous as ever," he sighed, pulling me in for a peck on the cheek.

"You're not looking too bad yourself." I grinned and gave him a mock kiss to keep from smearing my burgundy lip gloss across his face. My makeup was a little heavy tonight, in an attempt to draw eyes away from the pretty little scratches Atropos had left along my neck.

Bub pulled out a chair for me. No sooner than we had gotten comfortable, a demon waiter appeared with a bottle of wine and two glasses.

Bub raised a brow. "Shall I order, or do you have a preference?"

"Go ahead." Surely he knew that I wasn't a regular here.

He ordered our dinner in Latin. I had a hard time translating, but it sounded like some kind of fish maybe. When the waiter left, Bub reached across the table and took my hand. His smile was still in place for our gawking fellow diners, but his eyes were anxious. "Asmodeus told me about the Fates. Why on Earth would they suspect you of stealing from them?"

"Well, cut right to it, why don't you." I frowned. "I took Meng to the factory to meet with them yesterday, and Lachesis caught me snooping around in the records room."

His brow dropped into a humorless line. "And what were we snooping for exactly?"

"Next week's schedule." I shrugged, and took a sip of my wine. "Turns out, it's all I've got for an alibi. I'm fairly certain that Asmodeus is the only reason I made it out of there in one piece tonight."

Bub shook his head and laughed. "You are a ballsy one, aren't you?"

I rolled my eyes, trying to dismiss the whole incident.

Winston was the only one who needed to know what I had really been doing in the Fates' records room. I had a feeling Horus had probably figured it out by now, too. It's not that I didn't trust Bub. I just didn't like the way I felt about the situation. I didn't like thinking about it, and I didn't like talking about it. When people know all about the muck you're in, that seems to be all they want to talk about.

Bub knew about Wosyet, and to his credit, he hadn't mentioned her name again since he'd found out. I was sure he had some inkling about my uniqueness, but he kept that to himself too. Come to think of it, Bub was pretty exceptional at avoiding the subjects I was uncomfortable with altogether. Most of the time, I liked that about him. The rest of the time, I pondered over what his opinions might be, though I wasn't quite brave enough to ask.

"Well, I have some news," Bub said. "I don't know that it's good news, but it might be useful. Hades and Persephone finally finished inventorying what was stolen, and the item of most concern happens to be the Helm of Hades."

"The cap of invisibility?"

"One and the same."

"Well, that might come in handy for a thief."

Bub leaned in closer over the table. "Especially for a thief who's been to the factory recently, hmm?"

My jaw dropped in surprise. Of course, that made perfect sense. I felt a little dim for not catching his drift sooner.

I dropped my voice to a whisper. "So that should clear my name then, right?"

"Eventually." Bub winced at my frown. "Give it a day or two. We have Anubis coming in this weekend with his jackals to do a little tracking, and we don't want to scare the culprit off by announcing the discovery just yet."

We both gave the room a quick glance, taking inventory of the ears in range. A demon couple was busy eyeballing us from the dance floor that circled around the nephilim piano man. They turned their noses up as I paused on them, pointing their tango in the other direction.

Our food arrived. I had been right. Raw fish fillets were laid out over a bed of tangled herbs on my plate. I curled my nose up at Bub.

"Try it," he said. "It's to die for."

"What is it?" I picked up my salad fork, not really sure where to go with it.

"Yellowfin cutthroat trout. It's been extinct in the mortal realm for nearly a hundred years, but there's a little fishery in Summerland that keeps them thriving for the price they demand here."

I nudged a fillet around my plate until I noticed the bowl of caviar that had come with it. There was a little pearl spoon dipped down in the bowl of black fish eggs. Caviar wasn't my favorite, but I'd come to appreciate it since Bub had come along. I picked up the spoon and gave them a taste. They were different than the variety Bub served at his parties. They were larger too, with tinges of gold in them.

"What kind are these?"

Bub looked up. "Hmm? Oh, those are mermaid eggs."

I choked mid swallow and spit the rest into my napkin before reaching for my wine. Bub was almost in tears he was struggling so hard not to laugh when I looked up.

"Oh, you are evil." I glared over the table.

"And this is news to you?" he chuckled.

I shook my head with a laugh and took another drink of wine. Every now and then, he pulled a good one on me. I never saw it coming. Eventually, I would get him back.

"So, do you still think sticky-fingers is one of Persephone's sirens?" I asked.

Bub's brow furrowed as he swallowed a bite of trout. "I don't know. If it is a siren, I don't think she's affiliated with Eurynome anyhow."

"Really?"

"If the theft had been at Eurynome's request, she would have been more inclined to take credit for a job well-done. She's no chicken of the sea."

I considered his words for a moment, and then I had to ask. "How likely is she to attack me again?"

Bub reached across the table and rubbed the top of my hand. "I'm sure she'll keep to herself. She's made her point. I'm truly sorry that you were dragged into this mess."

"I've been in worse fixes." I bit my lower lip and braced myself. "In fact, I was in one today. A *winged* siren tried to sabotage my morning harvest."

Bub's fork clattered onto his plate. "What? Why didn't you tell me sooner?"

"Well, I was going to call, but then I was whisked off to be interrogated by the Fates. It all happened so fast, and then I had to get ready for our date. I just figured I'd tell you at dinner, like I'm doing now," I said, kneading my napkin in my lap.

Bub was quiet for a minute. "It was winged?"

I nodded. "You don't think Eurynome would be employing winged sirens, do you?"

"It's doubtful, but then, we really don't know why else it would have shown up at your harvest, now do we?"

"I didn't really take the time to ask. I did kill it though."

Bub's eyes widened. "Well, I suppose it's anyone's guess then."

I shrugged. "I could always call a timeout next time I'm attacked. Say, pardon me, but would you mind telling me whose dirty work you're doing?"

Bub snorted. "Well, I'd like to say that I'm relieved at the possibility that this attack isn't my fault, but that relief is a little stunted by the fact that we're now blind."

I sighed and went ahead and took a bite of the raw trout. It was better than I expected.

Bub sipped at his wine with a frown, his brow shifted up and down as he thought over our conundrum. "Limbo City has been rebel free for months now, but obviously someone is able to gain access to your schedule." His English accent came through thickest on the word schedule, and he said it like the *c* wasn't there at all. It tickled me and I had to hide a smile behind my napkin.

"What might their goal be?" Bub mused. "Did the siren make an attempt on you? Did you fancy her an assassin? Or did she seem more interested in the souls you were harvesting?"

"I really don't know. She surprised me. So I threw a spear through her chest and set her on fire." I didn't want to go into the finer details of my near heart attack. The siren hadn't seemed too interested in anything until she noticed that her song didn't affect me or the girl I was there for.

I'd managed to surprise Bub again. He was struggling to look concerned, but pride kept slipping through his expression. "Did you use one of the Latin incantations from the demon defense course?"

"I did."

Bub beamed and scooped up a spoonful of caviar. "You vixen you."

I patted my napkin over my mouth again. My lipstick was done for the night, but I was hoping it had been dark enough to leave a nice stain behind.

"So." I leaned in closer, lowering my voice again. "Any special after dinner plans?"

Bub winced. "I have to get back to Tartarus and see if anything is missing."

"Still waiting to see if the thieves will strike again?" I jutted my bottom lip out, disappointed that our fancy date was still half business.

Bub's phone buzzed softly in his pocket. He pulled it into his lap and frowned at the screen. "Well, the good news is that no one seems brave enough to make an attempt on our lives tonight."

"And the bad news?"

"We're going to have to skip desert if we want to make it out of here without getting trampled by paparazzi. They're already piling up outside."

Camera flashes flickered off the windows, confirming the update he had just received. I groaned.

The sidewalk was slick when we stepped out. The sea was churning roughly, and it sprayed a fine mist over the city. Two photographers in raincoats were arguing at the foot of the stairs. One was a nephilim. I could tell by the feathers sticking out of the yellow collar of his jacket. The other looked like he could be a soul. Some of them had side jobs in addition to working at the factory. They stopped when they spotted us and began clicking off pictures in between barking nosy questions, one after another.

"Captain Harvey, over here!"

Four or five camera flashes blurred my vision, and I lifted a hand up to shield my eyes.

"Ms. Harvey, look this way!"

" How true are the allegations that you stole Atropos' shears?"

"*Has Meng Po brainwashed you into doing her bidding?*"

"*How's the Lord of the Flies in the sack?*"

Bub took my free arm and helped guide me down the marble stairs. Two horned bodyguards moved in to flank us as we climbed inside the limo.

"The nerve of those ghouls!" Bub's nostrils flared as he pounded on the privacy class between us and the driver. The car eased forward, warning the vultures before taking off down Market Street.

"Atropos' shears. Of course! No wonder she was such a wreck." It made perfect sense now. Although, it did seem odd that the city news rats knew about it.

"The Fates are a noisy bunch, and the souls like to talk," Bub sighed, answering that question.

When the limo stopped outside Holly House, Bub walked me to the front door of the building.

"I'll call you," he said, giving my cheek a quick peck before I slipped inside.

Charlie, the deskman, gave me a friendly wave as I made my way to the elevators. It took all of my will to smile back at him, and even then, I knew it was a weak one. That was by far the most expensive and most disappointing date I had ever been on.

CHAPTER 12

"Don't cling to fame. You're just borrowing it. It's like money. You're going to die, and somebody else is going to get it."
-Sonny Bono

The picture on the cover of the latest *Limbo's Laundry* was not a flattering one. My mouth was gaping open in horrified surprise. One of my eyes was squinted shut from the harsh flashbulbs, and there was a spot of red wine on my pretty white dress. Bub was standing next to me, looking like his usual delicious self, even with the grimace. The headline read "Reaper de Jour: Is Beelzebub's new beauty a brainwashed burglar?"

I dropped my forehead on the edge of my desk and groaned. It never ceased to amaze me how many accusations and lies they could squeeze into a single headline. I couldn't even enjoy the fact that they had called me a beauty, not while they were insinuating that I was bespelled by Meng, and worse yet, a thief. The *de jour* part wasn't very nice either. I wasn't some new fling of Bub's. We had been out in public together plenty of times.

"Seriously?" Grim was standing in my doorway. He stepped inside and shut the door behind him.

"Seriously?" he repeated. His face was nearly purple, but his voice was even. I could almost hear him counting to ten in his head. "*What* the *hell* do you think you're doing?"

He slapped a stack of tabloids down on my desk, and I jumped. I had a vision of the guy at the paper stand pissing himself as Grim cleaned out the bin.

"Harvey." Grim sighed tensely and closed his eyes. "If you so much as even *think* about going back to that factory, I will personally terminate you. Are we clear?" He opened his eyes to pierce me with them.

I swallowed and nodded.

He straightened the lapels of his jacket and took a deep breath, trying to calm himself before opening my office door.

I wanted to cry. I hadn't even seen what the article had to say yet. I was contemplating whether or not I should even read it when Ellen slipped into my office.

She was dressed down for the weekend, wearing a pair of navy capris with matching loafers and a cream blouse with navy polka dots. A cream headband held back her springy curls. She peeked down the hall, making sure she hadn't been spotted and then closed the door softly behind her.

"Lana, Lana, Lana!" she said in a whispery squeal, bouncing over to sit on the edge of my desk with a couple candy bars in hand. She tossed one to me and picked up a magazine off the top of the stack with a giggle. "My god, that is a sassy dress."

"Yeah, and how 'bout that headline?" I rolled my eyes.

"Oh, pish, everyone knows they're full of baloney," she said, waving her hand dismissively. "The only reason anyone buys these anymore is for the pictures, and they definitely put the best one on the cover. You've got your hottest accessory on your arm." She turned it around for me to see and tapped a finger on Bub's chest. "Of course, the one of you in that green scarf was pretty spiffy too."

"There are more pictures?" I stood and snatched up one of the magazines, flipping to the article in the back. The headline articles were always in the back. That's how they made sure all the other bogus stories about sea monsters and premature council predictions stood a chance at being seen.

When I found the article featuring me I had to sit back down. It took up six pages in the book. There were pictures of me talking to Amy and a group of her demon friends outside of Purgatory Lounge. Another spread showcased Meng and me leaving the factory in a hurry. The last set of pictures was of the night before, outside the Hearth with Bub. I felt sick. I didn't even have to read the article to know the direction the anonymous so-called journalist was trying to lead everyone in. I really hoped Ellen was right and that everyone knew they were full of baloney.

Ellen admired the pictures and nibbled on her candy bar from her perch on my desk. She rotated the book around again and pointed at the picture of me in the scarf. "Athena doesn't carry those. Please tell me you got that at the market. I totally want one!"

I nodded, still speechless as I gawked over the skewed story of my life.

Ellen sighed. "Chin up, pretty. Next week they'll be picking on someone new, and you'll be old news."

"God, I hope so." I picked up the candy bar she brought for me, wishing I had a cup of coffee to go with it, but absolutely certain that I wasn't brave enough to risk going out in public yet. "How's the break room coffee?"

"You wanna cup?" Ellen hopped off my desk. "I'll go grab us some more chocolate too. You look like you could use it."

I'd never seen Ellen bring any of the other captains coffee before. If any of them saw her, it would probably just add to the long list of reasons they detested me. Today, I really didn't care. It was Saturday. I'd come in early to file some paperwork, but it could wait. I didn't have to be down to the harbor for another hour or so.

Ellen came back with our coffee and a stationery box under one arm. It was stuffed full of fat, caramel-filled truffles wrapped in pink and gold paper. She had the best hiding places. We sat on my desk and commenced to get high on caffeine and sugar. Ellen chattered on and on until she almost had me convinced that my life wasn't totally ruined. She had a human vibe about her, and I liked it. It was like the only things that mattered to her were the things that didn't really matter at all. Our conversations revolved around food, shoes, and unattainable men, but mostly unattainable men.

Ellen didn't have anyone special in her life, well, except for a pet toy phoenix named Duster. The breed was a rare mix that reduced the size of the traditional phoenix down to the size of a parakeet and enhanced it with the speech intelligence of an African Grey Parrot. Most of the features were still true to a regular phoenix, except for the gray belly and thicker, curved beak. The thing also experienced a shorter life cycle between resurrections.

Duster hated everyone who wasn't Ellen. The factory soul Ellen paid to come clean her apartment at Reapers Tower twice a week wouldn't go near his cage, so Duster was constantly covered in his own resurrection ash, which meant Ellen was often covered in ash too. She kept a lint roller in her desk to clean the little talon and tail prints off her clothes during the cuter, more youthful days of his life cycle.

It was easy to feel sorry for Ellen sometimes. She didn't have a lot of friends. She didn't have a career that would allow her to grow or advance, and she had to work in close proximity to Grim every day. I wasn't sure how she managed to always be in such a good mood. It couldn't just be the chocolate, though it was some really good chocolate.

When the time finally came for me to go, I began to panic. "Maybe I should just play hooky today. I could have Kevin pass out the harvest lists."

Ellen put her hands on her hips. "You'll just lend credit to that tabloid crap. Hold your head high, lady. You haven't done anything wrong. Heck, act like you haven't even seen it. If your unit knows what's good for them, they'll keep their mouths shut anyway."

"Kate Evans never passes up an opportunity to open her big mouth."

"Ha! Like she has any room to talk after the article they published about her last year."

I raised an eyebrow. "Yeah?"

"Oh, yeah." Ellen giggled and then lowered her voice. "You musta been too busy with that special harvest Grim sent you on to hear about it, but she and Artemis had a little too much fun at that dive bar on the west side, and someone snapped off a picture of them with their lips locked. Oh, Apollo was in an uproar! It was just after the Oracle Ball, and he was still in town. That poor Alex still took the harlot back, even after the public mockery. It's a wonder they're still together."

I grinned, feeling better about the day, until Grim interrupted our girl talk by barging into my office.

"Ms. Aries, I don't pay you to gossip. Get back to work."

Ellen gasped and hopped off my desk. "Yes, sir." She circled around him and rushed out of my office.

Grim watched her with a scowl that he turned on me once she was down the hall. "Change of plans. You're going to have to merge your harvest list for today with tomorrow's. The Recovery Unit is getting hit pretty hard this year with all the natural disasters, and they could use a hand harvesting an earthquake in Indonesia today. Paul Brom will be there with a few of his team members to recover the souls that are out of your team's reach, but you should be able to handle the rest."

He tossed a file on my desk and left without another word. And just when I was starting to wrap my mind around facing Kate. Now I was going to have to spend the whole day with her. Super.

CHAPTER 13

"A single death is a tragedy;
a million deaths is a statistic."
-Joseph Stalin

I could tell Kate wanted to say something once we were all gathered together on the ship. She was fidgety and kept pressing her lips together. I hardly stopped to take a breath, not wanting to give her an opening, as I made the announcement about Indonesia and sent everyone off to double check the holds of their ships. We'd be collecting around a thousand souls today, which was actually quite a bit lighter than our usual daily intake, but I needed the break from Kate already.

Josie stayed above deck with me while Kevin went to arrange the picnic tables and couches downstairs in our own hold. Josie and I hadn't spent much time together over the summer outside of work. Between the new paper pushing captain duties and dating Bub, my extracurricular activities had become a distant memory. There was no time for shopping or coffee dates, poker games or all-nighters at Purgatory Lounge. I felt like I hardly knew how to talk to her anymore. She was struggling to find words for me too.

"So, what was Kate's problem?" she said finally, taking a long pull from her travel mug.

"You mean you haven't seen the cover of *Limbo's Laundry* yet today?"

"The bin was empty, and I was running too late to make an extra trip to the one on the north side. I needed to stop and grab a cup of coffee. Jenni ruined another pot this morning," she grumbled.

I dug through my duffle bag and handed her the one copy I had saved. The rest had gone through the industrial shredder in the copy room at Reapers Inc.

I'm not sure that I'd ever seen coffee come out of Josie's nose before, but I wouldn't be forgetting it anytime soon.

"Those bastards! I'm writing a letter to the editor." She flipped through to the article and gasped. "No! I'm going to pay them a visit in person. Who the hell do they think they are, publishing crap like this!"

I laughed. "I imagine Kate is just waiting for an opportune moment to crack a joke at my expense today."

Josie scowled. "Let the bitch just try."

"It's okay. Just drop Artemis's name. That should shut her up."

Her eyes went wide. "I'd almost forgotten."

Josie was a tabloid whore. She pretended that she only picked up *Limbo's Laundry* when there was a review in there for one of the Muses' theater productions, but I'd seen the stash she kept under her and Kevin's bed, and she was constantly updating me on the latest rumors circulating through the city.

We stood on the deck together in silence for a few minutes, glancing out over the fog-frosted sea or looking down when the hounds tromped past us as they chased each other around the ship. It wasn't an uncomfortable silence, but it did bring a cloud of melancholy with it. We'd gone through spells before, losing each other to the excitement of a new lover or to the annoyance of our differences. This time was different. This time there was a wall of resentment she was trying to hurdle over on her way back to being good with me. For the first time, I ranked higher than she did in the reaper hierarchy.

There were so many other little things widening the distance between us, but most of them were of the mundane human variety that we all liked to pretend didn't affect us. I got to spend more time with Kevin, since I was his mentor. I dated more powerful men, whereas she had only been a fling for the likes of Horus and Apollo, eventually settling for the puppy love of a fresh academy graduate. Kevin was great, but he was still more tabula rasa than tall, dark, and mysterious. He was a safe choice, and maybe that's what Josie needed right now. She hadn't talked much about it, but there was plenty I hadn't talked to her about too. That alone was probably the biggest factor deteriorating our friendship. She had stopped asking questions, but it didn't matter. I heard them hanging in the air between us, like so many hopeful bubbles that I popped each time I rushed out the door for nothing so urgent that I couldn't have taken ten minutes to sit down with her and come clean.

Come clean. It sounded so easy. Oh, but it wouldn't be. It would be like lying out on an autopsy table and cracking open my own ribcage so that she could take a peek at my insides. Then I would hand her my heart, and it would be up to her to squeeze or put it back in my chest. I wouldn't be the same either way, and neither would she. You can't unknow something, no matter how wrong it makes you feel. That's what I kept trying to tell myself I was protecting Josie from.

She finished off her coffee and gave me a weak smile. "I better go help Kevin," she said, heading for the hold.

"Josie?"

"Yeah?" She stopped and turned back to me.

I opened and closed my mouth a few times like a fish out of water. The pause was about to get awkward, but I

101

couldn't get the words out. I took a deep breath and blurted, "I'm sorry."

Josie's tired eyes blinked at me. "For what?"

"For being a demon magnet. For putting Kevin in danger twice this week. For not being around more lately to do the girl things we used to do." I shrugged.

Josie's mouth curled up slowly. "Kevin's a good reaper, and I know you look out for him."

"What about the girl stuff?"

Josie rolled her head to one side. "Hell, Lana. We live together. When there's time for girl stuff, I'm sure we'll figure something out."

"Maybe we could do a poker game soon. We haven't done that in a while."

"Yeah, maybe." Josie nodded and went to check on Kevin.

I felt a little better. At least she was willing to talk to me, even if we weren't one hundred percent. Gabriel was still weighing heavy on my mind. I couldn't take Josie giving me the silent treatment too, and that's most definitely what I'd be getting if she were as critical about my choice in men as Gabriel was. Of course, Gabriel was more familiar with how attached I could get to a lover. Josie could look at Kevin and mentally gage the timeframe it would take before he would outgrow her desires or her desires would outgrow him. She could also do it without the heartache and anxiety I suffered through when I attempted to play Miss Cleo.

"We're immortal," she would say. *"That doesn't mean we're frozen in time. People grow. People change. It's nothing to lose sleep over. The afterlife will go on."*

The afterlife will go on. My mind circled back to all the secrets I was keeping. I had made my mind up to tell her, to tell her everything. I just didn't know when I would get around to it. Maybe that was another reason I was avoiding her lately.

Soon the crew was back in order. Kate wasn't as twitchy anymore, but now Alex was looking like she might be able to harvest all of Indonesia with a single look. Whatever their problem was, I didn't care. They could keep their drama to themselves, and I would keep mine to myself. I passed out everyone's coins and we left for the mortal realm.

Indonesia wasn't pretty. Rusted metal sheet roofs littered the ground. The town of collapsed shacks we had wandered into looked as if it had just been waiting around for the final straw to drop in and close the place down. The earth was uneven and split into chasms that had choked in their attempt to swallow the wreckage. The living rummaged around in the debris, pretending to look for survivors while they plundered their neighbors' homes. Reapers stepped around them, searching for the non-survivors. The hounds kept watch over clusters of dull-eyed souls waiting along the perimeter, far enough away to keep them from trying to interact with the living.

I noticed Paul Brom, the captain of the Recovery Unit, standing tall on a raw ledge as he supervised his people. Paul looked like Charlie Chaplin, but with a better, fuller mustache. He used wax to curl the ends out and upward so that he looked like a true Victorian gentleman. Grim might have required us to wear the traditional reaper cowls, but he hadn't enforced any rules about headgear. Paul started wearing a bowler hat soon after Saul paved the way with his Stetson. Grim had been annoyed, but then again, everything annoyed Grim.

"Captain Harvey." Paul gave me a polite nod as I joined him on the ledge.

I smiled back at him. "Morning, Captain Brom."

We hadn't really exchanged much more than reflex greetings at the office. Like the other captains, he couldn't seem to make up his mind about me. It wasn't generally safe to befriend anyone on Grim's shit list, or anyone who attracted rebel terrorists as well as I did. I was lucky that the few friends I had to begin with were actually sticking around.

"How are you holding up, kid?" Paul was being brave today. I'd always assumed he held the same contempt for me as the general reaper populous. The captains were just less obvious about it, maintaining their politically correct authority by not discrediting it with petty, jealous barbs.

"So far, so good." I shrugged and turned to look out over the crumbling landscape to see how everyone was faring.

Brom's unit carried little batons that lit up like light sabers when they located a buried soul. The batons were a special design that worked like an extension of a reaper's arm, allowing them to sift through wreckage and deep water and plenty of other sticky situations to recover souls that were trapped beyond our reach. Many of the bodies would eventually be unearthed, but some of them were lost to the mortals for good. The Recovery Unit made sure their souls weren't lost for good too.

Alex was still scowling, but she seemed to be keeping her charges in line, so who was I to complain. She was out-harvesting Kate and fiercely leading souls past her sulking girlfriend just to rub it in. At least it gave them something else to focus on besides harassing me. Kevin was holding his own, harvesting reasonably mild souls, while Arden took his time, seeking out the younger victims. I'd never actually seen him in action before, and I found myself quickly endeared to the new expression on his face as he pulled the soul of a girl from a collapsed shack. His big, dark hands engulfed her little face, cradling her cheeks and chin as he whispered something in her native tongue. She nodded and took his hand, letting him lead her through the waiting souls until she found a familiar face.

Josie spotted us on the ledge and pointed a few souls off to the sidelines before making her way up to join us. "Good morning, professor."

Paul reached out his hand to squeeze her shoulder. "Ms. Gala, always a pleasure to see you."

Josie had taken Paul's soul hypnosis class at the academy last spring. She was every teacher's pet. Unless Jenni was in class with her, then they battled for the title. Their shared enthusiasm for education was lost on me. It wasn't that I didn't understand the importance of it all. I just didn't thirst for it the way they did. I used to be embarrassed by that admission, but I'd learned to appreciate the honesty of it at least.

"I never got the chance to congratulate you on making the Posy Unit." Paul was still busy flattering Josie. He remembered me and nodded in my direction. "Both of you."

"Thanks." Josie beamed. "I actually applied for your unit too, but I guess I was needed here."

Paul nodded. "Yes, I suppose you were."

They both glanced at me, and I had the vague feeling that my work ethic was being called into question, though I wasn't sure why. As far as I could tell, I was doing a bang up job as captain. Besides, it wasn't like his team had been called in to help out on one of my harvests.

I cleared my throat and stood up taller. "Well, I think you all are handling this all right without me. I should really go try to put a dent in the extra workload we're going to have to make up for tomorrow." I gave them each a nod. "Brom. Galla."

I coined off before they could say anything. Josie would probably chew on me for my rudeness, but it was warranted. At least I could get a few hours to myself, harvesting souls who didn't know or give a crap about my personal life and who couldn't grind my self-worth into the ground with a single look.

I dodged around on the original Saturday docket, randomly picking harvests that didn't seem too challenging. I didn't have Kevin or the hounds, and my mind wasn't in the best of places, so I took it easy, picking a plane crash here

105

and a morgue roundup there. A girl in leopard print tights asked if hell was real and if that's where she was going. I lied and said I didn't know. I just didn't feel like dealing with the denial and chaos. Prostitutes are bold and high maintenance, even postmortem.

I took care of a nice chunk of souls, but Sunday was still looking bleak. I left my catch locked up in the hold of the ship for Josie and Kevin to deliver with their lot from Indonesia. It was around five when I made it back to the condo. I was surprised to find Jenni there. I was even more surprised to find her in my room, snooping through my closet.

"Looking for anything in particular?" I said, throwing my duffle bag on the bed.

"Oh!" Jenni turned around with a gasp, clutching a pair of boots to her chest. "I- I was just looking, you know, for a pair of shoes to borrow." She held the boots up.

"For what?"

"Hmmm?" She looked painfully confused.

"For what? Are you going on a date? Business meeting?" I sat down on the end of the bed and pulled my boots off.

"Oh. Uh, a date. Tonight. I was in a hurry." She tossed the boots back in my closet. "I don't think these are my size though. Maybe I'll check Josie's closet." She gave me a tight smile and backed out of my room.

So Jenni was dating. Maybe that's why she was acting so funny lately. I wondered if Josie knew, though I doubted it. She would have mentioned it me earlier. It felt nice to have some frivolous secret mixed in with all the life or death ones I was carrying around.

CHAPTER 14

"Life is just one damned thing after another."
-Elbert Hubbard

Between the tabloid accusations, the reaming from Grim, and the awkward encounter with Paul Brom, I was feeling pretty down in the dumps. The only thing that could fix that was whiskey. Lots of it. It was Saturday, but it was still early. I had at least a good two hours before the weekend crowd would begin to invade the city. I put on a comfy pair of jeans and a tee shirt, then I took the travel booth across the street from Holly House over to the one around the block from Purgatory Lounge. I pushed through the front door, ready to tie one on.

Purgatory felt like home. Red Christmas lights hung from the ceiling, dotting bright reflections across the brick walls and the glossy wood floors every time they twinkled. Tent menus were set out on the row of booth tables that separated the bar area from the dance floor. Back in the far corner, several nephilim were playing pool, while a pair of female souls watched from the jukebox, lazily slipping coins in the machine and trying not to look too obvious as they ogled the angelic half breeds. I was relieved to see that there was only one other patron sitting in front of the bar, until I realized who it was.

Ammit was a slobbering mess. Her eye makeup was smeared across her damp face, and her black braids were a tangled, frizzy mess. I couldn't believe my eyes, but she was actually wearing sweatpants. I'd never seen a deity have a complete and total meltdown before, but something told me that if she was wearing sweatpants in public, she couldn't be far off.

"Hit me, demon," she said to Xaphen, sliding an empty lowball glass across the counter to him.

Xaphen didn't look so good. It was one thing to deal with rowdy souls or reapers, but I couldn't imagine it would be easy for him to cut off a deity. He slowly filled the lowball glass halfway full of rum. Ammit locked eyes with him, and he went ahead and filled it the rest of the way before sliding it back to her. He frowned when he noticed me and tried to shake his head, but I was in no mood to be dismissed tonight.

I sidled up next to Ammit and took the barstool next to her, avoiding his glare. "Whiskey on the rocks, X-man."

Xaphen grumbled at me, sending his halo of flames into an annoyed little dance along his forehead. He pulled down another lowball glass and set it down hard in front of me before filling it with ice and whiskey. Misery loves company, and my presence would only prolong Ammit's stay, but that wasn't my problem tonight. Xaphen would get over it.

"Lana, Lana, Lana," Ammit slurred as she reached over to pat my leg. "You're my friend, aren't you? You can be honest with me, right?"

"You bet." It's always best to humor the gods, especially when they're drunk.

Ammit leaned in closer, too hammered to realize there was no one close enough to overhear us. "Am I a complete airhead?"

"Who would say such a thing?" Short and sweet. That was my usual tactic with upset drunks.

"Everyone!" she wailed, throwing her head down on the bar with a cry. "Horus! Anubis! Osiris! They all hate me."

"What are you talking about? They adore you."

"Nope. No, they don't." She lifted her head to shake it, and then stopped when she nearly toppled off of her stool. "Someone stole my headdress. I forgot to lock the office closet at the Hall of Two Truths. I'm nothing without my headdress! The Weighing of the Hearts ceremony is ruined forever, and it's all my fault." She burst into tears again, dropping her head back to the bar.

The Hall of Two Truths was in Duat, where souls of the ancient Egyptian faith went to be judged before either passing on to Aaru, their heavenly realm, or being eaten alive by Ammit's vicious crocodile headdress. In actuality, the headdress was more of a holding dimension. Ammit took the unworthy souls and dumped them into a lake of fire in Duat after the ceremony.

The Egyptians were pretty proud of their ceremonies, even though they rarely happened anymore. Their religion had been reduced to a small corner of the new age market. Neopagans who followed Osiris or Isis more exclusively would end up at their gates on occasion, and they would all make a big to-do about it. It was a precious ritual for the Egyptian gods. Sometimes, they could go as long as three or four years without a single soul being delivered.

Ammit's sobs escalated into wailing, drawing an unpleasant glare from Xaphen. I didn't really know what else to do, so I gently patted her shoulder in a pathetic attempt to soothe her. The next thing I knew, I had a hysterical deity in my lap. She threw her arms around my neck and rubbed her runny nose across my sleeve.

"What am I going to do?" She hiccupped in my ear.

"Uh." I could see Xaphen grinning from the corner of my eye. My whiskey therapy was not going as well as I had hoped. "Where are you staying tonight, Ammit?" I asked, gently pulling away from her.

"What?" She blinked at me and rubbed her arm under her nose before taking another swallow of rum.

"Do you have a room somewhere in Limbo?"

"Oh." She glanced over the bar, looking confused. "Is it closing time?"

"Not quite, but I thought you might want to share a cab back to your hotel. Which one are you staying at?"

"I don't know. Just drop me at the Pagoda Inn. I'm gonna need some hot tea in the morning." She pulled herself upright and downed the rest of her rum. Xaphen gave me a relieved nod before phoning the only cab company in Limbo City.

Bill Skipper was a troll, literally. He was the runt of his family, who all resided in a Faerie hill in Summerland. He'd run away from home at a young age, dodging his abusive older brothers, and started up a cab company in Limbo City. No one knew his real name, and most people just called him Skipper. He'd named his company a Hop, Skip, and Jump Taxi Service, but drunks couldn't remember all that. The usual closing time line was, "Call me a Skipper!"

Bill had three cabs. His other two drivers were a nephilim and a tree spirit who had taken up residency in the bit of woods on the northwestern coast of the city. I was glad to see Bill behind the wheel when the cab pulled up outside of Purgatory. He was quiet and that would give me a few minutes to talk to Ammit about things I didn't feel like discussing in the bar.

Ammit dove into the backseat, wiggling across the squeaky vinyl until she'd made it in far enough for me to join her.

"Where to?" Bill asked in his gruff troll voice that always made me think of Batman. Even as a runt of a troll he was still a big guy, squashed up in the front seat and holding on to the steering wheel with just his fingertips, like the thing might break if he wrapped his meaty hands around it. The top of his ball cap grazed the ceiling as he glanced over his shoulder at us.

"The Pagoda Inn, and then Holly House," I said, helping Ammit put her seatbelt on.

Bill pulled out onto Morte Avenue and headed east towards Market Street. The sky was just beginning to fade, and the sidewalks were slowly filling with factory souls and deity tourists. We passed Athena's Boutique and the melancholy that had been chasing me around all day took another stab at me. I needed to plan a shopping trip with Josie, but it would have to wait a couple weeks until the rumors about me died down a little. Athena was a gossip queen. She would be all over me about the tabloid article. Best to wait until the excitement had shifted to someone else or until the thief was found. Speaking of thieves, I was beginning to wonder if the same one had struck in Duat.

Ammit reached over and squeezed my hand, giving me a watery eyed smile. "Thanks for being so nice to me, Lana. No one else seems to care."

"I'm sure your headdress will turn up. You're sure you didn't just misplace it?"

She shrugged. "I've put it in the same closet for a few thousand years now. I don't know. Maybe it's a good thing that they fired me. I was really getting sick of that dead-end office job."

"They fired you?"

"Yeah," she laughed. "Any monkey could do that job, except for the ceremony part. I suppose they could always get that horn-ball Babi to take my place." She giggled to herself. "Any monkey. Well, he fits the bill."

Babi was the god of baboons. He was also known as being a horny death deity.

I leaned in closer to her, letting the sounds of traffic insulate our conversation. "I'm sure you've heard about Atropos' shears being stolen by now. Hades' place was ransacked too. Maybe it's the same thief. Maybe when they're caught, your headdress will be recovered too."

Ammit nodded slowly. "Yeah, that had crossed my mind. Even so, I doubt I'll get my job back. Osiris was pissed. Isis wouldn't even look at me." She welled up again.

"What are you going to do?"

"I don't know." She rubbed under her eyes, trying to repair the sad state of her makeup. "Maybe I'll move to the city. I could find a job that isn't in an office. I could start my own business. I think I could be good at other things."

"Yeah?"

I gazed out the cab window, wondering what it must be like to be able to walk away from a job and a life and start over fresh somewhere else. It was a fantasy that ached too much to indulge in most days, but I couldn't help myself sometimes. With Ammit sitting next to me so full of possibilities, it was hard not to fantasize right along with her, and it was hard not to resent her for the fact that her possibilities were more than just wishful thinking.

CHAPTER 15

"On a large enough time line,
the survival rate for everyone drops to zero."
-Chuck Palahniuk

I had really been looking forward to a nice, boring Sunday, but the added workload from Saturday's delayed list screwed that daydream all to hell. The harvests were boring enough, but they were stacked on top of each other so tightly that it felt like riding through a fast-forwarded slide show that consisted of only three slides; military memorial, illness epidemic, natural disaster, played over and over again. The whole team ended up skipping lunch. It was nearing eight o'clock before we called it a day.

Kevin and Josie went ahead and offered to deliver the souls without me again. I think they enjoyed their time together on the ship. It was the only real time they got to spend alone, seeing as how we all lived together. It made me wonder how clean the sheets in the captain's quarters were.

I waved them off and headed back down the dock towards Market Street, stripping off my work robe and stuffing it in my duffle bag as I went. The hounds had gone along with Kevin and Josie to keep guard over the souls in the hold. We had an extra heavy load tonight, and they were excited to be in charge of so many. Though I think Saul was staying behind more for the fact that he had convinced a few child souls to play fetch with him.

It was late, but I was still surprised to only see one guard waiting at the entrance of the harbor just off the dock. It was Abe. I gave him a tired smile and a salute. "Keep up the good work, Abe."

He frowned at me, but followed it up with a quick nod. "Yeah, you too."

I stepped out onto the street, thinking that was weird. Then a deafening crack splintered through my skull. I was out before I hit the pavement.

CHAPTER 16

"I'm not afraid to die.
I just don't want to be there when it happens."
-Woody Allen

I don't know why I was dreaming about Craig Hogan. We were back in the dirty alley around the corner from the thrift store on the west side of the city. The scenario had changed, but the conversation was still a familiar one.

"I could help you study for the big test coming up. You know, if you want," he said, kicking his foot at the curb. His pale skin glowed in the streetlight, drawing out the splash of gray freckles that trailed over his nose and across his cheeks.

It was the first time he had approached me outside of class. We'd been giving each other doe eyes across the room for months at this point.

I tucked a curl behind my ear and blushed. "Yeah, that'd be nice."

"Yeah?" He smiled, hunching his shoulders up.

The alley was full of other reapers. They pushed past us, crowding in like cattle. A few faceless women were sobbing softly.

Craig looked after them with tender eyes. "I hope they don't mind."

"Mind what?" I asked.

His eyes drew back to meet mine. "That I'm dead."

I looked down and realized that my hand was buried in his chest. The glow pulsed inside him, keeping rhythm with his heartbeat.

"Do you mind?" he said.

I took a step back, trying to tug free, but his insides stuck to me like taffy, coiling around my wrist. I tried to use my other hand to push his shoulder back, but it only sank through his flesh, becoming as entangled as the other. Craig closed his eyes and leaned in, as if to kiss me, and then I woke up.

My mind was going off in an exhausting loop of *oh my god, oh my god, oh my god.* I kept squeezing my eyes shut and opening them again, waiting for the scene to change, but each time, I found myself staring into the unconscious face of Clotho. There was a split across her forehead, crusted with dried blood, and a swatch of duct tape over her mouth. She was tied to a chair across from me, and we weren't alone.

Next to Clotho, I could just barely make out Atropos' silhouette. I felt someone stir beside me. It had to be Lachesis. My brain picked back up with the *oh my god* mantra. Someone had snagged me and brought me to the Fates' factory, and that someone was powerful enough to best all three of the Fates. Whatever they wanted, it was a fair assumption that they were going to get it.

My eyes adjusted to the dark slowly, until I realized we were up in the roost. A lamp hanging in the corner of the room cast out a shallow light that reflected in the pool, where a big black mass floated in the water. My heart skipped a beat, and then I realized it was the dead body of Shashthi's cat.

The rustle of feathers drew my attention to the outer wall of the roost. Dozens of storks huddled in against each other. I could only see the edge of a wing or gleam of a beak poking out of the shadows here and there, but their disgruntled coos vibrated through the room. The tall arched windows had been covered in chicken wire, trapping them inside with us.

The hatch on the far side of the pool opened, bringing new panic and light with it from the room below, and someone came up to join us.

He—she—it just didn't make sense. For a split second I saw strawberry curls like Lachesis', but they quickly fell into a wave of shiny black hair, and then shrunk up into a dirty blond crop. At the same time, I saw eyes flicker through a kaleidoscope of colors and a nose elongate and shorten like Pinocchio couldn't quite make up his mind on fibbing about something.

A flutter of black wings snapped me out of the hypnosis. Caim appeared in the room with the shifter, and my heart tried to crawl out of my chest and hide under my chair. I hadn't seen Caim since our last encounter on the Sea of Eternity. My team had slain quite a few of his demons, but he had also managed to wound us by claiming Coreen Bendura, a senior reaper whose death had essentially thrown me into my initial role of leadership.

Caim was minion numero uno for Seth, the Egyptian god bound and determined to destroy the structure of Eternity, all because he couldn't be king. No one had seen Seth since he fled Limbo City after his role among the rebels had been revealed. Of course, no one had seen much of any rebels since the travel booths had been put in place around the city.

I really hadn't been looking forward to seeing Caim again. It was easy to stand tall when he was across the sea and on a different boat. Being in the same room with him was a different story. His wings were no bigger than

Gabriel's, but they were black, thinner, and more sharply angled. Everything about him was dark, thin, and angular. He was a true protégé of Seth's. His skin was mostly a pale gray, except where it split into a tarry black at his chin and spread down his throat, disappearing beneath his black robe. His fingertips were stained the same sticky black, like he had dirtied his hands too many times for them to ever come clean again.

Caim's shifter companion looked bored, even through the constantly changing faces. "Where is my payment?" it growled in a raspy voice.

Caim snarled, exposing his broken teeth and tarry gums. "Your job is not yet complete."

"This job has taken long enough. I want my money now, or I blow this whole plan to hell and back."

Caim wielded Atropos' shears, pointing them at the shifter's belly, who promptly shifted into the image of Seth. I knew it was only a copy, but my stomach flip-flopped all the same at the perfect replica of the god.

Caim laughed. "Face it, trickster. I might be playing second fiddle, but you're just a pawn in this game."

My stomach turned again. *Trickster?* As in, the Norse god Loki? The rebels certainly weren't being picky about the hells they recruited from, especially considering how exclusive the Egyptians could be. The Egyptians were the smallest religion to hold a seat on the Afterlife Council, and their subcommittee, the Sphinx Congress, was a breath away from dissolving into the melting pot of the Summerland Society, the mixed pagan subcommittee.

Loki melted from Seth into a twin of Caim. "Perhaps you'd like to go fuck yourself?"

Caim huffed and stuffed the shears in his robe. He turned away from his double and noticed me staring.

"Sleeping Beauty awakes. Finally."

Every muscle in my body twitched and tensed as I watched him circle around the pool. He knelt down in front of me and paused, flashing his apocalypse campaign smile before ripping the tape from my mouth, letting it dangle from one side of my cheek.

"I don't suppose you're going to make this easy on us, hmm?" he said.

I swallowed, trying to slow my breathing down. At the rate I was going, I was bound to hyperventilate before even finding out what he wanted.

Caim sighed. "Usually I enjoy drawing out the torture, but we happen to be on a tight schedule."

Loki, still posing as Caim's twin, leaned back against a wall and crossed his arms. "I could go take a walk in her skin. That might yield something useful."

"Right. Useful. Because you've found out so much since you've been here." Caim sneered at the god.

"I'll be requiring payment first."

I gasped as Caim shoved his hand in one of my front pockets and retrieved the coin Winston had spelled for me. *Shit.*

"What do we have here? This is new." He rolled the coin between his blackened fingers and grinned at me with dark curiosity. I still hadn't found my voice, so all I could do was watch as he tossed it to Loki.

In that split second, while I held my breath, I envisioned the end of Eternity. Loki would vanish. He would close his eyes and open them in the throne realm. He would find Winston, and we would all be lost. Royally screwed. That's what we were.

Loki snagged the coin out of the air. I waited, still holding my breath, but nothing happened.

"There. Consider yourself paid. Now take a walk."

I almost passed out from relief. If I ever found my way out of this mess, I would have to ask Winston about the coin. Did it only work for me? Did the tosser have to be the catcher as well? It didn't matter. The debris of Eternity snapped back like a slingshot, stabilizing my horror fantasy, and all was right again. Well, except for the part where I was tied up with the Fates and at the mercy of a rebel demon.

Loki glanced over the coin and tucked it away. He waited for Caim to move aside, and then he took his place, kneeling down in front of me.

The moment our eyes locked, my head began to swim. The image of Caim that he had adopted melted away like a layer of wax, and for a split second, I saw his true face. It wasn't pretty. He looked like Marty Feldman with an underbite and out of control eyebrows.

My breathing took off again as he grasped my chin and rotated my face around. I squeezed my eyes shut, cringing against his touch. When I opened them, I was staring back into a reflection of myself.

"Is there anything duller than playing a reaper?" he groaned. "I swear, even the humans lead more entertaining lives."

Caim waited for Loki to disappear down the hatch before turning his soulless eyes back on me. "Why don't you be a good girl and just tell me where Grim keeps his prize soul, hmmm? You could save us both some trouble, and I could be gone before that worthless heap of Norse trash makes it back."

I tried to look confused, but I was numb, frozen in disbelief and horror. I couldn't have gotten the words out even if I had known what to say to him.

"Grim's. Prize. Soul," he said slowly, sliding his tarry fingers up my thighs and digging them in deeper with each word. His nails sliced through my jeans like razors and I felt my flesh split open. My breath rushed out faster. He drew closer, filling my line of sight with his black, broken grin. I turned my face away, closing my eyes. The storks cooed louder as the wind whistled through the chicken wire.

"Tell me," Caim whispered. "Tell me, so I have a reason to spare you." His fingers loosened on my thighs and crept up my stomach, snaking over my breasts, finally resting around my neck.

I opened my eyes again, taking in a shuddering breath before his thumb pressed into my throat. The room flashed darker and brighter, keeping time with my pulse as it throbbed in my temples. I thought that I might pass out. I wanted to pass out.

Just then, Clotho decided to come to. Her wide blue eyes flashed open, and she blinked stiffly like a toy doll. She groaned, taking inventory of her condition.

Caim released me and turned his attentions to her, dancing over to jerk the tape away from her mouth so she could join the conversation.

"You are so dead," Clotho roared at him. She pulled at her restraints more fiercely than I had, but they wouldn't give.

Caim threw his head back, howling in delight, almost in awe of his own boldness, and then he put that prize smile of his right down in her face. "Promises, promises."

"What the hell do you think you're doing? When Zeus hears of this, he'll hunt you down. Your head will be mounted on an Olympian wall by the end of the week."

The storks squawked at the voice of their fearless leader. One brave bird hopped closer, stabbing at Caim's arm with its beak. Caim hissed, snatching the delicate creature by the neck.

"No!" Clotho strained against her ropes.

Caim gave the bird a shake. It struggled in his grasp, losing feathers in a halo on the floor. The thing lit up brighter in its panic. It looked like it had been feasting on souls all day, and for all I knew, it had been. I could see the same thought creep across Caim's face as he retrieved Atropos' shears from his robe again.

"What are you doing?" Clotho shrieked at him.

121

Caim stepped away from her chair, taking the stork with him. He knelt down on his knees and pinned the bird's head to the concrete floor, shuffling in his robe some more. I immediately recognized Ammit's crocodile headdress. Caim set it on the floor and positioned it towards the stork. Then he took the shears and cut the stork's throat, severing its head in one quick motion.

Clotho lost it. The pupils and whites of her eyes went black like the night had just possessed her. She sucked in a ragged breath and screamed. I couldn't look away. It was too terrible. It was too incredibly awful to peel my eyes from the scene that would no doubt haunt my darkest nightmares for years to come.

Black blood pooled around the stump where the stork's head used to be, and from the blood rose a pale steam. It coiled and spiraled through the air, humming and gurgling the soft music of innocence that waifs through maternity ward nurseries. The eyes of Ammit's headdress slowly came to life, glowing green in the dark room. Its sharp jowls wedged open, and the freshly spilled souls were sucked down in a one long yawn of a swallow.

The room was suffocating. Clotho's grief and Caim's excitement spiraled around me, a nauseating blend that took my breath away. Caim was shaking with quiet laughter. He reached down and ran his fingers through the stork's tacky blood. The rest of the flock cooed forlornly, huddling in tighter to one another with a collective shiver. Clotho's screams finally tapered off, fading into a raw sob as her chin dropped to her heaving chest. She stared vacantly at the floor.

A door slammed downstairs and Caim's attention jerked away from his kill. A soft growl stirred in his throat.

"Clotho! You up there?" It was Asmodeus. I sucked in a breath, hesitating in my excitement, and it was a split second steeped in regret. Caim stood and slapped the tape back over my mouth so hard that I tasted blood mixed in with the bitter adhesive. I rocked in my chair, pulling against the ropes that bound me, until Caim's fist cracked against my temple. The chair rocked some more with the impact, but I stayed upright.

The storks were cooing anxiously again. Caim turned away from me and silently replaced Clotho's tape too. She didn't move, didn't blink. She had just abandoned herself, drifting off to wherever a goddess goes when she's lost her mind entirely. Caim wound around the pool, carefully avoiding the light cast into the room through the hatch. When he stopped behind the door, he loosened a satchel hanging from his robe and pulled out a helmet. It was silver with two short crested rows of black feathers. He pulled it over his head and vanished.

Hot tears filled my eyes and ran down my cheeks, wetting the edges of the duct tape before they trickled down my chin. I wanted to scream out to Asmodeus, but I could barely manage a whimper. A tiny fly rested on the end of my nose, and then a cool hand brushed down the side of my neck. I trembled.

Beelzebub looked over my shoulder and pressed a finger to his lips. "Shhh. This might hurt a bit, love," he whispered, just before ripping the tape from my mouth.

CHAPTER 17

"It is not the strongest of the species that survives, nor the most intelligent. It is the one that is most adaptable to change."
-Charles Darwin

My mouth fell open, and I choked down a painful breath. "He has the Helm of Hades. We have to warn Asmodeus."

I was too late.

Asmodeus stepped inside the roost with his fists in the air. He was dressed in black, from the skullcap on his head down to the combat boots laced up his claves. I'd never seen him without his faded fedora. His aura of cool, casual charm was missing tonight too. It had never occurred to me that the lust demon might be Bub's first choice for backup, but he looked plenty prepared for battle. Of course, no one is ever really prepared to fight the invisible. I watched helplessly as he doubled over, falling face first into the pool. The bony handle of Atropos' shears protruded out of his back, the blades angled in deep under one shoulder blade. Beelzebub exploded beside me, shifting instantly into a hoard of buzzing flies. He dispersed around the room.

The storks stopped cooing. The wind stilled outside the windows. The place grew quiet as a tomb, while I listened for some sign of anything or anyone. A single minute must have passed, though it felt painfully longer. Bub's flies assembled, and he took form again on the upper ledge of the roost. He was dressed the same as Asmodeus, in full combat apparel. His fist tunneled through the air, and I heard it connect with flesh. Caim reappeared as he plummeted from the ledge, Hades' helm falling from his head and bouncing across the concrete floor. It skittered to a stop at the edge of the pool. Caim's wings pulled in sharply, buffering his fall. He still landed on his ass, but he recovered quickly, rushing to snatch up the helmet. He snagged Ammit's headdress while he was at it.

"You sheep! You puppets!" He spat at us. "You're still letting them run Eternity according to the humans' desires. We are gods! You let the souls decide, but we don't have to. You see? I've taken these here. I've claimed them for Seth!" He held out Ammit's headdress and shook it. "We will remake Eternity, and victory will belong to the gods who claim it, not the ones who compete in your pathetic pageants!"

Bub took flight again, descending in a violent swarm, but by the time he pulled himself back together, Caim was gone. The coward slipped the helmet back over his head as he stepped through the hatch door. I could tell Bub wanted to go after him, but reason swallowed his fury. Instead, he rushed to my side, retrieving the knife from my boot before cutting through my ropes. Then we both sloshed through the pool to where Asmodeus's still body floated.

Bub laid a gentle hand on his back, wincing before he rolled him over. Asmodeus was sickly pale. He bobbed in the water, stiff and cold to the touch. My heart broke as Bub moaned softly, knotting his hands in Asmodeus's shirt. I'd never seen him so open and defeated. I didn't know what to do with my hands. I held them open over Asmodeus, almost too afraid to touch him. His unblinking eyes stared up at the ceiling. I moved to close them then jerked my hand back as a gurgle escaped his lips.

"Asmodeus?" Bub whispered. He ran a hand down his friend's face.

"Take it out," he groaned.

I wasn't thinking straight. I reached under his shoulder, gripped the handle of the shears, and tore them free of his flesh. Asmodeus gasped. His eyes began to work again, blinking sporadically as his blood seeped into the pool. It clouded around us, soaking into our clothes and filling the room with its sweet, coppery fragrance.

Bub's hands slipped as he tried to find the best way to take hold of Asmodeus, struggling to pull him through the pool. "Help me," he pleaded.

I looped an arm under Asmodeus's bad shoulder, and he cried out. More blood darkened the pool. I couldn't do it. He was too heavy. He was too injured.

I glanced around the room and noticed my duffle bag, abandoned by the hatch door. My work robe was in there. We could loop it under him and lift him out of the pool without causing him more undue pain. I stumbled out of the water. My clothes clung to me, dripping and cold against my skin. I unzipped my duffle bag with trembling fingers and dumped its contents; my soul docket, work robe, cell phone, and a clean shirt. The tea packet Meng had given me fell out on top of it all. I forgot the robe and tore open the packet, bringing the tea bag back into the pool with me.

Bub was still struggling to move Asmodeus. "What's that?"

"Hold his head up," I ordered him, cupping the tea bag in my hands. I squeezed my fingers together and dipped them into the murky pool, letting the tea bag stain the red water a rusty brown before tilting my hands up to Asmodeus's mouth.

"Drink."

Asmodeus opened his mouth and I let the tea spill from my fingers and down his throat. He began to cough, wincing as his shoulder jerked about. I dunked my hands down in the pool again, squeezing my thumbs over the tea bag to get a second dose. Asmodeus's lips trembled, and he frowned at me, but he took the second helping. He was still in bad shape, but he seemed to be breathing easier.

Bub looked up at me. "We need to get him to Meng's."

I nodded.

Someone else stirred in the room, and we both tensed. Lachesis was awake. She groaned and stretched against the ropes binding her. I waded out of the pool. The knife Bub had used to free me lay abandoned on the floor beside my chair. I used it to cut her free, letting her remove the duct tape on her own. Then I did the same for Atropos, gently squeezing her shoulder to wake her. I saved Clotho for last. She was still slumped in her chair like a ragdoll. Lachesis and Atropos stepped around the stork carcass, each sparing it a soft eye before wrapping their arms around their comatose sister.

"The shears?" Atropos glanced back at me.

"Caim had them."

"I know. Does he still?"

I shivered and wrapped my arms around myself. "They're in the pool." I glanced back and Bub and Asmodeus. "We need to get to Meng's."

Atropos nodded stiffly. "Do you have a phone?"

I dug through the pile I'd emptied out of my duffle bag and found my cell.

"Dial star five. It will ring you into the Nephilim Guard's station. Tell them to send everyone they can spare. Tell them to barricade the harbor. We might be too late, but there could still be a chance he's in the city."

I did as she said. The guard who answered didn't ask questions. He said they were on their way and hung up. I dialed Grim's private number next. It felt like the right thing to do if I wanted to keep my head on my shoulders.

He answered on the first ring. "What's happened?" He had enough sense to know that something was very wrong if I was calling him at this hour. We did not do social calls. It was a wonder he had even bothered to give me his private number at all when I made captain of the Posy Unit.

"I've already called the guard," I said, hoping his mind would calm before I laid the rest on him. "We have a serious problem."

CHAPTER 18

"The only way to keep your health is to eat what you don't want, drink what you don't like, and do what you'd rather not."
-Mark Twain

Asmodeus looked all wrong in Meng's guest room. The Nephilim Guard had spared two men to transport us to her temple in one of their fancy new SUVs. The Limbo City tax dollars were hard at work. With his lust demon wiles completely unguarded, Asmodeus had quite an effect on Jai Ling. After spilling a second cup of tea on the bedspread, Meng had to chase her out of the room.

The smell of her extra potent healing brew made my stomach grumble. Asmodeus turned his nose up, and gave the cup a questionable look. "Is this really necessary? I'm feeling much better. I'm sure I'm capable of healing on my own," he said, waving his hand in the air with a grimace.

Meng huffed at him. "You stabbed with death shears. Drink. No dead demons stink up my house."

Asmodeus took the cup from her withered hand, looking to Bub and me for sympathy.

I shook my head and grinned. "I've been right where you are a few times myself, and all I have to say is better you than me."

Meng shot me a dirty look. "See to it he drink that. I have others tonight."

"Really?"

Meng put her hands on her hips. "Did not know Grim put me on council just to run hospital. Sneaky illegitimate son of rabbit." The insult carried more weight in Chinese.

"Who else is laid up?"

Meng shrugged. "Nephilim guards. A reaper. Don't know what happen to them. They sleep still. This city troubled tonight." She shook her head and shuffled out of the room.

Loki must have been busy. I wondered if he was still walking around in my skin. I was fairly certain that the harbor guards were the ones snoozing down the hall, but I was curious about the reaper.

Jai Ling appeared in the doorway again. Her eyes roamed over Asmodeus with thoughts far darker than any young girl should have been capable of thinking. She licked her lips and timidly stepped into the room. A folded blanket and a suturing kit were nestled in her quivering arms. "Does he need to be stitched up?" she whispered to me.

"I think we can manage," I said, taking the supplies from her and laying them on the side table. Her bottom lip puckered out, and she left the room reluctantly.

Asmodeus was a charming fellow, but he wasn't so rarely beautiful in Eternity. Among the souls, however, he was a libido magnet. They'd throw themselves naked at his feet if he demanded it.

Bub was sprawled out in the corner chair beside Asmodeus's bed. Five o'clock shadow was filling in around his goatee. That and the tired circles under his eyes made him look a hundred years old. I knew he was ancient, but I was used to seeing him as a youthful, strong male in his

130

prime, not as a worn out refugee. His black military ensemble was still dripping pinkish water. I'd changed into the spare shirt from my duffle bag, but my jeans were still a disaster, rubbing my skin raw and making the cuts along my thighs itch. My hair was drying into an unruly catastrophe on my head. Mangy curls poked out around my face.

Bub caught my eye and stood up, walking around the bed to join me by the door. He pulled me into his arms. I let him hold me, not caring that my dry shirt was getting soaked.

I pressed my face into his neck and sighed. "How did you know I was in trouble?" I asked.

Bub grew brittle in my arms. I hadn't meant it as an accusation. I was so very grateful, but my nerves had settled enough that curiosity dug its way into my mind.

"Your phone," he said finally. "I tried to call. Twice. You always answer when I call. It has a GPS chip in it. I don't know why, but I decided to activate the feature and see what might be preoccupying you so late in the evening. When I saw that you were at the factory, I knew something wasn't right."

"Oh."

I wasn't really angry. It was hard to be when he had just flown in and saved the day. Part of me wanted to find his concern endearing, even if that concern was possibly at the notion that I might be stepping out on him. A darker part of me wondered how often he had checked up on me since I'd had the phone and if my location could be tracked inside the throne realm. I wondered if Bub could feel my pulse racing. I needed to talk to Winston, and soon.

Asmodeus whined through two cups of tea before he pretended to doze off, probably hoping to avoid any more of the liquid torture. Bub rolled him over and inspected the wound. It was black and oozing clear fluid. The infection extended half an inch around the opening, but it looked like it was receding. Atropos might not have used the shears anymore, but they still had a nasty smite to them.

I slipped out of the room, giving Bub and Asmodeus some privacy, before tiptoeing down the hall to check in on the other guests. I recognized one of the slumbering nephilim as Abe, confirming my assumption that it had been Loki waiting for me at the harbor. The other nephilim was a new face, but the reaper patient was oddly familiar. It took a minute to come up with his name.

Clair Kramer was Grace Adaline's apprentice. I remembered him from Grace's wandering souls course that Josie and I had taken last semester. He had been tasked with mundane duties like grading and handing out papers. Occasionally, Grace would send him out to fetch her some coffee. I imagined that she also took him out on harvests with her, but I'd never really asked. I was far more preoccupied with the fact that Craig Hogan was taking the class with us.

Clair stirred, waking to the hall light spilling over my shoulder and casting a long shadow over him and the bed. He jolted upright, gaping in horror as I stepped into the room.

"Hey, hey," I whispered. "You're at Meng's. It's all right."

"I-I didn't mean to bother you." He shook his head, clutching the bedspread up to his chest.

I snorted softly. "And here I thought I was bothering you. I just wanted to see who else Meng was taking care of tonight. What happened to you? I thought Grace only did low-risk harvests."

Clair looked confused and unsure of how to answer. "I was attacked on the street by... well, by you."

I shuddered, feeling utterly sickened by the thought of how much damage Loki could do while wandering around the city, wearing my face. "That wasn't me," I said, taking another step into the room. Clair squirmed and flinched away from me. I paused and lifted my hands up. "Honest. There's a shifter in town. He's part of the reason I'm here tonight too."

I watched the information roll around behind his eyes. He finally relaxed and gave me a reassured smile. "I believe you."

My shoulder sagged as I blew out a breath. "Where did you run into him anyway?"

Clair looked down at his hands. His long bangs slanted over his eyes and his cheeks flared a rosy pink. "In front of Holly House. I wanted to talk to you about the demon defense course starting up this fall. I thought since Kevin's your apprentice, he could vouch for me, and maybe you would put in a good word with Beelzebub. I'd really like to take the class."

"Ahhh. I see. Yeah, no problem." I shrugged.

"Really?" He looked up at me.

"Why not? It's the least I can do after you were attacked by my look-alike."

Clair laughed uneasily. My nerves were still raw, but the excitement had died down and I was feeling relatively normal again. It made me question the direction my life was spiraling into. A year ago, I wouldn't have been able to manage such a casual conversation so soon after a near-death experience.

I excused myself and went back to check on Bub and Asmodeus. Bub had reclined himself back in the guest chair. His feet were kicked up on the edge of the bed, and both men were softly snoring. I scratched a little note on a pad beside the bed and tucked it down behind Bub's folded arms, giving him a gentle kiss on the forehead.

It was well after midnight, and I had already made up my mind that I was going to make it to work in the morning. I loathed the idea of having another harvest heavy makeup day, and I told Grim as much after explaining the events of the evening. He had been livid, but at least it wasn't directed at me for a change.

Atropos had her shears back, though they were still minus a stork. They weren't plotting my demise anymore, so that was one plus on my list. Caim and Loki's appearance in the city was still eating at me. Anubis had finally arrived with his jackals, but the trail they picked up ended at the harbor. Caim had made his getaway. The jackals didn't pick anything up on Loki, so the nerve-wracking possibility that he was still in the city had everyone on the lookout.

I considered calling a cab, just to be safe, but it was highly unlikely that Loki would strike again tonight. Instead, I left Meng's on foot, walking down the long gravel drive that led back into the city. There was a travel booth just off Divine Boulevard, the main street Meng's driveway came out onto. It was a whole two blocks back to Holly House, but I was feeling lazy and exhausted, so I took the booth route.

When I exited the booth at the corner of Divine and Memorial Drive, I spotted a silver limo parked in front of Holly House. I didn't even have to wonder who it was there for. One of the back windows rolled down, and a small dark hand adorned with a cluster of beaded bracelets beckoned me over. Parvati, the Hindu representative on the council, opened the car door and slid across the seat, inviting me inside.

I'd become bolder with the council as of late, but one did not simply deny Parvati an audience. Through the War of Eternity, she had been a different deity entirely; the bloodthirsty Kali. She was a force of fury and chaos on the battlefield, one that the gods still whispered about fearfully when they thought no one else was listening. I'm not saying she won the war singlehandedly, but if she had been on the other side of the fence, Limbo City would be a different place indeed, and I might not even exist.

Beyond the deep-seeded terror, I didn't have much of an opinion about Parvati. She was nice and sweet, but she was also a politician. I never could quite tell where I stood with politicians. Their agenda always escaped me, as I'm sure they intended for it to. I was skeptical to say the least, but it never seemed to be enough to keep me out of their webs.

I climbed inside the limo, not wanting to induce the history book images of the dark, snake-tongued crazy I knew she was capable of becoming at a moment's notice. Parvati tapped the glass between us and the driver, and the car began a slow loop around the block. I cradled my duffle bag in my lap and waited, not quite ready for whatever she had planned, but I didn't have much of a choice in the matter.

Parvati, like most of the Hindu deities, was unsettling to be around. I think it had something to do with all their extra appendages. The Egyptian's animal natures had evolved until they simply became living headdresses, like Ammit's crocodile and Horus's falcon. They could take them off and leave them at home, setting the rest of Eternity at ease with their more normal appearances. With the Hindu gods, it wasn't so easy.

Parvati's brown eyes seemed too big and too bright for her delicate round face. She smiled placidly at me as she stirred two cups of tea at the same time, one with her two upper arms and the other with her lower set. She held out one of the cups to me, and I hesitated to take it from her.

"Please, dear reaper, let us make this a pleasant meeting."

I took the cup gingerly and balanced it on my knees, giving her a tight smile. She waited for me to take a sip of the sweet brew before beginning.

"Your involvement with the current events in the city has not gone unnoticed. I had theories of my own before Grim declined you as his new lieutenant, and I was not entirely surprised to find you in the thick of things after the fact."

I did my best to keep a neutral face and maintained eye contact with her, even when she paused to take a breath. She hadn't asked any questions, so I didn't feel inclined to answer any for her. She watched me carefully, like a cat watches a mouse, waiting for it to move.

"I am not typically a creature of deception or political strategy. I'm sure you know where my strengths lie. I am new in this life, and I wish to do my part in maintaining the peace. I will not deny that a sliver of me is seduced by the threat of a new war, but a larger more maternal voice commands my being now. Do you understand what I am saying?"

I nodded slowly. "I think so."

"Then take my words for what they are. No more, no less. I know the future of this world will rely on you in some way. I don't know how, and I don't need to know. The warrior in my heart recognizes the warrior in yours. The only question I ask is, are you prepared?"

I clutched the cup of tea so tightly that I thought the brittle china might crack. Anything I could say felt like it would be an admission to something that I wasn't sure I believed myself. I didn't want to think about the things that the future might hold. I wanted one day at a time. I wanted to fill my head with thoughts of John Wayne pajama parties and Athena's new spring line of shoes and accessories. I didn't want to think about whose path I might find myself in if Eternity decided to fall apart again.

I stared back at Parvati's passive gaze, feeling the sting of tears creep into my vision. "I don't know," I whispered.

Parvati nodded solemnly. I'm not sure when the thought slipped inside my head, but I realized that the real reason I found her so unsettling was because she reminded me of Khadija. She was softer on the outside, and much harder on the inside, but it was still right there. She had the wounded spirit of a woman who had paid the ultimate price to save Eternity, and I knew if she had it to do all over again, she would without a second thought.

She reached across the distance and rested a hand on my trembling knee. "That's good enough for me, child. Finish your drink."

I swallowed down the rest of the tea. It had gone cold, but I found it soothing nonetheless. The limo stopped in front of Holly House. I thanked Parvati for the tea as I stepped out onto the sidewalk.

"We'll talk again soon," she said, slipping me a business card and a polite nod before I closed the door.

CHAPTER 19

*"Friendship is a single soul
dwelling in two bodies."
-Aristotle*

My nerves were humming a tired tune when I stepped off the elevator on the tenth floor. I felt exhausted and rejuvenated, doomed and fortunate. I wanted to dance, and I wanted to cry. I felt like I had my own little Kali goddess living in my head, and she wanted to throw everything to the wind and go eat a steak and start a brawl at Purgatory.

Josie was sitting up at the breakfast bar when I came through the front door. Her yellow terrycloth robe was split open at the thigh, and her legs were folded up under her chin. Her raccoon eyes looked up from the pair of tea mugs waiting on the counter. The evening was full of tea it seemed.

"Lana, I thought maybe you were staying with Bub."

"No, I, uh." I swallowed. "I was abducted by Caim and Loki at the harbor after you and Kevin left. I've been at the factory, tied up with the Fates for most of the night."

"What?" Josie had to grab the counter to keep from falling off her barstool. "What?" She closed her eyes and shook her head, trying to rattle the words around until they made better sense.

I laid my duffle bag on the dining room table and pulled out a chair, dropping into it with a sigh. "They had Atropos' shears and the Helm of Hades and Ammit's headdress."

Josie looked horrified. "What the hell were they trying to pull off with all that? How did you escape? Were they captured? Are you okay?"

I held up a hand. "Slow down. I'm getting there. They escaped. We got the shears back, but they still have the helm and headdress. Caim was after the soul we harvested last fall, but when he realized... I couldn't help him, he killed one of Clotho's birds and sucked the souls out of it with Ammit's headdress. It didn't go over well. Fortunately, that's when Bub and Asmodeus dropped in. Bub realized something was wrong when I didn't answer my phone after he called several times. Apparently, my phone has one of those fancy GPS devices. So he and Asmodeus launched a little rescue mission."

Josie abandoned her barstool to join me at the table. She let everything I'd just told her settle for a minute. I could tell she had the hard questions that I'd been dodging on her mind again, but she looked too tired to pry tonight. So I saved her the trouble.

"That soul we harvested last fall controls Eternity." It came out easy, all in one breath. I was too defeated to even notice my conscious resisting.

Josie nodded stiffly. "I wondered as much. I imagine Grim would terminate anyone who tries to say it out loud though." She rubbed her hands up over her face and brought them to rest on the back of her neck, staring off into the depths of the hardwood table, but I wasn't finished yet. I was on a roll. Why stop now?

"The soul who ran the joint before him gave me something extra when she made me so that I could help find

139

her replacement. I'm able to see the potency of a soul. Grim didn't know about it until last fall, and neither did I."

Josie sat back in her chair and looked at me with new eyes. I watched her chest rise and fall like a tide while the news washed over her. "That makes sense, I guess," she finally said, nodding her head some more.

For my finale, I dropped the mother lode on her. "I also killed Wosyet."

Josie stared at me for a long minute without blinking or even breathing. Then she stood up and looked around the room like she had forgotten where we were. "Coffee. We need coffee."

"She was the nurse at the hospital—"

"Coffee first. I'm sleep deprived. I think I'm hearing things that you're not actually saying," she said, heading for the kitchen.

"Why are you still up anyway? I mean, not that I mind dumping all my deepest and darkest on you at two in the morning, but still. Here I am, hogging the conversation with my burdens. What is it you've got weighing on your mind these days?"

I slipped off my boots while Josie fumbled with the coffeepot, sloshing water across the counter. She snatched up a dishtowel and wiped at the spill compulsively, not looking up at me. "Jenni. I was waiting up for Jenni, but she's probably not coming home again. She stood me up today. We were supposed to meet for lunch. We'd planned the get-together over a week ago. I watched her pencil it into her day planner."

"New boyfriend?" I wouldn't drop that secret on her tonight. There was enough startling news in the air.

Josie laughed, but she still wouldn't look at me. "Right. This is Jenni we're talking about."

"Well, Grim has her working a lot of hours, I'm sure."

Josie sighed and leaned over the kitchen sink, squeezing both hands on the ledge of the counter. "I'm worried about her. She's been distant, and—" she looked up at me, "and you've been distant, and Gabriel doesn't come around lately since you're feuding. Kevin's a doll, but all he does is talk about how exciting the harvests are that you take him on. I'm about to strangle him."

I recoiled at her list of burdens, not liking how so many of them revolved around me. Josie's eyes watered. She swallowed hard and threw the dishtowel in the sink. "Well, there you have it. I'm a miserable wretch with petty problems that don't hold a candle to the shit you've been marinating in for the past year. How do you sleep so well?"

I shrugged and stared across the condo and out the darkened living room windows. "I really don't know." I laughed, hearing myself echo the answer to Parvati's question. "I'm not sure I know anything anymore."

Josie brought me a cup of coffee, all decked out the way I take it. She set her cup of straight black down next to mine and curled herself up in a dining room chair across from me, resting her chin on her knees again. "So, you're a freak of nature that can kill gods and spot special souls able to keep Grim in the business of playing the man behind the curtain? How's that working out for you?"

I smiled at her. "It totally sucks, but thanks for asking."

CHAPTER 20

"Surprises are foolish things. The pleasure is not enhanced,
and the inconvenience is often considerable."
-Jane Austen

I hadn't counted on wearing my coffee Monday morning. I also hadn't counted on seeing Loki in my kitchen. I almost pinched myself to be sure that I wasn't stuck in another nightmare.

"Are you all right?" he asked, filling a mug full of coffee.

"I'm not awake yet," I said, more to myself than him.

A soft growl stirred from under the table. Saul was curled around my feet. He was a perceptive little beast, and he always stuck close by when he knew I was feeling fragile. Loki eyed Saul, sizing him up before he turned back to the coffee pot.

"Well," he went on, adding sugar to his mug, "I have a busy day planned at the office. I better get going before Grim sends an escort."

"Jenni?" The surreal moment was fading.

"Yeah?" Loki turned back to me, and a hazy aura that resembled my roommate floated around him.

"Would you mind telling Grim that I'm going to be taking the day off? I had a rough night."

"I heard. Thank goodness you didn't tell them where Grim's hiding that soul." Loki might have been exceptional at chameleoning himself into other people, but he was a lousy spy.

I was quick to shrug. "Like Grim would tell me where he hides anything."

Loki's frown was deeper than the one he pasted on Jenni's face. I could see them overlapping, her glossy pout superimposed over his bulldog underbite.

"Right. You're sure about skipping work? Looked like you had quite the harvest list for today."

"The team can handle it without me. I really need to get some sleep."

He seemed disappointed. There was probably another ambush planned. "Whatever," he said, giving Saul another sour look.

I waited until he left and I heard the elevators ping at the end of the hall before making my way over the kitchen sink and vomiting up all the coffee and bile swirling around in my stomach. My head throbbed. I slid down to the tile floor and pressed my back into the corner of the cabinets. One day. That's all I wanted. Just one day where everything was blissfully mundane, and I didn't have to wonder if I'd still be breathing when night fell.

I had to dial Grim's private number four times before I got it right. My fingers didn't want to work. My hands were shaking so hard that the phone rattled against my hoop earring.

Grim answered on the second ring. "I really can't handle much more bad news, Harvey."

"How sure are you that this line is secure?"

"One hundred percent." His tone shifted. "What's this about?"

143

"Loki is posing as Jenni. You can't let on until we get her back, but we're going to need to get him out of the way in the meantime."

Grim was silent for a minute. "You're absolutely sure?"

"One hundred percent."

"Split your harvest list. Give out half to Arden, Alex, and Kate. Be here with the others by nine. I'll put together the rest of the team. Don't breathe a word of this to anyone else." He hung up without saying goodbye.

I swallowed and looked around the condo, wondering how long I had been living with a psychotic god. Then I wondered what had become of Jenni, and how we were going to find her. Rain splattered across the living room windows. It was a sudden downpour, and it hadn't been announced. My first thought was Winston, and my heart seized up. I thought of the coin Loki had gotten his hands on.

"No, no, no," I sighed, clutching the phone to my chest. It couldn't be Winston. My heart sank even lower when I realized that there was no way for me to check in on him. I stared helplessly at the numbers on my phone's keypad, trying to pull it together before dialing Josie's number.

"Captain?" Josie was out of breath. She and Kevin had been taking full advantage of the gym at Holly House. She sounded chipper, despite our late night confessional. It felt good to have the secrets out in the open between us, even if they did bring all kinds of new and terrifying possibilities with them.

I hated to drop another nasty surprise on her so soon, but some things just can't wait. "I need you and Kevin to cut your workout short this morning. We have a crisis. I need you both up here now." I wondered if Loki was still in the building and added, "Don't stop to talk to anyone. Not even Jenni if you happen to see her."

"You mean Jenni finally showed up?"

"I'll explain everything when you get here." I hung up before she could ask any more questions. I had enough of my own to tend to. I had five minutes tops before they would make it back up to the tenth floor, so I made one more phone call.

"Greetings, reaper," Parvati answered.

"What was in that tea?"

I could feel her smile through the phone. "Already proving useful? It's good to know that my timing is still impeccable."

"Well?"

"It's called Divya Drishti, or divine perception. The effects won't last forever, but I thought you might benefit from the increased focus it generates. I have always found it helpful in troubled times. It can light the true path through many a delicate circumstances."

I thought of Loki and then of mine and Josie's conversation the night before. I nodded to myself. "Thank you," I said, wondering if there was going to be a political catch to the gift, though I was so grateful that I almost didn't care.

"You are very welcome. Farewell, reaper." It felt too easy, like any second she might call back and request that I go pick up her dry-cleaning or assassinate someone.

Josie and Kevin clamored through the front door, right past the protective Latin prayers engraved in the framework. That was the other big question weighing on me. How had Loki gotten into the condo in the first place? The prayers didn't prevent demons from entering Holly House, but they were meant to keep those with foul intentions at bay. If Loki had only dropped by to snoop for information, the spells might not have been strong enough to detect him. Grim had demanded my silence, so I couldn't very well dial up Holly and tell her that her security measures were lacking.

"What's the deal? Did Jenni show or not?" Josie asked, rubbing a towel over her face.

"Not exactly." There was really no delicate way to put it. "I think I know why she's been acting so off though. Loki's taken her place. I'm guessing she was grabbed by rebels."

Josie swallowed, clutching the towel in front of her. "How long ago?"

I shrugged. "It's hard to say. I just found out this morning." It was hard to think about too. It could have been days, or it could have been weeks. If Jenni was still alive, it was hard telling the condition we'd find her in.

Josie and Kevin were still standing in the dining room, frozen in place.

I cleared my throat. "Josie, I'll need you to deliver the rest of the team's dockets today. Kevin can go with you and take the hounds down to the ship. Don't tell the others that we're not going to be harvesting with them. Meet me in Grim's office at nine. Bring all the firepower you can carry. I have a feeling it's going to be a long day."

CHAPTER 21

*"If all the world's a stage,
I want to operate the trap door."
-Paul Beatty*

I didn't ask Grim what he had done to get Loki out of the way. It skipped my mind when I entered his office with Josie and Kevin and found a familiar pair of silvery white wings nestled into one of the office chairs.

I didn't want to see Maalik, and I could tell he wasn't exactly thrilled to be in the same room with me either. He didn't turn around to greet me. He didn't look at me when I took the seat next to him. His brow was set in a firm line, and his jaw tightened, looking foreign against the soft, dark curls cascading over his shoulders.

A moment later, Beelzebub entered the room, dressed in a black ops getup like the one he had worn the night before. He looked tired, but he'd found time to shave and clean up before the meeting. He gave me a small smile that quickly vanished when he noticed Maalik.

My recent choice in lovers had shifted about as drastically as my job titles had in the last year. The choice really hadn't been mine to make though, on both accounts. I suppose I could have refused the men. The career change would have been more difficult though. I liked breathing.

Maalik was definitely the safer of the two men. He was also the more archaic and old-fashioned. When he had first moved to the city, he hadn't had much cultural knowledge of the modern world, but he gave it a fair shot. He wore jeans and went out to Purgatory Lounge a few times with Apollo. He'd even taken an interest in modern cuisine and rock music.

The one thing he did have trouble shaking was his inane protector complex. In addition to giving me the hellhounds, he had also set me up at Holly House, and then tried to micromanage my career in order to keep me out of harm's way. After our split, he'd drifted back into his old ways, avoiding the social circles and wearing his standard issue black robe.

It was hard not to feel a little responsible for his lack of luster, but I just wasn't prepared to become his Rapunzel playmate that he seemed to have less and less time for. Even if I had been okay with that, circumstances wouldn't have allowed it. Horus was blackmailing me, and as much as I hated to admit it, Winston was depending on me too.

Beelzebub had been my saving grace, which seems entirely wrong to say about a demon. He didn't pry into my trunk of secrets. He didn't treat me like an invalid and try to protect me from the reality of my work, not that he hadn't saved my ass a few times. The difference with him was that he would sit back and let me fight my own battles until I cried uncle, and then he'd lend a hand. Afterwards, we might discuss my technique, but he'd never suggest that I just go hole up somewhere safe until the big boys took care of the bad guys. I adored him for it.

Beelzebub was also more in touch with society. He threw parties regularly and dressed to the nines in the latest European fashions. He was still somewhat entangled with the politics of Eternity, but he was far more causal and subtle about it than Maalik.

The fact that they were both from hell didn't even seem like a good comparison point. Bub loved the hells. He maintained homes in several of them. Maalik had an apartment in Jahannam that he had gladly given up when he moved to Limbo City. He was an angel of Allah, and he still considered Jannah, the Islamic heaven, his true home.

Grim's office was feeling crowded all of a sudden, and then Ammit joined us, breaking up the awkward silence with her cheerful smile, packed full of hope. I took a wild guess and figured that Grim had told her about the headdress sighting. I was relieved to see that she had traded in the sweat pants for a pair of jeans and a black turtleneck. Her braids were tidier, and she had them pulled back into a low ponytail. She had also reapplied her eye makeup in bold Egyptian fashion, complete with Eye of Horus teardrops and long, curling tails.

Josie and Kevin gravitated over to her, distancing themselves from the fuming triangle I had become the focal point of. The tension in the room boiled until I thought I just might have something left for my stomach to give up.

Grim gave us all a bored sigh and folded his hands over his desk. "This is how it is, kids. Maalik has a thorough knowledge of a large portion of the hells. Beelzebub has a thorough knowledge of another portion, and Ammit another portion still. You three reapers have a history of working well together and overcoming extraordinary odds as far as battling demons is concerned. Plus, Lana has special training in demon defense. I'm hoping she's passed a bit of that on in some way or another to the lot of you.

"I'm fairly confident that you all are trustworthy and dependable enough to track down Caim and retrieve the Helm of Hades, as well as Ammit's headdress and the souls stolen from the factory last night. Finding Ms. Fang and bringing her home safely would be the cherry on top of this shit-filled Monday, but I'm not holding my breath. Any questions?"

Maalik tensed at the mention of the demon training. None of us said a word.

Grim sighed again, the only indication that he had some inkling of the discomfort he was subjecting us to. He raised an eyebrow and ran a hand down the front of his tie. "Well, I have a question," he grumbled. "What's the plan of action, Captain Harvey? Do you have some idea of how to get this search party off the ground?"

It was the first time he had addressed me formally as a captain. It was also the first time he had sincerely welcomed my leadership. It took me a minute to find my voice.

I stuffed my hand down in the pocket of my robe and pulled out one of Jenni's scarfs that I'd fished out of her closet. "The hellhounds can track Jenni with this. Wherever she is, Caim is sure to be nearby." I wanted to ask him to reconsider about Maalik. I was pretty sure we could pull the mission off without him, but I was too proud to spoil my small victory with Grim by protesting.

Grim nodded. "All right then. Next order of business. How are we going to keep your merry men under the radar?"

Bub held up a finger. A little fly circled around his knuckle and perched itself along the edge of his fingernail. "I'll send a few of my foot soldiers ahead to serve as lookout."

Maalik rolled his eyes. He lifted his hand nearest to me. Hellfire ignited into a startling ball of flames in his palm. I flinched at the closeness of it and wondered if he had done it intentionally.

"Or I could just turn anyone who gets in our way to ash," he said flatly.

Let the pissing match begin.

Grim considered their methods with a nod, purposely ignoring the conflict. He didn't have time to play Dr. Phil today. Instead, he turned to me and raised an eyebrow. "I'd like to hear some good news when you call me next."

"I'll do my best."

No one else felt brave enough to inject themselves into the conversation. Instead, they all followed me out of the office and past Ellen. She gave us a lopsided smile and slid a bag of coins across her desk. "Grim said you might be needing these today," she said in a hushed voice. Her eyes roved over our grim party, pausing on the brooding men.

"Thanks," I said.

Ellen learned early on how to skim over the heavier issues at Reapers Inc. She was more inclined to ask about my sex life than about work. I was sure she had some notion of the importance of what we did, but she didn't let it keep her up late at night.

I took the coins, and we piled into two separate elevators, Maalik and Ammit taking one, and the rest of us taking another. I knew it was more than likely going to be the last comfortable moment I had all day, so I took the opportunity to pull Bub in for a long kiss, not caring that Kevin and Josie were in the tight space with us.

Bub pulled away with a grin. "What was that for? Not that I'm complaining."

I smoothed my hands down the front of his shirt. "That was for being my hero last night, and because I probably won't get the chance to do it again most of the day."

"*Most* of the day? How is your night looking?"

"I'll know after we find Jenni."

"If we find Jenni," Josie said softly.

I put a hand on her shoulder, and Kevin mirrored me on her other side. "We'll get her back."

We took the travel booths down to the harbor and quickly boarded the ship. The nephilim guards didn't give us a hard time, and most of the other ships were quiet, their owners having already left to begin harvesting for the day.

151

The hounds were waiting for us on deck. The new crowd excited them. They could tell today was going to be different. For them, it was an adventure. For the rest of us, it was a great big nervous question mark.

When the city faded through the fog and the open sea filled our line of sight, the reality of what we were doing finally sank in. The fit was about to hit the shan, and I was leading the way.

Josie, Kevin, and I had all stripped away our work robes. They would only be in the way when the fighting began. Josie had brought her new crossbow. Kevin had inherited her longbow, though he'd also brought my old scythe, since I'd disposed of his in the chest of a rebel siren. He and Josie were both dressed in dark jeans and lightweight black tank-tops, inconspicuous and cool enough for the warmer climates we'd be making our way through soon.

I was wearing a similar black tank top, but I'd chosen a pair of thin leather pants. They were an old pair that had survived a few other demon attacks. Well, they'd mostly survived. The bottom hems were a little rough where acidic demon blood had eaten through the leather, and a few claw marks had been stitched up above one knee. The strap of throwing stars Bub had given me during my training was fastened around my thigh, and I'd brought along a second hunting knife so that I could tuck one down in each boot, where I had also wedged a couple canisters of angelica mace. I'd also worn a pair of thick leather wrist guards that laced halfway up my forearms.

My double-headed iron battle axe was polished and ready to go. I hadn't found much use for it in my daily activities, which I could only be thankful for. Still, the thing was beautiful. I propped it up in a corner of the navigation room so it would be close by while I manned the helm.

Josie and Kevin were making the rounds, double checking all the sails. I wasn't sure where Bub and Maalik had disappeared off to, but it was a safe bet that they were avoiding each other. Ammit stayed up on the quarterdeck with me.

"Nice boat you got here." It was the first thing she had said all morning. She was sitting on the railing with her legs dangling out over the ghostly waters.

I walked over and folded my arms over the railing next to her. "Yeah. It's taken care of us through some interesting events."

"So I've heard."

Horus's niece Kabauet, the goddess of cold water, had cleaned up our ship last year after we were attacked by Caim's demons. We'd been transporting one of the rejected throne candidates to Duat. It also happened to be the battle we lost Coreen in.

I frowned at the memory. "How good are you in a fight?"

Ammit tilted her head around to look at me. Her eyes flickered, the pupils narrowing to a more reptilian shape. "I can hold my own. Don't worry about me, reaper."

I had to remind myself that Ammit had been around for the War of Eternity too. She might not have been as memorable as Kali, but she was still formidable. I just wanted to be sure that her fighting skills hadn't gone stale during the sedentary millennium that had passed since then.

Beelzebub and Maalik were survivors of the war too. I hadn't paid much attention to the brief history lesson I'd received at the academy as a fresh reaper, and I was suddenly sorry for it. I wanted to know more about everyone's roles. I wanted to know who I should want at my back if war broke out again. Maybe I could ask Jack to give me a proper history lesson in the study at Bub's Tartarus manor. There had to be some good books on the war in his collection.

CHAPTER 22

*"We owe to the Middle Ages the two worst inventions
of humanity – romantic love and gunpowder."*
-Andre Maurois

Saul's coffee can paws were flopped over the deck railing. Little toenails poked out in between the black tuffs between the pads of his feet, but he was careful not to scratch up the woodwork. Strings of slobber webbed down from his jowls and his wet muzzle bobbed in the wind, sniffing the breeze along the coast of Jahannam.

Coreen was curled up towards the back of the main deck, halfway sulking about Saul being the better tracker and halfway napping to be ready when we got to wherever we were going.

Josie and Kevin had disappeared off to the captain's cabin. Maybe the anxiety of the upcoming battle had excited them, and they wanted to wind down with a quickie. Maybe they just weren't comfortable wandering around the deck with Beelzebub and Maalik shooting eye daggers at each other from opposite ends of the boat. It was no picnic for me either, but as the chosen leader of the group, I felt it was my responsibility to keep an eye on things and be ready when

Saul picked up Jenni's scent. Besides, if I couldn't handle a little tension between the two men, I really had no business rushing into a demon hideout.

Beelzebub and Ammit were getting along fine it seemed. They were both technically hell-born, so it wasn't much of a surprise. Maalik resided in Jahannam, the Islamic hell, before joining the council, but he wasn't really hell-born. He was an angel, and he was a servant of Allah. He had hated being stuck in Jahannam, and he'd been thrilled when he was first voted onto the council last year and was allowed to move to Limbo City. That afterglow was long gone now.

I found Maalik hiding out in the crow's nest, the basket lookout at the top of the main mast. It had probably taken him all of two seconds to fly up there, but it took me a bit longer climbing up the ratlines to join him. I was out of breath when I finally reached the top.

"What do you want?" he asked evenly, still refusing to look at me. There wasn't a thing to see in any direction, but he kept his eyes narrowed at the horizon anyway.

"I wanted to apologize for you getting dragged into this. I had no idea Grim was going to ask you to join us."

"Why shouldn't he have? He was right. I know the hell regions better than most, and I'm more than proficient in a battle."

"Of course you are. I know that. I just know that this is uncomfortable for you, and it is for me too."

"Uncomfortable," he scoffed. "Yes, babysitting my former love and her new demonic consort is... uncomfortable."

I frowned at him. "Babysitting? I'm trying to be civil here. There's no need to be hateful."

"Save it, Lana. I'm not here for your insincere apologies. We have a mission. I'd like to get it over with as soon as possible so that I can return to my council duties. I don't have lackeys to pass my work off onto when I'm not around like you do."

I opened my mouth, but before I could deliver a witty retort, he cut me off with a harsh swish of wings as he dove out of the nest, gliding effortlessly down to the forecastle deck where Saul was grinning in the wind. I stood there gaping after him, wondering when he had become such an asshat. Lackeys? Really?

"That went well."

I almost fell out of the nest when I heard Beelzebub behind me. His army of flies reassembled, and he reached out, grasping my elbow to steady me.

"Just trying to keep the peace." I took my arm back.

"I know, love." Bub gave me a tender smile. "He was an ungracious lout."

"Yeah." I looked back below and spotted Coreen trotting off to where Maalik had landed. She wagged her tail and snuggled herself in next to him at the head of the ship. He scratched her behind the ear. Saul dropped down from the railing for a quick greeting pet too. Maalik had given me the hounds when they were only puppies, and he had been around them, off and on anyway, while we dated. It annoyed me that they were still fond of him.

The ship slipped on past where Jahannam's border met that of the Christian Hell and carried on along the rocky coast. We were far enough out that no one would be able to recognize the ship. I could just barely make out the gates of Hell and the Styx Stop where I had met up with Bub for my first day of demon defense training. The Styx River was a thin, gray line behind the café. Soon, the rocky ledges of Tartarus would swallow the coast. If Jenni's trail led us there, we were going to have to use one of the tender boats to make it to shore. It seemed incredibly inconvenient that coin travel was so limited on the sea, but then I remembered that also meant demons couldn't just appear on my ship. Can't really complain about that.

The wind was stronger from the crow's nest. I trembled against it. Bub stepped in behind me and wrapped his arms around my waist, warming my backside with his chest. "You want help down from here, pet?"

I cringed. "I'm not really sure that I want to be covered in flies right now."

Bub almost looked hurt. "You'll be in my arms the entire time. Not a single one will touch you."

"Okay." It was hard to refuse. I was already feeling like a jerk for offending him.

He took me in his arms, cradling my back with one and looping the other under my legs. A swarm of flies appeared and wrapped themselves around his legs, taking particular care to stay away from me. They were gentle, slowly lifting us from the lookout perch and descending down the length of the mast. We landed so softly on the deck that no one even noticed.

The flies disappeared as Bub regained his footing. He set me down with a pinched brow. "I hadn't realized that the flies bothered you so badly."

"They don't. I'm just extra twitchy right now, that's all," I said, squeezing his shoulder. Grief, I couldn't seem to say the right thing to anyone today.

Bub nodded and gave me a small smile that didn't quite reach his eyes. "Is there a spare cabin around here that I might be able to catch a quick nap in? I didn't sleep well last night."

"You're probably better off on one of the couches in the hold. The other cabins haven't been touched since Josie and I bought the ship. That's been forever ago."

Bub nodded. "The hold it is."

We took the stairs off the main deck next to the cargo access hatch. The hold on mine and Josie's ship was originally the gun deck. The actual cargo hold was a deck below that. We hadn't really had much use for a gun deck, seeing as how we didn't have a full-fledged crew to run it, and even if we had, there were only a few rare occurrences I could think of that an operational gun deck would have even been useful. The cargo hold had been full of miscellaneous rigging equipment and rats, so we'd closed it off and converted the gun deck into a hold for our harvests. It was easier to access too, so it just made good sense all the way around.

A dozen rusted cannons sitting along the outer walls next to boarded up gun ports were the only signs as to what the space had once been used for. Everything else was intended to make the place cozy. Our mismatched sofa collection had grown quickly after we'd joined the Posy Unit. Josie, Kevin, and I had spent a couple evenings hitting thrift stores in Limbo City and various afterlives. Our daily harvest count had jumped from a few dozen to several hundred overnight, so the couches had been necessary. Souls are less inclined to cause problems if you keep them comfortable. In addition to the sofas, we had several picnic tables. Kevin had become somewhat of an amateur carpenter. It was his first real independent interest outside of his academy studies, so I was in full support of it, even if the benches were a little off kilter.

There was a separate cabin off the main room, with several sets of shackles welded to steel plates set into each of the walls. We didn't have to use the room often, but every now and then we would get ahold of a real mess of a soul and have to lock it up. The vast majority of our catches were easy to manage. We had several decks of cards and board games set out for them, along with a bookshelf containing a full set of religious texts for all the afterlives, in case they wanted to brush up on their scripture before getting quizzed at the gates we dropped them off at.

Bub took in the room with a comical grin. "I don't think I've ever been down here before. It's not quite what I expected." He chose a long, floral print, corduroy couch and stretched out, kicking his feet up on one of the arm rests and folding his hands behind his head. His black shirt strained over his chest, and I could see the lines of his abs and pecs pressing through the thin material. I had the sudden urge to pounce on him, but I contained myself. He needed to be well-rested, and I needed to be on deck to keep an eye on things. The thought of Maalik walking in on us made for pretty powerful motivation to behave too.

"I better get back upstairs."

Bub nodded and closed his eyes. "Thanks, love."

"Sweet dreams." I was afraid that if knelt down for a kiss that I would end up on top of him, so I gave his leg a quick pat before heading back up to the main deck.

Josie was at the helm on the quarterdeck when I resurfaced. She was talking with Ammit, but she paused and gave me a little wink. Apparently, she was feeling better after her and Kevin's little rendezvous. It made me wish that I had stayed down in the hold with Bub, but there would be time for that after we rescued Jenni and reclaimed Hades' helm and Ammit's headdress.

There wasn't much to do besides wait. Thinking about what might lay ahead for us was taking up too much space in my head. Bub's request for a place to nap redirected my busy mind away from the harder thoughts and onto more simple things, like the sorry state of the ship. Josie and I only really used the captain's quarters and the navigation room, but there were lots of other rooms, all outdated and in need of serious renovation. We had been planning on fixing up the cabin behind ours, now that Kevin was on board with us too, but we had all been too busy lately to get started on the project. There was also a nice sized room under the forecastle deck, and stacked under the navigation room there was a kitchen, dining hall, and an infirmary, complete with antique surgical instruments like bone saws and cauterizing irons.

I ambled around the dusty, abandoned spaces of the ship, wondering what they might have looked like in their prime, and wondering what they might look like if we ever got around to fixing them up. There didn't seem to be much need for it most days, but there really wasn't much need for a lot of things other people did either. It seemed like it might be a nice hobby to have, and Kevin could help, now that he was the carpenter on hand.

When I wandered back to the main deck, the sky above us was a bright, clear blue. Noon had come and gone, and we were still floating around without a clue. The rocky ridges of Tartarus were coming to an end along the coast. If we made it all the way to Naraka, the Hindu hell, we would have to turn back. If Caim had somehow found sanctuary there, there was no telling how long it might take us to track him down. We'd need more people and more supplies.

I had just dragged out one of the target dummies to give my throwing stars a test run, when Saul's bellows sounded like a trumpet over the deck. He leapt away from the railing and ran excited little circles around Maalik, who hadn't moved from his spot since our unfriendly run-in.

Kevin stepped out of the captain's cabin at the same time Bub came up from the hold. Their hair was tousled, but they both looked rested. Ammit and Josie came down to join us on the main deck. Josie had grabbed my axe from the navigation room. She tossed it to me.

With the monstrous weapon in hand, I felt more like the leader of a gang of Vikings getting ready to go pillaging. "Looks like we've found the trail. Josie, best get a tender ready. Kevin, steer us in a bit closer and then drop anchor."

Ammit's eyes had gone reptilian again, and her hands looked strange. They were larger, but her fingers were shorter and the nails were black and pointy. Golden fur spiraled up her arms. Caim might have stolen her headdress, but she still had the power to invoke other fearsome creatures. "I'll meet you on shore," she said, disappearing over the railing.

She broke through the surface of the sea without a sound, and when she didn't come up for air, I almost panicked, until I noticed the small trail of bubbles leading away from us. She reached the shore before we had even finished lowering the tender. She clawed her way through the soggy sand with her new hands, and when her lower half became visible, I realized it had shifted into the bottom of a hippopotamus. Now I was really curious about her part in the war.

Bub stayed behind with our group, but Maalik flew ahead to join Ammit on the coast. The hounds perched themselves at the front of the small motorboat, letting the wind whip their slobber back on the rest of us, in a mist of sticky dog breath.

There were several downed trees along the beach, stretching out into the water. We pulled the boat in between some of the thicker roots, hoping to disguise it from spying eyes. The ship was a good distance out. In fact, it was so far out that it was hard to tell if it was moving or not. I couldn't even see the target dummy I had left on deck. I was hoping it would be a good deterrent for any other ships that happened to cruise by.

Once we had all made it ashore, Saul put his nose to the ground and took off, heading inland through the tall weeds and brush with Coreen on his heels.

Beelzebub took the lead after them, being the most familiar with the realm. A handful of flies buzzed around his head and shoulders. They seemed to be constantly coming and going, like they were reporting back to him. I caught him nodding to them every now and then, like he understood their buzzy monotone hum. It made me giggle to think that flies might actually have a legitimate language. Would it be called Buzzish or Buzzinese?

Josie, Kevin, and I followed Bub. Kevin pushed through first, clearing away brush and grass with his scythe. Bub didn't even seem to notice. He wove through and around the foliage and roots like he had been the one to plant them there in the first place. He was fun to watch, skipping up and kicking off trunks to leap over smaller shrubs. He made it look easy. We didn't have such a fun time trying to follow his footsteps.

Maalik flew low above us, keeping a lookout for any surprises that might lie ahead and doing his best to avoid making eye contact. He was determined to keep his distance. I was starting to realize that he wouldn't be letting go of his grudge anytime soon. I was done being angry at him for the past, but it takes two people to bury a hatchet.

Ammit brought up the rear of our merry party, tucking me, Josie, and Kevin in neatly between her and Bub. Her hands were still more lion than lady, but she had shed the hippo bottom for her more human looking legs again.

I wasn't very familiar with the outskirts of Tartarus. Mostly, I'd only caught little glimpses along the Styx when I was out with Bub on his houseboat. The wilderness we hiked through was a far cry from the landscape that surrounded the desert mountains near his manor. Thorny shrubs and trees were packed in thick. The mountains we were migrating towards looked like broken piles of charcoal and ash, and the sky was a deep orange, tinged by the dusty purple horizon where evening would be creeping up on us soon.

After an hour of hiking, my axe grew heavy. I wanted to roll a coin and jump ahead, but the footing was too uncertain, and it was hard telling exactly where the hounds were leading us. Saul stopped periodically and sniffed a long, careful circle before picking the trail back up. I think it was more for Coreen's benefit. She would use the small break to loop back around, encouraging us to hurry along. Trails always seemed so urgent with hounds, and I guess they were. Time, rain, or even a good wind could disperse a scent.

We trudged through swampy grasslands, infested with screeching locusts and invisible critters that rattled and chirped a haunting warning that we were all far too nervous and on edge to acknowledge. When our line of sight opened again, we passed several steaming tar pits, carefully navigating over scattered rocks and boulders that hissed when we stepped on them. At one point, Kevin slipped and nearly lost a boot. Maalik dipped down and seized him under the arms, yanking him free of the tar. He growled an annoyed sigh and tore off again before Kevin even had a chance to thank him.

I wasn't really sure where the trail was going to end. I had visions of a dilapidated shack or a medieval fortress, maybe something along the lines of Snake Mountain. What I hadn't expected was for Saul to lead us through a gap in the crumbling mountains and to the mouth of a cave.

We had maybe another hour of daylight left, but it was fading fast, and a smoky fog was beginning to rise up from the earth. Something told me that if we took too long, we weren't going to be able to find our way back to the coast. Saul whimpered softly near the entrance, refusing to go any further without us. I couldn't blame him. It didn't look promising. Kevin stepped inside the cave, timidly toeing the line where the light sharply faded into darkness.

Maalik finally swooped down to join us. "Move aside," he said, pushing past Kevin as he ignited hellfire in his palm again. He held it above his head, casting a shallow light into the cave.

The walls were dripping with moisture. They gleamed with a rainbow of undertones and sparkled where sharp chunks of crystal crusted rocks reached out from the walls, ready to maim uninvited guests. The path was narrow, so we followed Maalik in single file.

As we ventured deeper, the scrambled hum of some distant noise echoed down the passage to us. It sounded like an out of tune radio, with different languages overlapping each other and random grating static filling any silences. It grew louder with each slippery step we took, until the racket drilled through my skull like an icepick.

Josie stopped in front of me and put a hand carefully to the cave wall, steadying herself as she shook her head. Kevin stopped with her. He squeezed her arm and slipped her a pair of earplugs he had tucked away in his pocket. After having his eardrums blown by the siren, he wasn't taking any chances. He put a pair of plugs in his own ears and turned to offer me a set too. I took them with a nod of thanks, but I stashed them away in my pocket for safekeeping. There was still a chance that I might be able to decipher some of the demon static, and I didn't want to hinder that by muting everything just yet.

Bub, Ammit, and the hounds didn't seem bothered by the noise at all, and Maalik only seemed mildly annoyed. Of course, it could have just been residual annoyance from having to be so close to me. I was beginning to find his attitude annoying. It wasn't like I had insisted that he come along. I hadn't made out with Bub in front of him. I wasn't being unkind or rude. He really needed to get over himself. We had bigger problems, and they were right around the corner.

CHAPTER 23

*"No one can confidently say
that he will still be living tomorrow."
-Euripides*

Saying that we were outnumbered would have been a gross understatement. There were too many demons to count. The tunnel had led us to an upper ledge that circled and overlooked a pit, and it was overflowing. There was a party in full swing below. The rebels were celebrating. I wondered whose birthday it was.

The crowd consisted primarily of the generic, low grade demons of the Christian Hell. Some of them resembled humans, and they even wore clothing, but most of them were naked, with scorched, scaly flesh. Their rib cages pressed tightly against thin, scabby skin, and spaded tails darted around dangerously, striking out like they had a mind of their own. Tusks and talons gleamed from heaving orgy piles scattered around the room. Their moans and inhuman howling echoed and bounced off the cave walls. I tried to avert my eyes, appalled at the demonic peep show.

Bub squirmed behind me. His hand came up to rest on my hip, and it occurred to me that this might actually look like a good time to him. The thought made me a little queasy.

When my stomach had settled, I stole another glance around the pit. A few smaller circles of Egyptian rebels were sitting off to themselves, looking about as unnerved by the demon activities as I was. They were a broody, cocky bunch, eyeing their new brethren with enough contempt that I was almost certain they were reconsidering their alliance.

A random selection of Pagan beings and deities peppered the crowd. A few winged sirens were entangled in one of the orgy piles, adding their hypnotic shrills to the tortured moaning. I noticed Kevin from the corner of my eye as he pushed his earplugs in tighter. A satyr was charming a circle of succubi with eerie music from his panpipes. The sounds of evil at play were mashed together in a migraine inducing song that was more than fitting for torture chambers.

Ammit was panting beside us. Her eyes were doing weird things again, and she looked hungry. Maalik had extinguished his torchy hellfire hand, and we all retreated back into the passage a little ways.

"What's the plan, boss lady?" Kevin asked, popping out one of his earplugs.

Maalik snorted, like the very thought of me being in charge was comical at best.

I ignored him and slung the leather strap of my axe over my shoulder, letting the heavy blade rest against my back. "I say we watch awhile from the ledge. Keep an eye out for Caim or anyone else of importance like—"

"Seth?" Maalik injected.

"Yes," I hissed back at him, rolling my eyes. "Like Seth or Tisiphone."

Maalik's eyes widened.

"Didn't you know she was with them now too?"

He folded his arms with a scowl, but he managed to keep his mouth shut as I continued.

"When a good opening presents itself, I'll take Saul down to finish tracking Jenni's scent, though it could be difficult with so many sweaty bodies down there."

Bub tensed again beside me.

I swallowed and tried to focus, wrapping my mind around all of our options. "If an opening doesn't present itself, we'll have to make one. I think you five and Coreen could manage a big enough distraction for me and Saul to finish tracking down Jenni."

"What about the helm?" Bub asked.

Ammit stepped up closer. "And my headdress."

I thought it over a minute. "Bub, you didn't have any trouble with Caim the last time he had the helm on. Do you think you could locate him if he's wearing it again?"

"I can try. It was easier at the factory. There weren't so many other... distractions."

"Okay." I swallowed again and pressed my lips together. "I imagine Caim's keeping the headdress somewhere safe. If Bub manages to subdue him, maybe we can beat the location out of him?"

"I'll eat his face off if he refuses," Ammit said in a low growl.

"Okay then. Looks like we have a plan. Sort of." I made way back to the ledge, glancing down at the crowd from the shadow of a low boulder.

Maalik followed me, his wings tucked in tight against his back and out of sight from the demons below. "That's a really weak plan, you realize," he whispered.

"Yeah? You have a better one?"

He sighed. "Look around the base of the cave. What do you see?"

Past the party of heathens, the floor dipped off, sinking into a lower wall. There were a handful of openings roughly carved into the rock. I could see barred gates a short distance inside some of them, secured with heavy chains and padlocks. It wasn't the cleverest of hiding places, but it was a safe bet that we'd find Jenni and maybe the headdress somewhere beyond one of them.

Maalik leaned in closer to me. "If we managed to get ahold of Caim or Seth or whoever, our best chance at interrogating them would be in one of those rooms. The fighting, if we have to resort to that, should be saved for very last. We are vastly outnumbered. If we don't use the element of surprise against them wisely, we won't make it out of here, let alone back to the ship." He had a point, but I wasn't sure if it was going to do us much good.

"We need a distraction that isn't us," I said, just as Caim emerged from one of the gated openings, carrying Ammit's headdress by the snout. He circled around the pit and perched himself on a lower platform that jutted out into the crowd.

Soft growling trickled out of the passage behind me. Ammit was losing her mind. Her eyes glowed and rolled around furiously in her skull like they were looking for a way out. I wanted to reach out to calm her, but something told me that I would probably lose an arm if I tried.

The time for careful planning had passed. I grabbed Maalik by the sleeve and pulled him out of Ammit's path.

Below, Caim commanded the crowd's attention. He shook the headdress like a trophy above them, drawing thunderous cheering and laughter.

"Tonight, we commemorate our first victory against the tyrants of Eternity! We lay claim to the souls they have hoarded away from us. Soon we will wield the power to suck them from the very sea, and we will use *this* to funnel them into the new world we will create in our own image, a world where we will not be denied and suppressed by a government built on human politics, a brave new world, where power will not be distributed by popular vote but by the strength and will of those who should have rightfully ruled from the beginning!"

The crowd roared to life, which is probably the only reason they didn't hear Ammit coming. Her lower half had shifted into that of a hippo again, and her torso and arms were fully lion. Her face was still her own, aside from the slatted, reptilian eyes. She barreled down the passage and leapt from the edge, soaring over the crowd and landing on the ledge just behind Caim.

I wanted to wait and see his face. I wanted to watch him piss himself, but time was precious and our task was great. Instead, I looked back to the others waiting in the cave and pointed out over the crowd. "Give her five minutes, and then have at it," I said, feeling my breath tighten in my chest. "I'll find Jenni."

I slipped off around the other side of the ledge, looking for a way down to the lower floor. It was dark and slippery. I had to feel my way along the rock wall with both hands, but every so often I would catch a sliver of light, peeking in through gaps between the boulders. I could still hear everything going on in the pit below.

Miraculously, Ammit was still in control of herself, enough to address Caim anyway. "Thief!" she hissed. "Coward! You speak of strength and will like you have any, hiding behind Hades' helm. You sneak in at night and steal what is mine, and you call that bravery?"

Caim's reply didn't quaver nearly as much as I had hoped it would. I guess being surrounded by a few thousand demons gave his confidence all the boost it needed. "I call that a necessary evil. I call it being wise. I do not presume to be all powerful, and I wouldn't dream of taking on the mighty Devourer of Souls on my own." The bastard was actually trying to flatter her.

Ammit smelled his deceit. The growl in her throat hummed behind her words. "Wise? Did you not think I would come for it?"

"I had hoped you would," he lied. "We could use your kind on our side. You too have been denied your rightful place among the gods."

"I do not doubt my strength and will as you do. That is why I have no need to prove it by destroying the peace of our evolved society."

Caim grew weary of playing nice. "Or perhaps you don't prove your strength because you have none without your headdress." He was taunting her now.

I could hear the demons stirring, growing hungry for blood and chaos. My hand slipped from the wall as it found an opening in the rock. I almost lost my footing and went down, but a strong hand reached out and caught me under the arm.

Maalik had followed me down the passage. Hellfire swirled softly in his eyes, lighting his face just enough for me to make out the hard lines of his features in the dark. "Hurry. We're almost out of time."

I nodded and ducked through the opening and into the new passage. It spit us out before the row of openings along the lower edge of the cave. I hesitated at the end of the wall, sensing the demons just beyond.

The demon defense training I had gone through with Bub was really going to be put to the test today. I opened my mind out in all directions. The crowd on the other side of the wall was one big pulsing red light. The heat washed off of the demons in waves and curled up along the cave walls, fading as it tapered off into the depths of the ceiling. I shuddered at the magnitude of their union. To my right, I felt for signatures through the wall that separated off the locked rooms. They were mostly empty, except for a deep red pulse that flashed from a room near the end of the hall.

Then I felt her. The pulse was so faint that I had missed it with my first pass. It came across my mind as a soft green light, blinking off and on like a distant radio tower from the third room down. For a second, the demon chatter faded to the background, and my focus honed in, pinpointing Jenni's location. The only sound I could hear was labored breathing. I couldn't tell if it was mine or hers. My fingertips itched and my palms grew clammy. She was near death. It made every harvesting instinct in me creep to the surface. I pulled myself out of the daze and back into the present.

Maalik was watching me carefully. "What was that?" he mouthed.

I shook my head, not entirely dismissing him, just letting him know that this wasn't the time or place to be getting into specifics. He wouldn't have liked the explanation anyway.

The little trick was something I had learned from Bub, right before he had kissed me for the first time. I had still been seeing Maalik, and even though I'd turned Bub down, guilt found its way into my stomach all over again, fluttering its way up to scrape along the edges of my heart, bringing the memory back in a bittersweet rush that still felt tainted by betrayal. I shook my head and threw my attention back into the moment.

Just beyond the wall where we waited, Ammit was growing tired of Caim. "This is your final warning, traitor. Release the headdress," she said in a voice that cracked and strained against her animal natures.

Caim chuckled at her. "There are better than three thousand demons gathered among us. Do you really expect to leave here alive tonight?"

Apparently, five minutes had passed. A howl went up from the crowd, followed by another. The hellhounds bellowed in harmony amidst the demons, shocking them into momentary silence.

Ammit returned Caim's laughter with her own gravelly chortling. "The real question is, do *you* expect to leave here alive tonight?"

The hiss of Kevin and Josie's arrows were unmistakable. I could tell they hit true by the screeching that followed. I took the cue and bolted for the room that I knew Jenni was being kept in. There was a gate located a few feet past the opening, and it was locked. The small bit of hope I'd managed to scrape together was fleeting. My first instinct was to use my axe to hack through the lock, but that would have made enough commotion to draw someone's attention, even with the battle breaking out in the pit.

Maalik stepped up beside me. His eyes swelled with flames. He pointed a finger at the lock, and it simply melted away with the touch of his hellfire. His eyes were still smoldering when he turned them to me. "Get what you came here for. I will find the helm," he said, with a look just as cold as it was hot.

I didn't waste any time as I pushed past him and into the room. The only light I had to go by was the red glow stretching in from the doorway. It took my eyes a minute to adjust to the darkness, and when they finally did, I wished they hadn't.

Jenni hung from the back wall of the room. She was sickly thin and naked. Her arms twisted up behind her at odd angles, suspended by shackles that cut into her flesh. Blood ran down from her wrists in trails so old and so thick that they had begun to crust and flake away. Her skin had an orange tint to it, and it took me a minute to wrap my head around the fact that it was because she was covered in a wash of her own blood.

She looked at me with abandoned eyes, like she had seen me before, but I wasn't really there. Maybe she had been hallucinating. Maybe Loki had been up to his tricks here too. Maybe she was just broken.

I pushed all the maybes away for a later time and took my axe over to the chains connected to the shackle on her right hand. Adrenaline hummed through my system, but I had enough focus to aim true. When the metal sparked and gave way, Jenni slid diagonally against the wall, hanging from her other bound hand. She groaned and blinked a few times, but still didn't look entirely aware of her surroundings or me, even after I had chopped through the other chain that held her to the wall.

I set my axe down and squeezed her shoulders, shaking her gently. "Jenni? Jenni, we have to go now. Everyone is waiting for us." I looked around the room for something to cover her with, but there was nothing. The room was perfectly empty, save for the broken chains dangling from the back wall.

Jenni finally looked up at me with some sort of recognition. "What are you doing here?"

"Saving your ass. Well, trying to anyway. We need to go."

She laughed hoarsely. Tears streaked down her cheeks, turning pink as they gathered blood from her stained skin.

"Jenni, I really need you to pull it together right now."

Her shoulders slouched forward, arms hanging limply between her knees. "We've done this before, you know? Lots of times. Sometimes it's Josie who comes. Once, it was even Grim."

Loki had definitely been pulling his tricks.

I shook her again. "Loki. He's with the rebels. He's been imitating us to try and get information out of you."

She still didn't look convinced.

I reached down in my boot and retrieved one of the hunting knives and a can of angelica mace. "Here," I said, thrusting them into her numb hands. "You're probably going to need these. It's not going to be pretty getting out of here."

Jenni was placid for another minute, and then she launched herself at me, wrapping a naked arm around my neck and pressing the edge of the hunting knife up under my chin. "Did you really think giving me a knife was a good idea? Breaking the chains was a nice show, but I'm not falling for your game again. You'll have to kill me before you put me back up on that wall," she hissed into my face with breath that smelled like stale blood. Her lips peeled back, and I could see the red stain across her gums.

"Jenni," I rasped through gritted teeth.

She pushed me away suddenly, and I got a facefull of angelica mace.

"Damn it, Jenni! There are a lot of fucking demons out there. Don't waste that."

"Lana?" she whispered, really seeing me for the first time. She looked down at the mace and the knife in her hands. "I'm so sorry. I—"

"Forget it. We need to get the hell out of here, like now." I grabbed her arm and pulled her up with me as I stood.

She took in her surroundings more thoroughly now, taking particular note of her nakedness with wide, dilating eyes.

"Sorry, I didn't think to bring clothes. We've got some back on the ship," I said.

"Yeah. Okay." She nodded and tested out the knife in the air. "I can work with this. Who all did you bring?"

"Josie, Kevin, Bub, Maalik, Ammit, and the hounds."

"That's it?" Jenni looked sick.

"Well, we didn't really know what we were walking into. Hadn't planned on the party out there."

Jenni swallowed. "We won't be able to take them all."

"We don't have to."

"Gonna duck tail and run?"

I raised an eyebrow at her. "You better believe it."

We both squatted into a fighting stance as someone shuffled into the room.

Maalik appeared out of thin air, the Helm of Hades in hand. "What are you still doing in here?" he growled.

"There were complications. Hey, you've got the helm. Give me your robe."

Maalik's glare dropped as he took in Jenni's naked flesh. He quickly stripped off his black robe and tossed it to her. My eyes were instantly drawn to his bare chest. His skin was firm and smooth and it dipped inward just before disappearing beneath his drawstring pants. Even in the middle of the mother of all crises and after all of his jackassery, he could still make my blood boil.

He caught me staring and pasted his scowl back on. "Time to go," he said, slipping the helm back on and vanishing from my roving eyes.

Jenni pulled the robe over her head. It was enormous on her small frame. She took the hunting knife I had given her and slashed through the fabric just above her knees and elbows. She ripped a small strip from the leftovers and tied it around her waist, cinching the material in and out of the way. With her wits intact and her confidence restored, she looked more like the Jenni I knew and far less like the shriveled prisoner that had been chained to the cave wall.

"Let's go kill some demons," she said.

The pit was in raw shape when we spilled out into the open. I didn't see Caim, but Ammit had obviously reclaimed her headdress. The thing wasn't posing as a hat anymore. It had grown and melted into her flesh, taking over her entire head. She was no longer the cheerful demon goddess, but rather a beast crawled up from the bowels of Duat, formidable and glorious in her outrage. She thrashed her way through to the center of the pit, taking demons down by the dozens in her wake. Some were crushed in her reptilian jaws, and others trampled under her hippopotamus stampede. Her lioness claws slashed across bellies, spilling intestines and bile where more erotic fluids had been spilled mere minutes before.

Beelzebub was doing almost as well as Ammit. I only caught little flashes of him as his flies transported him from one side of the pit to the next. He formed only long enough to strike a fatal blow or two, and then he was gone again, off to surprise another rebel, usually at strategic moments when they looked like they just might have the upper hand against one of our comrades.

I didn't see Maalik, but I did see his hellfire spreading its way across the cave from one demon to another. Kevin and Josie were still on the upper ledge, raining arrows over the pit. Saul had stayed behind to stand guard over the passage at their backs, while Coreen blocked the passage that Maalik and I had come through. One of the Duat rebels tried to get past her, and I watched as my sweet little hellhound crunched through his middle, splintering ribs through flesh in a single bite. She pressed one of her hefty paws over his throat, cutting off his screams as she chewed out his heart.

Jenni gazed over the battlefield with eager eyes. There were still too many demons, even for the likes of our brave and motley crew. I couldn't see an out for us yet, but we were going to need one pretty damn quick. For all I knew, Caim had run off to fetch reinforcements.

A stray demon spotted Jenni and me along the outskirts of the pit and made a running leap at us. Jenni stepped in front of me, running her knife up under the creature's rib cage and into its heart. She pulled it out just as quickly, shucking the demon aside and wiping the blade clean on the edge of her robe.

She gave me a smile that was just a little too wide. "I'm going to get in there." She nodded to the pit. "Let me know when it's time to go, kay?"

I nodded to her, still a little too shaken to return the smile. I thought about joining her for a minute. My axe was aching in my hands, just ready get in on the action, but I couldn't lose my mind to the battle. I needed to be thinking our way out of there, and I couldn't do that with demons on my back.

Winston crept into my mind. I felt guilty for considering him, but he was probably our only shot at making it out of there alive.

"What are you waiting for, love?" Bub slipped away from the battle and formed beside me.

"Maalik found the helm," I said, breathless from the very bad plan forming in my mind.

Bub nodded. "I figured as much."

"I need you to track him down. I need his help with something."

Bub frowned, but he didn't waste time protesting. "I'm on it." He vanished again, dispersing into a swarm of flies that circled through the bloody bodies waging war in the pit.

Our people were losing steam, and Kevin and Josie were running out of arrows. Kevin had switched to his scythe. He pressed his lips to the side of Josie's temple before leaping from the ledge. Josie shouted after him. He landed firmly in the center of the pit, pulling the blade up in a long arc around him. It leveled half a dozen demons, but more filled in behind them. Josie had been pacing herself, but now she tore off arrows one after another, pushing back the wall of rebels falling over themselves to get to Kevin as he sliced and diced.

I forgot my plan and jumped in with my axe, hacking away at the demons from the backside. I hadn't trained much with the axe, and while it was an impressive blade with enough weight behind it to split a skull in half with the ease of slicing an apple, it was still awkward and slower than using a scythe. The demons approached me carefully. They calculated the swings I took, looking for a gap in my technique. My breath was tight in my throat, and I squeezed the iron handle of the axe so tightly that I could feel it grating my palms pink.

A scaly female demon was the first to break my defensive circle. She was one of the few with clothing. She also carried a short sword in one hand and dagger in the other. Her hooved feet slammed into my gut as she delivered a flying kick, but I managed to throw my axe handle up in time to block her sword before she put my eye out with it. She pressed down on top of me, darting her forked tongue out as she shrieked in my face. Her dagger slipped under my axe and I wasn't quick enough to dodge it. It scraped along my hip, and I screamed back into her face with a bloody war cry of my own.

The demons behind her burst into flames as Maalik appeared. He rested the helm under one arm and stepped up behind the demon on top of me, kicking her under the ass hard enough to topple her over my head. She squatted low to the ground and hissed Latin curses at him. I was still on my back, but I twisted around and smashed her in the face with the top edge of my axe, running the tips of both blades and the spiked shaft through her gnarled expression.

Maalik held out his hand and helped me to my feet. "You're injured," he said softy, looking down at my side.

"I'll heal. We need to get out of here."

His eyes pulled away from my hip reluctantly and back up to meet my gaze. "How?"

"Winston gave you a coin, didn't he?"

Maalik's eyes lost their softness. He stared hard at me for a minute. "This is not the time for such discussions, Lana."

"It's the only time for such discussions. Go. Give Winston our coordinates. Ten minutes. That's all we need to get clear. Tell him to activate coin travel in the outer passage only. He can cave the place in after that."

Maalik's shoulders sagged. "You know the condition he's in. What if he can't handle it?"

I didn't want to tell him, but I didn't have a choice. "He has another soul to help him now."

Maalik was stunned. I was certain that I'd never seen that particular look on his face before. He was so stunned that he didn't even notice the demon coming up behind him. It was a scrawny, scabby male with needle teeth and bloody fingers. He launched himself between Maalik's wings, dropping the angel to his knees. He hung on, flailing about as Maalik rocked his shoulders, trying to shake the heathen loose. The thing bit down, crunching along the bend of his wing in a quick, tight line. Blood sprayed from the puncture wounds, misting down over Maalik's feathers. His teeth ground together and he reached aimlessly over his shoulder.

"Get down!" I rolled the handle of my axe around and swung the blade sideways just as he flattened himself to the cave floor. It sliced through the top of the demon's head. Half of its skull slid away, sloshing to the ground and leaking steaming brains while the thing's torso twitched and crumpled in a pile behind Maalik.

"Where's your coin?" Maalik said through gritted teeth, struggling to focus his eyes at me. "We can both get out of here." It didn't occur to me until just then that he was mad at me because he still wanted me. Through all the anger and political secrets and bullshit, he honestly still thought we had a chance, and he honestly still wanted to protect me.

I put a hand on his shoulder, steadying him as his consciousness waivered. "Loki stole my coin last night at the factory, and besides, I can't leave the others here."

Maalik pulled away from my hand. The Helm of Hades was still tucked under one arm. He thrust it at me. "Fine. I'll go, but you put this on."

"You should take it with you—"

"Put it on," he growled at me, forcefully pushing it into my chest. I winced at his outburst but went ahead and took the helmet. Maalik's consciousness was flickering again. "I don't care if there's another soul. Make it home. You're still needed." He took Winston's coin from his pocket and flipped it in the air, vanishing on his last word.

The battle wasn't going well anymore. Jenni was dancing in a circle in the middle of the pit, making quick slashes in the air around her with the hunting knife. The demons had thinned out, but that meant they were being more careful about approaching her, taking their time and easing in little by little as she tired.

Kevin's back was pressed up against one of the outer cave walls. Six demons had him cornered. His swings with the scythe were slower and less accurate. He took a limb where he should have disemboweled or he thrust the blade when he should have decapitated. His arms didn't have enough strength to follow through with the blows anymore, and he knew if he tried to he would only end up leaving himself open.

Josie had run out of arrows. She leapt down from the ledge and snapped the neck of the first armed demon who turned his back on her, seizing up his weapon to join in on the battle in the pit. She was carefully making her way towards Kevin, but she was moving slower now too. She wouldn't make it to him in time.

Coreen and Saul were growing fat and weary after feasting on so many demon hearts. They were lazily pacing the entrance to the pit, swatting only when a demon came close enough to be a threat.

Ammit stationed herself on the ledge where Caim had addressed the rebels. She was looking as swollen and nap ready as the hounds.

I hadn't seen Bub since I'd sent him off to fetch Maalik. I thought of him eavesdropping on the ship and wondered if he had seen Maalik disappear from the cave. It didn't really seem to matter now. If we didn't make it out of there soon, we were all going to end up in a rocky grave right along with the demon rebels.

There were several demons working their way down the curve of the cave wall towards me. I decided to take Maalik's advice and lifted the helm to my head just as a familiar whip curled around my wrist.

Tisiphone, the Greek fury who had fled Tartarus to join the rebels, hovered above me on leathery wings. Her black eyes oozed blood, staining her pale flesh like war paint.

Tisiphone and I had a history. It wasn't a friendly one. She had tried to kill me, on more than one occasion. I'd survived by a thread each time. It hadn't set well with her.

"We meet again, little reaper," she purred, jerking my arm and the helm away from my head. With a quick flap of wings, she wrenched me into the air with her whip, catapulting me against the cave wall behind her. The helm and my axe were rattled out of my grasp, and I felt my spine crack and crunch as all the air was knocked from my lungs. My skull throbbed, shooting sparks of white and red across my vision, and I tasted blood in the back of my throat.

Caim took the opportunity to emerge from the shadows he had been lurking in while his minions took the brunt of the assault. He scooped up the helm with a hoot of triumph and looped his arm around Tisiphone's bare waist as she landed next to him.

"Let me keep her in one of the chambers. Please," she pouted. "We already know that she's not useful. Let me have my fun. The other one has gone stale. We can kill her now." She was talking about Jenni.

I glanced across the cave at my waning team. The thought that we weren't going to make it out of there alive found me again, settling into a dark, sour place in my heart.

A tiny fly rested on the tip of my nose.

"Get everyone out of here," I whispered to it. "The place is about to cave in. You can use the coins in the outer passage."

The fly circled the tip of my nose twice with a series of short buzzes before taking off.

"What's that, reaper?" Tisiphone stepped in closer to me, watching my mouth as it moved.

"I said you look like shit. What's Caim been feeding you, rats?"

Tisiphone snarled at me. Her whip coiled around my neck. It tightened as she placed one of her heeled boots dead center on my chest, pushing me back into the wall, because I wasn't having enough trouble breathing apparently. I was beyond being afraid of her. I don't know if it had to do with the familiarity of our past encounters or if it was because I was just so damned sick of getting my ass handed to me. Either way, my mind was sharply clear and serene as I lifted my knee up just high enough to dig the hunting knife out of my boot and stabbed it through the thickest part of her calf.

Half the hells must have heard her. The tip of my blade poked through the other side of her leg. It oozed dark blue blood that splattered across me as she retreated, lifting herself into the air with her leathery wings. The spell that held her beauty intact quivered. Her hair coiled in on itself, and snake heads appeared at the ends of each lock, hissing and snapping. It was enough to respark the terror in me. I shrank away from her.

Caim watched Tisiphone, almost in awe of her true form. It was distraction enough for Beelzebub. He reassembled midair, landing on Caim's back and crushing the demon king to the ground. The helm bounced against the rock floor, still locked in his grasp. He was quick to roll away, throwing Bub off as he scrambled to put distance between them.

Bub's expression was made of stone. "We have unfinished business, cousin."

Caim snarled at him, flashing his tarry chompers. He lifted the helm, positioning it over his head. "Ready when you are, bug boy."

"Still afraid of a fair fight?"

"Fair fights are for sore losers." Caim pulled the helmet down on his head, vanishing from sight.

Beelzebub dissolved into an army of flies, and their invisible battle began.

I was struggling to keep myself upright against the cave wall. My senses hadn't all returned just yet, but I did notice the rest of the team making their way towards the exit. Ammit had found her second wind. She and the hounds were guarding the others backs as they hurried for the passage leading to the upper ledge. Kevin was carrying Jenni over his shoulder, and Josie followed them with backward steps. She had scavenged another weapon during the battle, a short, forked trident. She glanced at me from across the room and shouted to Ammit, pointing in my direction.

I pushed away from the cave wall, just in time for Tisiphone to drop in and slam my back against it again. My hunting knife was still lodged in her leg. She clawed talon fingers down the cave wall on either side of my head.

"Where do you think you're going?" she said through fanged teeth. She wasn't even trying to keep up her beauty spell anymore. Snakes snapped at my face as she leaned into me.

My breath came out in a tight rasp as I tried to push her away. She squeezed in closer, drawing our bodies together like a vice. My lungs ached as she pressed all the air out of me. Her mouth opened, and she tilted her head down to bite into my shoulder. I panicked and kicked my foot up, catching the handle of my hunting knife. It tore deeper through her leg, and we both screamed as she ripped away from me, taking a handful of my hair with her.

I didn't give her a chance to recover. She rose a few feet into the air, and I sprang forward, grabbing the knife in her leg and jerking it free. The blade was slick with blue blood, but I held fast to it and slashed it across her opposite shin.

Tisiphone howled. She spun away from me, snatching up her whip from the ground. I was so sick of that goddamned whip. She lashed out, but I was ready for her this time. I let the tail end of it wrap around my wrist. She jerked me into the air, and I let her, kicking off the cave wall behind me.

I launched myself at her, burying the hunting knife in her chest all the way to the hilt. Her black eyes drooped and blue blood gurgled up from her chest and splattered across my face. I smiled at her, taking a bittersweet sigh of relief before her leathery wings gave out. We plummeted back to the ground. I landed on top of her, sending a fountain of blood up from her lips before she twitched and went limp. One less devil to haunt my nightmares.

The cave was still crawling with demons. I retrieved my axe just as Ammit surfaced on my side of the battle.

"Time to go," she said through sharp crocodile teeth.

The cave trembled. Rocks rained down on us from the darkened ceiling, pausing the battle long enough to draw leery eyes skyward, before the fighting picked back up with desperate intensity.

"Where's Bub?" I asked.

"Here, love." Bub appeared at my side, the Helm of Hades in hand.

"Caim?" I looked around the room.

Bub growled. "Gone."

"We should be too," Ammit grumbled beside us.

The remaining demons were creeping in on us and blocking our way to the opening that led up to our escape route. Coreen was still waiting at the mouth, trapping the heathens inside the cave. She howled a warning note as more rock crumbled down above us.

Bub handed me the helm. "Put it on. Ammit and I can make it across faster than you will without it."

I didn't argue. I pressed the helmet down over my sweaty hair and swung my axe up to grasp it with both hands.

Bub dispersed into a swarm, and the three of us plowed our way through the hoard of demons. I was careful to step around the rebels, only striking when my path was obstructed or when too many of them fell on Ammit. Bub reached Coreen first. A demon came for him, but he seized the thing by the throat, snapping its neck and tossing it aside to help clear our path.

When Ammit and I reached the opening, she threw her hippo bottom against one of the supporting boulders of the wall. It broke loose and rolled into the pit, sending demons screeching for cover.

We raced up the trembling passage, ducking into the one that led out of the mountain just before the ledge circling the pit gave way entirely. Ammit shifted back into her human body. Our exit was looking uncertain, but then I remembered that coin travel was supposed to be active in the outer passage now. I slipped off the helm, and Coreen wedged her slick body up against my leg. Then I coined us the hell out of there. Bub and Ammit were quick to follow.

We hadn't paid especially good attention to the grounds surrounding the mountain. When we emerged outside, we tumbled down a rocky hill and landed in a patch of coarse weeds.

"Lana!" Josie ran over to help me up. The others were waiting on the cleared path we had made from the shore.

"Where's Maalik?" Kevin shouted over the rumbling. Jenni was out cold over his shoulder still.

The mountain was coming down behind us. A few winged demons and sirens had managed to find a way out. They spied us from a cloud of dust creeping up from the destroyed mountain.

"Maalik's fine. We're not yet. Let's go," I said, lifting my coin again.

We bypassed the tar pits and haunted grasslands, resurfacing along the coast. I could hear the sirens screaming their outrage in the distance. The song wasn't as alluring from so far away.

Josie pulled the tender boat out of its hiding place, and we all piled on board. It was the longest ride of my life. My heart didn't stop racing until we were back on the ship, and even then, I kept watch behind us, sure that the demons would give chase, but they didn't. We had defeated them, and it was time for everyone to lick their wounds.

I found Kevin, Josie, and Jenni in the captain's quarters. Jenni was laid out on the bed, still unconscious.

"What happen?" I asked.

"I'm not sure," Kevin said. "She was fighting one minute, and then she just went out."

Josie was holding her hand. She pressed soft fingers to the cuts along Jenni's wrist. "Blood loss. Maybe infection. She's in bad shape."

I wrapped my arms around myself. "We'll get her to Meng's as soon as we dock."

CHAPTER 24

*"Life's tragedy is that
we get old too soon and wise too late."*
-Benjamin Franklin

Meng didn't even look surprised to see us. She had us bring Jenni into a back room and ushered us out so she could get to work. The rest of us weren't in too bad of shape. Minor scrapes and burns. The place where Tisiphone had bitten my shoulder felt sore, and my back and chest ached. I probably had a few broken ribs. The cut along my hip itched too.

Jai Ling was busy mixing up tea for everyone. Meng had finally banned her from Asmodeus's room, but all the new patients were making for a nice distraction. She was starting to sound just as cranky as the old bat whenever she had to mix up a special batch of tea.

Bub slipped off to Asmodeus's room to check in on him. I was surprised that he was still laid up, but Atropos' shears were pretty wicked.

I found Maalik in the room where Clair had been the day before. His wing was wrapped up tight, and he was stretched out on his stomach over the bed, trembling with each breath he took.

"You made it," he sighed when I came into the room. "Thank Allah. How are the others?"

"Meng's seeing to Jenni now. Everyone else seems okay, for the most part."

He looked down at my hip and then up at my shoulder. "Meng should see to you next."

"I'm all right," I said, shrugging and then wincing at the pain that followed. "I've been in worse fixes."

"I wish you hadn't been," he groaned.

"I know. I know." I took the chair beside his bed and folded my arms over my legs. "You were great today. Thanks."

He frowned. "I was stupid today, letting that demon sneak up on me, leaving you behind in the middle of battle."

"If you hadn't left, none of us would have made it out of there."

He squeezed his eyes shut against the tears I could hear in his voice. "You are too important to be put in such situations."

"Another just like me could be made tomorrow. I'm not so unique."

"No, not just like you." He opened his eyes and looked at me with more tenderness than he'd spared me earlier in the day. "Not just like you."

For some reason, his kindness made me even more uncomfortable than his rudeness had. I broke eye contact first and cleared my throat. "I'm a lot more durable than you give me credit for."

His wings trembled as he laughed, and then he flinched in pain, still wearing a soft smile. "I'm beginning to see that. I never should have doubted you. I just didn't know how else to show you that you were precious to me other than by keeping you safe from harm."

"It's water under the bridge now." I tried to smile at him, but the room was getting warm. I needed some air. "I better let you get some rest." I stood to leave, but Maalik called my name as I reached the door.

"Yeah?" I asked softly, turning around again.

He gave me a pained look, like he wasn't sure he wanted to ask, but he just couldn't help himself. "Do you love him?"

I hadn't expected that. I didn't really know how to answer. Bub and I hadn't made it to that stage in our relationship yet, and I wasn't sure we ever would. My first instinct was to say that I didn't know. He was being too nice to tell him that it wasn't any of his business. Telling him no wouldn't have been entirely honest, and it would only give him false hope that I knew good and damn well wasn't real. So I did the only merciful thing I could.

"Yes," I said. "I do."

Maalik blew out a slow sigh. "That's all I needed to hear."

"I hope you heal quickly," I said, backing out of the room.

I halfway expected to find Bub waiting outside. His eavesdropping on the ship seemed strange to me, and I didn't know what to make of it yet. Maybe it was accidental. At least, that's what I wanted to believe. He never seemed like the insecure type to me before.

At the end of the hall, I noticed Meng coming out of Jenni's room. She wiped her hands over her stained dress. It was a light blue color today, and it reminded me of scrubs typically worn by OR doctors and nurses.

"How is she?" I asked.

Meng looked up at me, too tired even to scowl. "Not good, but she heal. You can see her now." She shuffled off down the hall without another word.

Jenni was curled up on her side facing the wall. Her breathing was ragged, and I almost thought she was asleep, until she coughed and reached for the tea on the side table.

"Jenni?" I circled the bed and sat in the wicker chair in the corner.

"Lana," she whispered, setting the tea down and reaching out to squeeze my hand. Her fingers were purple and swollen, and her wrists were bandaged, but she held tight. "Lana, I was so stupid." Tears streaked down her face.

"No." I shushed her, but she wasn't having it.

"So stupid. It was Apollo—"

"Apollo?"

"Only, it wasn't Apollo. I should have known it wasn't Apollo." She pushed her head back into the pillow, closing her eyes. "I didn't tell Josie. I know how she feels about him. I don't know why I said yes. I've never been asked out by a god before. He wanted me to meet him at the harbor. Said a boat ride would be romantic. So stupid." She sobbed, turning her face to the door so I couldn't see her.

"Jenni, you listen here. He *was* a god. Just not a very nice one. Anyone would have accepted an invitation if they thought it was from Apollo."

"I'm Grim's second-in-command. What was I thinking? I don't have time for dating. I haven't dated in two centuries. Two centuries! I'm supposed to be past that phase."

"Phase? Come on now, there are plenty of deities who have been in relationships for thousands of years."

"Yeah, but they have scriptures and believers to hold them together, and most of them bicker and cheat on each other. So what's the point?" She sniffled and rubbed the back of her hand under her nose. Then she rolled back over and gave me a hard look. "Why are they so interested in you, anyway? I swear, the only name that was mentioned more than yours was Grim's."

I said the first thing that came to mind. "That special assignment last fall. Grim put me in charge after Coreen died. You remember? I can't believe they're still making a fuss over it." It was getting far too easy to skim over the truth. I didn't like the way it made me feel, but it was still the lesser of two evils. Keeping my head on my shoulders was still my number one priority.

Jenni nodded stiffly, like she wasn't quite sure if she believed my story, but I planned on sticking to it.

My wounds were really starting to burn and itch. It was time to see if Jai Ling had the tea ready and to find some clean clothes and bandages.

Jenni gave me a small smile as I stood. "Thanks for coming for me. It had been so long, I thought you guys had given up the hunt."

I blushed. "We'd only just started the hunt this morning. Loki was posing as you, so we didn't know you were gone until then."

Jenni frowned. "Really? No one could tell that wasn't me? Not even Josie?"

"Josie kept mentioning how oddly you were acting, but no one could have guessed that you weren't actually *you.*"

"Who finally figured it out?" she asked.

"I did."

Her eyebrows shot up in surprise.

"I had a little help." I shrugged. "How long did they have you anyway?"

Jenni shook her head. "I'm really not sure. It felt like forever. What's today?"

"Monday."

She shivered. "Five days. I went to meet Apollo Wednesday night."

"I'm so sorry, Jenni."

She stared up at the ceiling as her eyes watered again. "No, you didn't know. No one knew. I'm safe now. I'm okay now."

I watched in awe as she tilted her cup of tea up with trembling hands and finished off the brew. It couldn't have been the same crap Meng was serving the rest of us. There was no way.

Jenni waved the cup at me. "Think you could send Meng back this way when you see her? I could use a refill."

"Sure." I quietly slipped out of her room.

Meng was already on her way down the hall with another tray of tea. She stopped and looked up at me. "You next. Go wait."

I nodded at her and hobbled down the hall. The adrenaline had fizzled out of my system, and I was feeling everything far more than I wanted to. I found an empty room and lay down on the bed, hoping to catch a quick nap before Meng arrived with the abominable tea.

I had just dozed off when I heard her tsk over me.

"Fine mess you are," she sighed, rinsing her hands in a bowl of water on the bedside table. She tossed a cotton hospital gown over my lap. "Get rid of you clothes. They stink." She pointed to a wicker hamper in the corner.

I was too exhausted to care about modesty. I kicked off my boots and peeled away my tank top and leather pants.

Meng shook her head as she took in my wounds. She folded a towel over the bed and waited for me to put on the gown and lay back on the bed before helping me roll onto my side. She cleaned the cut along my hip and applied some ointment before taping it up with a gauze bandage. Then she did the same for the bite on my shoulder. There wasn't much she could do for the bruising, but she did wrap a good section of my torso after she found several broken ribs.

When Meng finished, she stepped away from the bed and yawned. "Jai Ling bring tea soon. You can go in morning."

"Thanks, Meng," I said, following it up with a yawn of my own.

Meng nodded as she left. "Goodnight, reaper."

I hated to admit it, but the old bat was starting to grow on me, even with her cantankerous attitude. She had fixed me up so many times, it was hard not to feel grateful, even if she did gripe most of the time.

Bub appeared in the doorway. "All right, pet?"

"I'll live." I grinned.

Jai Ling squeezed past him and moved a few things around on the bedside table before setting down a small tray of tea. She looked about as ragged as Meng, in a matching scrub-blue dress. "Hey, Lana," she said meekly. "Mind if I leave the pot here with you, so you can pour your second round later?"

"Sure."

"Thanks," she sighed, letting her shoulders sag. "It's been busy around here." She gave me a little bow and turned to give one to Bub too before leaving.

Bub came around the bed and sat in the chair against the wall. He was still in his black ops outfit, and aside from a small bruise along his jaw and a scratch above his brow, he looked pretty good.

"We kicked arse today," he said, smiling broadly.

"And we got our arses kicked in the process," I laughed.

"So, there were kicked arses all around, but we still won the day."

"That we did. Hades come by to collect his helm yet?"

"On his way now. I left it with Asmodeus for the time being. I thought he might appreciate an invisible nap. It's hard to sleep when he's constantly worrying about that little bird popping in on him. Oh, and Ammit just left for the factory. The Fates are pretty eager to get their little souls back in the pond," Bub said, slipping his boots off and setting them next to mine.

"Are you staying the night here too? You don't look so bad."

"You don't look so bad yourself." He winked at me. "My two favorite people in all the worlds are here licking their wounds tonight. Where else should I be? Scoot on over, lovely. I'm tucking in."

I lifted the covers and Bub nuzzled in next to me, careful not to bump any of my injuries. He gave me a light peck on the nose and his goatee tickled my chin. Meng was going to have a fit in the morning.

CHAPTER 25

"The best proof of love is trust."
-Joyce Brothers

I slept in Tuesday morning and woke alone. There was a small pot of daisies on the bedside table and note from Bub, letting me know that he had left to find us some coffee and to fetch some clean clothes. Another note in Josie's frilly handwriting told me that she and Kevin had felt well enough to harvest today and that they would take care of passing out the harvest dockets again. Meng's temple was quiet, and after wandering down the hallway, I realized it was because almost everyone else had checked out. Even Maalik and Jenni were gone. Asmodeus was the only guest left.

"Lana!" he greeted me as I shuffled into his room. "Bub's out hunting down some joe. If I have to choke down one more cup of tea, I'm going to lose my ever-loving mind."

"I hear ya," I said, taking the corner seat.

Asmodeus was looking better. His coloring was coming back, and he was breathing easier. "I'm getting outta here today, no matter what the old gal has to say about it," he said, folding his arms over his chest.

"I'm sure she's ready for us to be gone. She's gonna need another soul to help out around here if things get much worse."

He huffed. "Yeah, I hear there was one helluva fight. I always miss out on all the fun."

"Fun? Right, we were having fun last night. Oodles and oodles of fun." I gave him a playful scowl.

Asmodeus unfolded his arms and leaned closer, lowering his voice. "Hey, how 'bout that cute little thing you all brought in here in bad repair last night? Who was that?"

"You mean Jenni?"

"Is that her name? Boy, she was a gem."

"She was unconscious and covered in blood." I raised an eyebrow.

He just shrugged. "I'm a demon. A little blood doesn't detract from beauty."

I snorted.

"She single?"

"Yeah, I guess she is. She's not much for dating though, and I think she's probably less interested now than ever."

"Why's that?"

"That's how they nabbed her. Loki impersonated Apollo and asked her down to the harbor."

Asmodeus shook his head. "Dirty bastard."

Bub appeared in the doorway with a cardboard carrier holding three steaming coffees in Phantom Café to-go cups. My duffle bag was hanging from his shoulder and he had a box of donuts in his other hand. "Miss me?"

I suddenly realized that I hadn't eaten since the night before last. "You have no idea," I said, taking one of the cups from him.

"Gravely decadent for the lady and I, and a dark brew with two sugars for the lady killer who was almost killed," Bub announced, handing out the drinks.

Asmodeus quivered as he chugged down his coffee. "Ahhh. Hellfire, that is some good joe."

Bub held out the box of donuts, and I grabbed an apple fritter and a custard-filled chocolate long john, wolfing them both down in under thirty seconds. The sugar rush hit me instantly, and my fingers began to tingle.

Asmodeus bit into a glazed donut with a chuckle. "You should feed that girl more often."

Bub nibbled on an apple fritter. "I've got some catching up to do in that area." He turned to me. "Why don't you take tomorrow off too and come stay the night with me in Tartarus?"

Just the name of the place turned my blood to glue in my veins.

Bub touched my shoulder. "The rebels are scattered for the time being. My home is far from that cave, and it's well guarded, but we can stay in Pandemonium if you'd rather."

I loved Beelzebub's Tartarus home, and I hated that a bunch of scabby demons had the power to scare me out of a good time. I hated it so much, in fact, that I was even more determined not to give them the satisfaction. "No. It's all right. Could we take the houseboat?"

Bub's face broke into a wild grin. "As you wish, love."

I was going to have a good time, even if it killed me.

CHAPTER 26

*"Life is like stepping onto a boat
which is about to sail out to sea and sink."
-Shunryu Suzuki Roshi*

I called Reapers Inc., but Ellen informed me that Grim would be tied up for the rest of the day. She struggled to maintain her professional air, but finally broke and whispered into the phone, "Romantic rendezvous with your demon lover?"

"Yes," I whispered back with a laugh.

Ellen gave a little excited squeal. "I'll tell the boss that you needed more time to heal up. I want all the juicy details when you get back Thursday morning. Oh! Good job retrieving the helm, by the way. Hades and Persephone were ecstatic."

"Thanks." I hung up with a smile and joined Bub at the travel booth around the corner from Meng's place. He had already packed my duffle bag for me, and the hounds were with Josie and Kevin. I thought about stopping by the condo to check on Jenni, but knowing her, she was probably already back to work like the others. For all I knew, she was the reason Grim was going to be tied up all day.

Bub and I took the travel booth straight to the gates of Hell. He kept his houseboat docked near the Styx Stop most of the time. We ducked into the little café just long enough to order a couple sandwiches for the trip.

It had been several weeks since we'd made time to lounge down the river, and even at the thought of rebel demons on our trail, I was still excited to be slumming it with him. Out of all the fancy cocktail parties and Hearth dinners, floating down the river in that beat up houseboat was still my favorite place to be with the Lord of the Flies.

I'd switched out of the patient gown Meng had given me and into a pair of cutoff shorts and a lacey camisole, using one of Bub's old flannel button-ups to cover all my bandages. The sleeves were too long, so I rolled them up to my elbows. I didn't bother with shoes.

Bub hadn't even bothered with a shirt. He stood at the steering wheel on the covered front deck wearing nothing but a ragged pair of jean shorts. The hems were uneven and unraveling at his knees. The light breeze over the river blew his dark bangs across his eyes. He ran a hand through his hair and smiled as I came out of the cabin of the boat.

Tartarus was sticky and warm, but it was more than bearable over the Styx. The red mountains that I preferred were waiting in the distance, and thin strips of thorny trees poked into view whenever the beach was visible. The Styx was fairly wide, and with Tartarus being more rural these days, we rarely ever passed another boat.

"I've already called Jack, and he can't wait to receive us. Said he's preparing the feast of all feasts," Bub said.

I closed my eyes to smile into the breeze. "We can eat tomorrow. Why don't we sleep on the river?"

"I suppose we could." Bub nodded.

The sky was a bright purple today. It was late afternoon, but it looked like a storm might be brewing. Lines of orange and gray cracked up the horizon from the mountains, and thunder drummed in the distance. I loved a good storm, and we so rarely got them in Limbo City.

Bub's eyes softened, soaking in the melancholy sky. He let out a slow, thoughtful breath. "It's been so long ago that I first ventured out here, I sometimes wonder if this is all as magnificent and beautiful to me now as it was then."

I rested my head on his shoulder, wondering if how he felt about me would tarnish over time too.

He lay his head on top of mine. "Am I a bad lover for not worrying about you more?"

The question startled me, and I lifted my head to look at him. "You mean for not smothering me and trying to lock me up in a tower?"

His shoulders bobbed in a quiet laugh, and the white of his eyes and teeth glowed softly in the near-dark. "I do worry about you, you know?" he said. "More and more it seems."

"I'm done worrying. We're immortal. We'll have plenty of time to worry later. Let's not bother with it tonight."

"There's only one thing I want to bother with tonight," he said, pulling me in closer by my flannel collar. He dipped in for a long kiss, flicking his forked tongue over the roof of my mouth.

I loved that he tasted like hot chocolate. It always made me think of campfires and marshmallows. He tugged me gently back into the boat cabin, kissing and stroking me the whole way.

Bub was gentle with me at first, careful of every bruise, every cut. He laid me down like a China doll and took his time, removing the flannel shirt first so that he could outline the faded burn scar along my neck with his lips and hot breath. Then he carefully peeled away the bandage over my shoulder and ran his tongue over the wound. My breath hissed out in surprise.

He slowly worked his way down, unbuttoning my shorts and slipping his hands under my camisole to bunch the fabric up under my breasts. Then he tugged up the edges of the bandage over my hip and ripped it free, drawing another sharp sigh out of me. His tongue darted out, licking at the gash. I moaned, full of ungentle thoughts.

I slid my hands up the back of his neck and tangled them in his hair, pulling just sharply enough to encourage him. He pulled against me, grazing his teeth along the bandages over my rib cage until I arched into him. Then he grasped the waistband of my jeans and jerked them down my hips. My skin rippled with heat, anticipating his touch. I dug my nails into his shoulders and pulled him closer, wrapping my legs around his.

Our little power play teeter-tottered back and forth until we were both finally naked and so full of longing that if the boat had caught on fire, we still couldn't have been persuaded to leave that room.

Bub wasn't being gentle anymore. He had checked over every inch of me with his mouth and found no discernible reason to be. He pulled me into his lap and held my arms in place with one hand at the small of my back. I wrapped my legs around his waist and squeezed, holding on as he rocked us into a desperate rhythm. Our hearts pulsed against each other, faster and faster, like a drum circle building energy, just waiting for the perfect moment to release. Just when I thought the boat might tip over, we did instead. Bub rose up on his knees, taking me with him, and we collapsed back into the pillows, gasping from sated desire.

The cabin had grown darker, and rain splattered against the row of small round windows that lined the top edge of the walls. It was a plain little room. There was no clock, no fancy furniture, just a frameless bed and a tiny closet in the corner with squeaky hinges. It was rustic and simple, not at all like his manor in Tartarus or his flat in Pandemonium. When we were here, it felt like we were nameless, like there was nowhere we needed to be and nothing we needed to do, except each other. I wanted to stay on that boat and keep floating down the Styx until the whole thing fell apart and sunk to the bottom. And when it did, I hoped we went down with it. It sounded like a meaningless human existence, but it was still the most meaningful way I could think of to live out my life. Often, when we lay there, tangled in musty sheets and sweaty from making love, I would trace Bub's skin with my fingers, drawing little hearts on his balmy flesh before it dried, and I would daydream about a life we would never have.

My chest heaved and tears ran from both of my eyes, disappearing back into my tangled hair. My grief was silent, but Bub noticed anyway. He propped himself up on one elbow and laid a gentle hand on my chest, right over my frantic heart.

"What's this about, love?" he whispered in the dusky light.

I pushed the heels of both hands into my eyes to fend off the tears and sighed. "This isn't going to last, but I so want it to. It just makes me feel hopeless at times." I tried to laugh, but it turned into a sob halfway through.

"Shhh." His hand moved over to my uninjured shoulder and he squeezed me in tighter. "You don't know these things. Don't spoil what we have by fretting over some imagined expiration date."

"I'm trying my best not to. It's easier said than done." I rotated around in his embrace and nuzzled against his neck, pressing myself against his bare chest and thighs. I felt safest there. I felt safest when I was naked and alone in the dark with a demon. Imagine that. How warped had my life become?

I breathed in the warmth emanating from his skin and sighed.

"Better?" he asked, rubbing his arm across my back.

"All better." I closed my eyes and wished for morning to never come, but it did, and I got over it.

When I woke, the boat was already tied to the dock in front of Bub's Tartarus manor. The storm had passed, and the sky had bloomed into a rich pink with curly gray clouds. Bub was standing naked on the deck of the boat, drinking a cup of coffee like it was the most natural thing in the world, and I suppose it was.

I dropped the flannel shirt I had picked up off the floor and joined him on the deck, just as naked and unashamed as he. He grinned when I approached, and our lustful evening flashed boldly across his eyes. I took the cup of coffee he offered and folded my arms over the deck railing next to him.

We stood there for a few moments, drinking our coffee in silence as we gazed out at the mountains behind his manor. Then Bub turned to me. Our eyes met, and a little unspoken dare passed between us. We forgot our coffee and leapt for the dock, stumbling over each other as we raced into the desert.

On land, Tartarus was like the inside of an oven. There was a little wind, but it was too dry and hot to really count for anything. It did feel nice though, pushing along my skin as we ran across the desert floor, barefoot and panting, giggling at the absurdness and rightness of it all.

The ground wasn't as rough as it looked, and the run wasn't as exhausting as it had been the first time Bub led me to the mountaintop, where he had laid a forbidden kiss on me as fast and hard as a piano dropped from a second story window. It hurt resisting him. I didn't have to anymore, and my skin puckered at the thought, breaking out in gooseflesh right in the middle of the desert.

The day felt stolen, like it almost shouldn't exist, like I had cheated fate. It made everything brighter and sweeter and sharper. I wanted to drink the neon sky. I wanted to rub the red sand into my skin until it was raw and bruised in a mad attempt to hide in the moment. I wanted time to overlook me and leave me here to bake in the sun until all that was left was a memory of my beating heart and my aching smile, floating in the sky like the remains of a mad Cheshire cat.

Bub called out my name in the middle of a breathless laugh. He was trailing behind me. I turned around, slowing down as I skipped backwards. My lungs burned like hot air balloons ready to lift me right off the ground and carry me over the mountains. Bub sprinted to catch up to me, not slowing once he did. He scooped me into his arms with a joyous howl, sending a dusty sand cloud up around our feet.

I leaned down for a salty kiss before pushing away from him and taking off up our mountain trail.

We ran for hours, stopping every mile or so to pounce on each other for a kiss or to laugh like loons at nothing in particular. When we reached the top of the mountain, we collapsed together on the ledge overlooking the plateau that stretched between the range and Bub's manor. It didn't seem possible, but we had enough energy leftover to make love on the hot, rocky ground, right in the blazing light of day.

Bub rolled onto his back next to me, breathing hard from our tireless play. "If only I knew your mind the way I know your body," he laughed.

"What makes you think that you don't," I laughed back at him.

Bub's laughter trailed off and turned his head to me. "Come now, pet. I'm a demon. I know a thing or two about secrets, and any fool can tell you've got enough to fund your own trade."

I pulled away from his knowing eyes and looked to the sky. "My secrets aren't so glamorous."

We caught our breaths and Bub stood, helping me to my feet. He reached out and tugged at one of my curls, wiping the sand from my hair.

"Don't you trust me?" he asked, looking wounded again, fragile and uncertain. A few months ago he would have asked the question in jest, not caring what the true answer might be.

A simple yes wouldn't do. I leaned into him, running my hands over his shoulders and up his neck, tangling them in his sweaty hair. Then I pressed my mouth up to his neck, just below his ear. "Catch me," I whispered.

I tore away from him, sprinting to the edge of the cliff. It was a tremendous drop. It had taken us half the day just to get up there. I didn't think long on it. I would have lost my nerve if I had. I just leapt. I threw myself to the open air and let the rush of the fall dry the sweat to my skin. I didn't even close my eyes. Halfway down, I twisted around to look up at the pink streaked sky. Then I heard the buzz of thousands of tiny wings surround me. Bub's arms followed, wrapping slowly around my middle. One of his legs nudged between mine.

The fall slowed, but it didn't stop until we had made it back to the foot of the mountain. When the deafening buzz of flies faded back into nothingness, Beelzebub turned me around in his arms. He crushed me to his chest. I could hear his racing pulse beating in time with my own as it thrummed through my head and chest, echoing out in an adrenaline infused wave to the rest of my limbs.

"You've lost your mind, you realize?" Bub finally said, leaning back to grin down at me.

I answered him with panting laughter. Maybe I had lost my mind. It felt too good to get overly concerned about it though.

When we arrived back at the manor, Jack had lunch waiting for us on the back patio. He didn't comment on our nakedness, but he did bring out a pair of khaki shorts for Bub and a blue sundress for me, that we gleefully ignored while we snacked on tea sandwiches and grapes and more wine than we should have been allowed to.

We spent the rest of the afternoon in the garden of horrors behind the manor. Every plant had come from the human realm, which was really hard to believe, considering the fact that they all looked perfectly suited for hell. There was bleeding fungus and white baneberries that looked like clusters of doll eyes clinging to bloody stems. Porcupine tomato and devil's claw thistle circled a clearing in the center of the garden, with voodoo lilies and Venus flytraps rising up behind them in all their traumatic beauty.

There was no straying from the path here. A foul step wouldn't be easily corrected. It made me feel all the more naked. Bub and I sat together on the black iron bench that rested in the center of the clearing while he told the story of each plant and how he happened to come by it. It made me wish I had spent more time exploring in the human realm.

As night fell, I struggled to stay in high spirits. The thought of returning to the city and to work was an annoying little distraction encroaching on the ease my mind had settled into.

Bub and I humored Jack and put on some clothes, after we showered to wash away the sand and sweat from our baked flesh. Jack left some ointment and bandages in Bub's dressing room for me to touch up my battle wounds. I was healing up nicely. Anymore, I wasn't sure if it was from Meng's tea or if it was because I was a more potent kind of immortal than my fellow reapers. It made me suspicious of my own skin.

Jack hadn't been kidding about the feast of all feasts. Since it was just Bub and me, he had prepared the smaller, more intimate dining room, situated just off the kitchen in a little windowed alcove. The spread between us was better than anything the Hearth could have dreamed up. Fancy deviled eggs, stuffed potato skins, caviar, French bread, and a dozen other tasty side dishes lay in a spiral pattern around the table, circling up to the main course, a roasted duck. Jack brought out an exceptional red wine that he had made himself, over three hundred years before.

We were so full after dinner that we couldn't even bear to look at the dessert spread Jack had prepared and had to promise to sample it for breakfast before departing for work.

Bub and I wobbled on our way back to his bedroom, the wine and food making us slow and lazy. We collapsed on his bed, and though it was only eight in the evening, we were out in no time.

I woke before Bub and lay in bed, watching him sleep and thinking about the retirement plan Jenni had signed me up for earlier in the year. She hadn't mentioned much about the retirement investments since being made Grim's new second-in-command. It was just as well. The minimum timeframe for most of the plans was five hundred years. Even just daydreaming about it felt premature.

I had signed up for one that would allow a fifty year hiatus after six hundred years, but that was before I had been made captain of the Posy Unit. I was seriously thinking about renegotiating my contract with her and setting up something in the way of an indefinite hiatus after five hundred years. It was still a long ways off to be thinking about, but it was the only thought that made getting out of bed and getting ready for work even remotely tolerable.

Bub finally woke, and we had coffee and leftover crème brûlée and chocolate mousse before he walked me out past the front patio where coin travel was active. He looked almost as disappointed as I felt about our time together coming to an end.

"When can I see you again?" he asked as I pulled away from our goodbye kiss.

"Maybe Friday? I'll call you," I said, leaning in to brush my lips against his once more.

I took one last look across the desert and up at the mountains in the distance, over the Styx and down by the dock where the houseboat rocked gently in the water. Then I looked back to Bub's face, full of longing.

"Let's do this again soon," I said, grinning at his overly eager nod.

I rolled my coin and stepped out of the travel booth across the street from Reapers Inc. The sidewalks were full and angry horns chimed over the congested morning traffic.

"Watch it!" a pair of Greek nymphs bumped past me.

I tucked my duffle bag under my arm and hurried across the street.

CHAPTER 27

"Dying is easy.
It's living that scares me to death."
-Annie Lennox

There were directories inside the elevators at Reapers Inc. They detailed what could be found on various floors of the skyscraper. In three hundred years, I had never really paid attention to the list. Floors thirty-five through thirty-nine were labeled as under construction. The letters were yellowed and a few had been replaced over the years.

I punched the button for the thirty-seventh floor, like Ellen had directed me to, in order to meet with Grim before beginning the day's harvest.

Like most of the floors at Reapers Inc., the thirty-seventh was unfamiliar to me. The elevator opened into the shell of a lobby, with an unfinished receptionist desk and dusty plastic painting tarps hanging from the ceiling. A saw squealed to life in the background, and I had a comical vision of Grim in a pair of overalls, doing a little renovation in his spare time. What I hadn't expected to find when I circled the walled off lobby area was Loki.

The trickster god was tied to a metal autopsy table. Grim had it tilted up on its side and propped against a taped off sheetrock wall.

Loki was a mess. The ropes splaying him open dug into his flesh, leaving purple burn marks in their wake. His chest and abdomen were raw and raised and looked more like hamburger than flesh. A sloppy pile of skin lay on the work bench next to him. He noticed my horror and smiled at me. Half his teeth were missing, replaced by gaping, bloody pits in his gums. One of his eyes was swollen shut, but the intent in the other was more than enough to make a statement. If he survived this, I was history.

"Captain Harvey," Grim greeted me without turning around. He wore a black, leather butcher's apron, and his focus was narrowed on a table laid out behind him.

Loki's long, bug-eyed face shifted into Grim's, and he sing-song mocked him. "Captain Harvey."

"Keep it up," Grim said softly to him.

Loki shifted again, this time into Coreen, Grim's late lover and former second-in-command. "Keep it up," Loki purred, panting erotically.

I was entirely unnerved, but Grim didn't even flinch. He turned around with a serrated knife in one hand and pair of needle-nose pliers in the other. His eyes were black holes, distant and unmoved by the horrors of the room. Dark, tarry blood dotted his brow. He very deliberately and slowly ran the blade down the length of Loki's arm, and then quickly stabbed the pliers into the bend of his elbow with the intensity of a cobra's strike.

That got a jolt out of the trickster. The resentment immediately soaked into his expression. He slowly faded from Coreen into Jenni. "Looks like we'll be working late again tonight, boss," he said in a girlish voice far more flirty than my roommate's.

Grim's stony expression didn't change. Instead, he retrieved a jar of squirming scarabs from the work bench. He unscrewed the jar and pulled out a handful of the fat green and black beetles. A few wiggled free from between his fingers as he crammed them in Loki's mouth. "Lend me hand, would you, Harvey? Tear off a piece of that duct tape on the table there."

I swallowed and walked around the outer edge of the room to the opposite side of the table from Grim, dutifully tearing off a piece of tape without a word. Grim took it from me with a nod of thanks and slapped it over Loki's mouth.

Loki tried to look unmoved, but after a few more seconds, the beetles began to feast on him from the inside. The sneering grin left his eye as it rolled back in his head and he gargled his annoyed discomfort.

Grim turned to face me. "There, that's better. Now we can talk in peace."

"Okay." I didn't know what else to say to him.

I'd never seen Grim with blood on his hands before. I'd never seen him with a look of such cold darkness before either. I didn't know if it was a ruse to spoil Loki's fun, or if he found the trickster so disheartening that he had shut off any semblance of humanity he might have possessed.

"You can keep the leftover coin Ellen gave you for the mission on Monday. Do you find that payment to be sufficient?" he said in a dry, even tone.

"Yeah, sure."

I hadn't really expected anything additional. Just having Jenni back was good enough for me. Besides, I wasn't about to argue with him while he was covered in blood and looking about as sane and emotionless as a serial killer.

"The Fates have their souls. Hades has his helm, and Ammit has her headdress. My second-in-command is back to work. No one important died," he said.

"I killed Tisiphone."

Loki's eye focused back on me for a second before rolling away again in agony.

Grim shrugged. "Like I said, no one important. This one I would have been disappointed to lose." He tapped his blade against the trickster's shoulder. "He made a mockery of me. Prancing around in another's skin. Lying through another's teeth. I don't have the time or patience for deceit. Of course, it's to be expected from his kind. Imagine my disappoint if the deceit had come from one of my own," he said, flashing his dead eyes on me.

I didn't say anything as he turned back to Loki and ripped away the duct tape. Loki choked out an alien scream, and the scarabs swarmed from his mouth, scrambling over his face and down his chest. He quickly regained his arrogant sneer and shifted into Tisiphone. "Perhaps you'd like to try again, little reaper," he hissed at me.

My throat went dry as I stood there, unable to blink, frozen by the demented anguish in his imitated smile.

"You can go now," Grim said with his back to me.

I hurried away from the nightmarish scene, only briefly turning back to catch one last look at what it meant to be on Grim's shit list. Loki caught my eye. He smiled, shifting into a perfect image of me, just as Grim buried the serrated knife in his gut, and the screaming began.

I pushed through the hanging plastic tarps and pressed the elevator button with trembling fingers. The ride down in the elevator took entirely too long.

I didn't want to think about why Grim had felt the need to show me what he had done to Loki, but I couldn't help but do anything else. Even though the secrets I kept from him weren't intended to usurp his authority, they were still heavy with deceit and tinged with white lies. He knew it, too. The little torture show had been a warning, but it was a warning I wasn't sure I could heed even if I wanted to.

I could understand Grim's desire to keep the throne a secret. I could understand that it was for the good of all, and I could even understand his goal of reigning supreme. What I didn't get was how he could be so afraid of losing his

211

position of power or of the threat of war, that he was willing to ignore the dangers of having a weak soul on the throne until it was too late.

That's why I had been made in the first place. And while I had initially resisted the responsibility, it was now becoming quickly engrained in my consciousness. This was what I was meant to do. Before harvesting, before being a captain of a specialty unit, my purpose was to make sure that the right soul was on the throne. I couldn't let things like death threats from Grim set me back, because if I did, the rebels had more than mere threats in store.

I left Reapers Inc. in a hurry, wanting to put more distance between myself and the thirty-seventh floor than the city would allow. I didn't stop shaking until I reached the harbor.

I was early, so I closed myself into the captain's cabin and spent the next ten minutes hunched over the small toilet in the adjoining bathroom, dry heaving in a sorry attempt to keep my breakfast down. I couldn't decide if it had been more Loki or Grim that had done it for me, but I wouldn't be forgetting either of their faces anytime soon.

I thought of Craig Hogan again, and I wondered if Loki's fate would be the same as his. If Khadija had given me all of the same powers as Grim, did that mean he could reach his hands inside Loki and pull him right out of space and time, making it appear as though he had never existed at all? I didn't really remember seeing anything about that particular gift in my history books, but I wasn't a prize pupil by any means. Maybe I had missed that part. It didn't seem like something I was likely to forget if I had learned about it.

Josie and Kevin had been managing the harvest dockets for the past few days, and I felt like letting them handle it again. But since I was the one making the big coin, I decided I should man up and resume my responsibilities.

Kate Evans was waiting for me when I found my way back to the main deck. I was surprised to see her without her better half, but maybe she had decided to distance herself, seeing as how Kate was bent on pushing her luck.

She was wearing a light blouse and a silk scarf, much like the one I had worn to work the week before. On anyone else, I wouldn't have thought twice about it, but on her, I could tell it was a pathetic attempt at mockery.

She tossed her bangs back and looked down at her nails. "You think I could cut out a little early today? I've got a hot date at the Hearth, but I need to go stick my nose in the council's business first," she said with a grin.

"By all means. In fact, feel free to take the whole day off. I think we can handle the day's harvests without you. I'm feeling rather limber."

"I bet. How was your vacation in hell?"

"Lovely. Thanks for asking." I wasn't giving in today.

"Heard you saved the day and found everyone's lost treasures."

"I had a good team."

Kate frowned. I think she had expected me to toot my horn and take all the credit. She fingered the scarf around her neck and finally pulled it off and stuffed it in her pocket.

"I still don't think you deserve to be captain of this unit," she said.

"I think you've made that plenty clear, but let me make something clear too. I didn't apply for this job. I applied to join this unit, but only because an acquaintance on the council was pushing me to. This isn't my idea of fun, but I'm doing the best that I can. I haven't let the authority go to my head, and I think I've been pretty fair about dividing the harvests, except for the days that you taunt me, of course."

Kate huffed, but it was less hateful than I was used to. "I guess I can agree with that much."

About then, the rest of the team marched up the ramp and came on board. The hounds trampled over each other to greet me, rubbing their muzzles sloppily under my hands.

"Morning, boss lady," Kevin said.

Josie gave me a smile and lightly nudged my shoulder with hers. "Feeling nice and rested?"

"Yeah, I am," I answered, letting my mind skip over the gruesome scene with Grim and Loki and settle on the days I'd spent with Bub instead.

"Good morning." Arden loomed behind the rest of the team, like usual, but he attempted a smile. "Congratulations on successfully thwarting the rebels."

"Yeah, thanks. We didn't do too bad."

Kevin's brow furrowed. "Didn't do too bad? I was awesome."

"Yes, you were, Rambo," I laughed.

Josie slugged Kevin's arm. "You were awesome all right. You were almost awesomely dead, too. Lucky you had me watching your reckless ass."

"So you admit it! You do watch my ass," he said, rubbing his arm with a grin.

Alex was being especially quiet. Kate sulkily went to stand by her, even though she was obviously still angry about something.

I passed out the harvest dockets, being extra generous and taking most of the crap jobs. I'd been out of the field for a few days, so I felt obligated. Everything felt peacefully mundane, and I could only hope it would stay that way, at least for a few hours.

I sent Kevin off with a harvest list of his own for a change. If he could handle jumping into a pit full of demons, surely he could handle a few light harvest sites on his own.

Josie stayed behind, waiting for everyone to coin off before she approached me. "Did you know that you made the news again?"

I groaned. "What are they saying now?"

She grinned and handed me the latest copy of *Limbo Weekly*. "Nothing so terrible, since it's a more reputable publication. People only buy *Limbo's Laundry* for the pictures anyway."

Atropos was on the cover of the magazine, sitting on the edge of her desk with her legs crossed and her shears in hand. She looked far saner than she had the last time I had seen her. The headline read "The Inside Scoop on the Fates, Their Factory, and Who Really Took Atropos' Shears."

I huffed. "That hardly counts as making the news."

"Page twenty-two," Josie said.

I flipped to the article and skimmed through it, stopping on the section Josie was obviously talking about. It was a question and answer interview between Atropos and Downy Dale, a nephilim journalist.

DD: Other reports have claimed that reaper Lana Harvey, the new captain of the Posy Unit, was responsible for the theft of your shears, but now it appears that rebel spies were behind the heist all along. Is that correct?

A: Yes. The reaper visited our factory on the same day that the shears went missing, so you can see how we might have come to that conclusion.

DD: That's pretty rare for a reaper to visit your factory. What was she doing there?

A: She had accompanied Council Lady Meng Po, who had requested a meeting to go over our soul purification methods.

DD: I've heard Meng's teas are pretty potent. I imagine they'll be a great addition to the reinsertion process.

A: Oh, well, we're still considering adding her teas. We have so many steps already. I really don't see how our process could be improved.

DD: I see. Now, the word on the street is that it was that very same reaper who accompanied Lady Meng, who led the mission into enemy territory to retrieve the souls that were taken from your factory. Can you confirm that for us?

A: Yes, I suppose it was the same reaper.

DD: That seems rather ironic, wouldn't you say? To have the same reaper you accused of theft, recover stolen property? Have you issued any special reward as of yet?

A: Well, no. Not yet, I mean. Getting the factory back in working order has been our top priority.

DD: Of course. I'm sure you'll be able to come with something suitable to show your gratitude in time. Since she's friendly with Lady Meng, perhaps it will be enough reward to simply reconsider her teas. With a gift like that, everyone wins.

A: You may be right.

I looked up at Josie. "I'm sending Downy Dale a gift basket tomorrow."

"I think he has the hots for you," she said, taking the magazine back with a grin. "You never did tell me why you went to the factory with Meng."

"I owed her a favor for patching me up so well last spring." I shrugged. "That scar on my neck could have been a lot worse."

Josie narrowed her eyes at me, still smiling. "How about that soul that was missing from our harvest lot last Friday? What happened to her?"

"Grief, woman. I tell you a couple of my secrets, and now you wanna know them all. I swear."

"Like a sailor sometimes," she laughed and ran a hand over her cropped locks. "On second thought, I don't really want to know. I'm still trying to forget the ones you told me Sunday night."

"Yeah, me too." I sighed.

"Hey, how 'bout a poker game Friday night?" Josie raised an eyebrow.

"Yeah, that sounds nice."

It felt good having a normal conversation with her. It felt even better knowing that she was still my friend after I had let all of my skeletons come spilling out of the closet to dance the hokey pokey around her. It was nice being able to really trust her again. I knew the absence of that trust had been entirely my own doing, but it still felt justified.

Laying my burdens on another wasn't just a matter of trust. There was a certain measure of risk and responsibility that came with knowing my secrets. Josie seemed up to the challenge, and I was ready to be thankful for a change instead of paranoid.

CHAPTER 28

*"May the forces of evil become confused
on the way to your house."*
-George Carlin

The day's harvests finished up at a fairly reasonable time, considering that we were backlogged due to Monday's adventure and my short vacation. Paul Brom's unit had picked up a little of our slack. After he heard about us going up against the rebels, he was more than happy to lend a hand. I think he was also feeling like evening the scales after we had helped him out.

Kevin and Josie took Coreen with them to deliver the souls, but Saul had insisted on staying close to me. He was the needier of the hellhounds, and he didn't like being away from me for so long. We left the harbor and took a long walk around the city, stopping off at the park to wander around the rose hedges and the memorial statues of the reapers I had named him and Coreen after.

I hadn't seen Winston since I'd dropped off the potential throne replacement, and I didn't have the means to, now that my coin was gone. I had been too distracted by the mess Grim was making of Loki to even bother wondering what the trickster had done with the coin. It wasn't like I could just ask Grim if he had come across it.

Saul sniffed a long circle around the clearing while I stood between the two bronze memorials. As dusk crept up on us, a sensor clicked on, and the light tucked inside the erected hand of Coreen's statue blinked to life. It represented the concentrated mirrors she had used when demons tried to breach my ship and claim the soul we were transporting to Duat. The plaque at the foot of the memorial dubbed the battle "Coreen's Last Stand."

I was somewhat surprised that Grim hadn't ordered the sculptor to place Saul and Coreen in the traditional reaper robes he was so insistent that we wear while harvesting, but I guess he decided that the least he could do was allow them some sliver of individuality, now that they were gone. Besides, Saul had looked ridiculous wearing his robe and cowboy hat at the same time. When I served my apprenticeship under him, I always wondered if the absurdness of it didn't shock most souls in to behaving.

I smiled sadly at the image of my dead mentor. "Boy, I sure could use your advice right about now," I sighed.

The lampposts scattered around the park buzzed and flickered on. It was starting to get darker earlier in the evening, and the trees in the park were dotted with yellow and red leaves. The seasons in Limbo City were pretty mild, but they still followed the typical pattern of the human realm, since Grim and the Fates had decided that would make the factory souls feel more at home. I shivered against the early bite of autumn.

My trusty hound nudged my leg with a whimper. I lazily scratched behind his ears, and we turned around to head home.

Just then, a portal decided to open behind me and suck me through backwards. I landed flat on my ass in Winston's front yard. Saul landed on top of me, knocking the air out of my lungs in a single bound.

"Lana!" Winston ran over to help me up. "God, I've been waiting for you to visit the memorial for days," he said, dusting off the sleeves of my robe as he chattered away. "I wanted to go find you, but it's just been too risky with the guard swarming the city and the rebels having Hades' helm. When Maalik showed up and told me that your coin had been stolen by Loki, I destroyed it."

"Destroyed it?" I asked, still trying to find my equilibrium.

"Yeah," Winston said, throwing his hands in the air. "Poof! It's gone. Just like that. I can't have evil minions showing up on my doorstep, now can I?"

"Sure. Right. Why didn't you tell me that Maalik's been visiting you?"

Winston frowned at me. "What business is it of yours who I choose to visit with?"

I felt my face flush. "It's not. I just don't see why you had to hide it."

"Look, Lana. I'm stuck here on a very secluded little knoll all by my lonesome. You're great and all, but do you really think your visits are enough to pacify me? There aren't many people I can trust, and of the few that I can, there aren't many I can tolerate. You and Maalik happen to be two of them. I know you two had a falling out, so what good would it have done to tell you that I visit with him too?"

I nodded. "Okay. Point taken."

"You want to come inside?" Winston asked, softening his tone.

"Sure."

We crossed over the lawn, leaving Saul outside to sniff out the realm. He had crossed over with me a few times before, but he always liked to explore the tiny domain anew when we visited.

"I wanted to thank you," I said as we stepped inside the little cottage, "for caving in that mountain and saving our asses."

Winston looked back at me with a grimace. "Yeah, about that…"

Egyptian belly dance music grew louder as we rounded the corner and walked into the open great room of the house. Decorated rugs and pillows were piled about. Beaded curtains hung from the doorways and thick incense curled through the air.

"Winston?" I glared at him.

He put his hands up. "I couldn't do it, Lana. But you all were going to die if I didn't do something. So, uh, so I put her on the throne." He smiled apologetically.

"You did what?" I shouted over the music.

"I had to," he shouted back.

"How?"

Winston kicked at a pillow on the floor and waved his hands through the smoky air. "It was easy. I had Horus talk Meng into giving him some of her special tea. I told him I wanted to hang on to it for safekeeping. You know, just in case we found a replacement."

"He doesn't know?"

"No one does. Well, except for you." He shrugged.

"Shit. Shit. Shit."

This was a catastrophe. Grim's vacant, soulless eyes came to mind, right before he stabbed Loki posing in my skin. It didn't seem like such a stretch anymore. If Grim found out that I had brought Winston a replacement and that he had gone ahead and switched places with her, he was going to kill me dead.

A young, Egyptian girl trotted out of the kitchen and plopped down on the sofa with a plastic bottle of soda. She threw her skinny legs up on the coffee table and happily waved to us. Winston gave her a big, toothy smile and waved back.

"I'm going to be sick," I said.

"It's all right. She's really great. You did good finding her."

"Who is she anyway?"

"Her Egyptian name was Amunet. She was the daughter of some ancient tribal king who ruled before Egypt was united. The name she had in her last life was Naledi."

The look on Winston's face when he watched her was curious. It took me a moment to see it for what it was. Love. Winston was in love with the new soul.

"I am so very screwed," I said.

Winston put a hand on my shoulder, trying to calm me. "It's okay. We don't have to tell Grim yet. I'll stay until the time is right. I can help her adjust and keep her company for now. I can hide her when Grim stops by and pretend that I'm still on the throne. He won't even know the difference. Horus isn't expecting me to leave with him for another ninety-nine years anyway."

Ninety-nine years. If I was lucky, I might live that long. So much for that retirement plan.

CHAPTER 29

*"The best way to destroy an enemy
is to make him a friend."
-Abraham Lincoln*

Liberty Park was full of humans on Friday. They ran and
played and fished as if they were hanging onto summer for
dear life. It was a beautiful afternoon in this particular part
of the mortal realm, even though it was early evening in
Limbo City. I had one harvest site left to take care of yet, but
it was three states over.

I sat at a picnic table near an arched concrete bridge that
a few people were fishing off of. None of them could see me,
of course, so I had to overlook little things like the kid
picking his nose and the old man cursing the squirrels for
throwing nuts at him. For the most part, it was an enjoyable
view.

Horus had finally learned his lesson and decided to
schedule an appointment with me, instead of doing the old
surprise meeting in a dark alley. Those rarely went well for
him. He was running late, but I had shown up ten minutes
early. Becoming captain had done wonders for my
punctuality — not that Grim appreciated the effort.

"Captain Harvey." Horus rounded the table and gave me an exaggerated bow before taking the opposite bench. He was in a dark blue business suit and shiny brown loafers, and his hair was slicked back in a low ponytail. "How goes the quest?"

"Surprisingly well," I answered.

That got his attention.

"Really? That's terrific." His grin stretched to consume his face. "I take it my little prank call to the factory had something to do with your success?"

I rolled my eyes. "Maybe." Leave it to him to try and take credit for my hard work.

"No need to thank me. Your dedication to the survival of Eternity is reward enough." Horus beamed, until I staked him with a glare. He had a lot of nerve praising me for a job he was blackmailing me to do. He cleared his throat and sat up straighter. "So, who are the candidates so far?"

"Don't worry about it. All you need to know is that we're covered when the time comes for you to leave with Tut."

Horus's smile plummeted, and a scowl quickly drew the lines of his face into a darker light. "Playing Grim's little game of secrets, are we?"

"Unless you have plans of overthrowing him, I don't see why you're so concerned," I said, meeting his sour expression with one of my own.

"You forget how well I've kept *your* secrets, reaper."

"Oh, please. You really think you have enough ground to stand on to see my head on a pike?"

Horus blinked at me. "If you're not afraid of being exposed and executed, then why are you tracking down replacement souls?"

"Because I like Eternity how it is," I sighed. "I don't want to see it ruled by the rebels, and I don't want to see war break out. Also, I like Winston."

"Tut," he corrected me.

"Whatever. I'm doing this for him. Not you."

Horus nodded. "I'm all right with that. I like that."

Birds chirped above us. We sat in silence awhile, enjoying the sun and watching the children at play.

Horus knocked his knuckles against the picnic table. "Does this mean that I don't have to pay you anymore?"

I snickered. "Council not paying you enough?"

"No, I'm just cheap like that."

I didn't really like it when Horus tried to be funny or nice. It was confusing and annoying. I had to keep reminding myself that he was blackmailing me, not asking for a friendly favor. I would have liked to say that I would have still helped him out if he had approached me differently, but I'm not entirely sure I would have. There was a lot to lose, and my head was at the top of the list.

Horus gave me a warm smile, but I refused to return it. I looked down at my hands instead. "I'm going to need your help in a big way when it comes time to tell Grim. Don't throw me to the wolves, and we'll call it even."

"Deal." He actually reached his hand out to shake on it.

I gritted my teeth and stuck out my hand to clasp his. "We might get through this without killing each other, after all."

CHAPTER 30

*"Forgiveness is like faith.
You have to keep reviving it."
-Mason Cooley*

There were far too many people at the condo Friday night. We almost didn't have enough room to set up for the poker game. The junker table in my old apartment had barely fit Josie, Gabriel, and I around it. It felt all wrong having such a big crowd, like maybe I should have been wearing a frilly little skirt and carrying around a tray of cigars and a decanter of brandy.

"Here." Josie handed me a spare deck of cards she had found buried in a kitchen drawer. She looked around the room and sighed. "This isn't right."

"I know." I frowned. "We might need to borrow a couple chairs from Warren."

"No, I mean *someone* is missing." She picked up a kitchen towel and set to work wiping down the table. Again.

I knew the someone she was referring to. Gabriel hadn't been over to visit in months. It's crazy how a full room can still feel so empty at times.

Kevin and Beelzebub were exchanging the typical guy small-talk over a cricket game playing on the big screen. Jenni and Ammit were sharing a bowl of chips on one of the other sofas, mindlessly watching the game. They both looked like their thoughts were buried in faraway places, neither pleasant. They were completely ignoring Ellen sitting on the opposite sofa, chattering on about Duster's last birthing.

Asmodeus came out of the guest bathroom and cast a quick glance at Jenni before jumping in on the cricket discussion.

The doorbell rang out a churchy tune, and I jumped.

"I'll get it." Josie tossed the kitchen towel to me over the breakfast bar before getting the door.

"Gabriel!" she squealed.

The angel filled the doorway, fanning out his wings to balance himself against Josie as she threw her arms around his neck.

"Hey," he laughed. "Nice to see you too. Think I could talk to Lana a minute?"

"Are you staying for the game?" Josie asked.

He tossed his curls back and gave her a meek smile. "I really can't."

"Oh," she pouted.

"Hey, Gabe." I came out of the kitchen and stood in the dining room.

Gabriel cleared his throat and waved his hand at me, motioning for me to join him in the hallway. "Think we could talk out here in private?"

"Sure. Why not." I stepped out of the condo and quietly closed the front door behind me. "What's up?"

His wings fluttered nervously, and he wrung his hands in front of his chest. I was surprised to see that he was wearing one of his nice, white work robes instead of a pair of drawstring pants. His hair was even combed. I couldn't remember the last time I had ever seen him look so nice. He also appeared to be perfectly sober. On a Friday night.

"What is it, Gabe?" I prompted him again.

His bushy blond brows bunched up in a pained expression. "Amy left me," he blurted out.

"Oh, man. I'm sorry." I wanted to hug him. I wanted to offer him a beer and invite him in to watch John Wayne movies until we passed out on the couch, but I couldn't do that with a full house ready to play poker, and I still didn't know what kind of shape our friendship was in.

Gabriel sighed. "Look. I've been a real ass. To everyone. Not just you, but you especially. Amy just kept pushing and pushing, trying to get me back into politics, but I don't want to be back there, Lana. I've been there. I've seen the hoops, and I've jumped through them long enough. I know it's been a few centuries, but it still doesn't feel like enough time has passed. Top that with my continuous ranting about your recent choice in men, and well, you can see how she might have taken offense and kicked me to the curb."

"Yeah, I suppose I can." I wasn't trying to be mean, just honest.

Gabriel lowered his voice. "Lana, it's not just the fact that he's a demon. He's in with the Hell Committee. I know, I know," he said, raising his hand before I could say anything. "So was Amy. But that's part of the point I'm trying to make. When did our lives begin to include so many politicians?"

My voice was barely a whisper. "Last fall. A lot happened. A lot is still happening."

Gabriel forgot our feuding and pulled me in for a tight hug. "I can't believe you didn't tell me before you took off on that crazy mission Monday. What were you thinking?"

"I couldn't tell you. I couldn't tell anyone."

"I could have gone with you."

"We did all right," I said, breathing in the frosting scent of his robe. The demons would have smelled him coming from a mile away.

"I don't want to fight with you anymore," he sighed.

"Then don't."

"I still don't like that you're dating Beelzebub."

"You don't have to."

Gabriel leaned back to frown down at me. "And I don't want to play poker with him. I bet he cheats anyway."

228

"Like you don't?" I snorted. "Why are you wearing your work robe? Did you get in trouble with Peter?"

Gabriel stepped back from me and turned solemn again. "I told you that I don't want to get back into politics, but with everything going on, I don't see much of an option. I'm no good to you as I am. I want to be a real friend to you, Lana. Not just a buddy that hangs out with you and crashes on your couch on occasion. I want to be the kind of friend you can trust to watch your back, and the only way I'm going to be able to do that is by infiltrating the political system again so I can keep an eye on the powers that be and what they have planned for you."

"You don't have to do that, Gabe," I said, shaking my head.

"You're living at Holly House. You're captain of the Posy Unit, because you're in with Horus—"

"I wouldn't go that far—"

"You're Grim's go-to reaper for the hard assignments, and you're a prime target for the rebels because of that."

"Really, Gabe. You don't have to get mixed up in the politics just because I am."

"It's already done. I was instated onto the Board of Heavenly Hosts today."

"Wow." I gaped at him. "That was fast."

"Yeah, well, they've been after me for a while."

"Does this mean no more Purgatory?"

"Yeah right." He rolled his eyes. "You seem to have cut back though."

"Yeah," I groaned. "Being captain is a lot more work."

"And you've been spending time with Bub," he added, lowering his brows again. "I stopped by your office Wednesday."

"What for?"

He shrugged. "I dunno. It was right after Amy dumped me, and right before I went to the board and signed away my free as a bird lifestyle. You might have stood a chance at talking me out of it at that point," he laughed.

Kevin poked his head out into the hallway. "Hey, Gabe! We're about to get started in here, Lana."

"I'll be right there," I said over my shoulder.

Gabriel sighed. His wings fluttered and folded over his back again.

I ran my hand down the sleeve of his robe. "You sure you don't wanna stay for the game? I think we have one more chair in there."

Gabriel grimaced. "I really shouldn't. Maybe another time. Maybe when you've got a smaller crowd. I miss when it was just you, me, and Josie."

"Yeah, I do too sometimes. We'll have to plan a night like that again."

"Yeah?" He perked up.

"Yeah." I smiled and gave him another hug. Gabriel gave the best hugs. "Call me tomorrow. Maybe we can get together after work and watch a John Wayne, and you can tell me all the gritty details of the last few months."

"We might end up with more tears than beers."

"What are friends for?" I walked with him down to the elevators and waited for one to open.

"Oh," he said, "I almost forgot to tell you. I'm on the fifth floor."

"You're still staying at Holly House?"

He grinned. "Correction, I am *living* at Holly House. Just signed a five year contract on a two bedroom with the captain of the Nephilim Guard." He winked at me as he stepped into the elevator.

I stood in the hallway smiling for a minute. Things were looking up. I was still on the verge of having a meltdown over the wrath of Grim, but at least I was in a better place with my friends again.

I made my way back to the condo and to the waiting poker game. Josie had saved me a seat between her and Ellen. The cricket game was over, and John Wayne was belting out a tune in Riders of Destiny.

Ellen leaned into me as I sat down and whispered, "I've never played poker before. You'll have to teach me."

I nodded and helped Kevin divvy up the chips.

Bub was dealing. He passed the deck to Asmodeus who cut it five ways. "Sneaky devil, I'll not fall for your hoodwinking this time," he said, thumbing the rim of his fedora.

Bub laughed. "Don't be a sore loser, chap." He took a closer look at the cards as he dealt them, squinting at the coffins, scythes, souls, and daisies printed in place of the traditional suits. "What sort of trick deck is this anyway?"

Acknowledgements

This was a really fun book to write. I got to research all kinds of awesomely creepy things! It's highly possible that I was flagged by the FBI during some of that... just saying.

There are so many people who have not only taken time out of their busy lives to read my books, but have also come to signings, tracked me down online to tell me how much they enjoy my series, written really nice reviews, and on occasion, pointed out typos. Thanks! You all are the greatest! Justina, Alice, Teresa, Bilan, Tommy, the Cupcakes girls.... the list goes on and on.

Special thanks to Professor George Shelley, whose editing skills ensured that this book wasn't riddled with silly errors. Nothing like an Egyptian god *wondering* around in a blue *suite*.

I am extra thankful for the new friends I've made lately. Alice, it is so refreshing and exciting to meet someone as cheerfully creepy as I am! Thanks for inviting me to join the book club, and thanks to all the book club ladies for the fun conversations over books and coffee!

I've also recently found some kindred spirits within the online book community, so I owe special thanks to Toni and Chelsea, who run the Paranormal Addicts blog, Carla with Book Monster Reviews, Michelle with Literal Addiction, and Clare Davidson, as well as all the indie authors who were part of the Indie Giveaway that Clare arranged. I had a lot of fun getting to know everyone, and I'm really excited to be working with some of you on upcoming anthology projects.

Last, but certainly not least, I would like to thank my husband, to whom this book is dedicated. You really take the cake, Sir Captain Sargent General. You not only tolerate the fantasy world I live in half the time, but you come hang out there with me. Thanks for being my sounding board, for letting me read chapters to you out of order, for plugging my series and bragging about me every chance you get, and for dressing up like the Grim Reaper for my book signings. I couldn't have asked for a better man.

ABOUT THE AUTHOR

ANGELA ROQUET is a great big weirdo.
She collects Danger Girl comic books, owls, skulls, random craft supplies, and all things Joss Whedon. She's a fan of renewable energy, marriage equality, and religious tolerance. As long as whatever you're doing isn't hurting anyone, she's a fan of you, too.

Angela lives in Missouri with her husband and son. When she's not swearing at the keyboard, she enjoys painting, goofing off with her family and friends, and reading books that raise eyebrows. You can find Angela online at
www.angelaroquet.com

If you enjoyed this novel, please leave a review on Amazon, Goodreads, or wherever possible. Your support and feedback are greatly appreciated. :)

Catch up with Lana in book 4, *Psychopomp*,
now available in print and for Kindle.

CPSIA information can be obtained at www.ICGtesting.com
Printed in the USA
LVOW08s1517060416

482439LV00001B/229/P